I0624735

Rivka's Revelation

By Gregory T. Glading

Chapter 1

The sun blasted the second Jewish Temple of Jerusalem's high, arching boulder walls. Its marble and gold sparkled with the lapis lazuli above, meshing the Temple mount with the Heavens. The stone-paved street amplified the clash of oxen hooves and hardwood wheels.

"Halt!" The Roman overseer shouted.

The cart stopped in the center of the Temple's Court of Gentiles. Decanus Gaius surrounded the cart with his contubernium force of eight soldiers. The overseer had a team of six slaves remove a fabric covering from the five-meter-long marble statue.

"Tip the cart." He pointed to the slaves.

Two slaves released latches on each side of the cart's rear axle, causing the bed to drop. The statue then slid from the cart and sat on its edge. They unlashed the four oxen from the cart. Next, they attached ropes to the statue and the oxen yokes.

"Pull!" The Roman overseer raised his arm. Four slaves held ropes lashed to each ox. The two others stood beneath, holding stabilizing ropes. The statue creaked upright as the oxen tread forward.

Barabbas hid behind an Ionic column of the courtyard colonnade. He flashed sunlight from a mirror, signaling to two Sacarii archers hidden behind the parapet of a flat-roofed building. The first arrow killed the overseer. The second archer slayed the Decanus. Their screams and death throes panicked the slaves and spooked the oxen. The statue of Jupiter tipped. Three seconds later, it fell and crashed on the stone pavement, shattering into boulders and pebbles.

The felled statue crushed two slaves like grapes. The other four fled.

Barabbas sprinted from behind the colonnade and attacked a Roman soldier with his sicae dagger. The soldier deflected his thrust with his shield and countered with a strike. Barabbas turned his body in evasion and, in a circular motion, sliced open his throat with his sicae's curved blade. The soldier's blood spouted like a fountain. An archer killed another soldier.

A legionnaire spotted the archer and hurled his javelin. It impaled him. The archer screamed, fell from the roof, and hit the pavement. Barabbas attacked the legionnaire from behind, killing him by slashing his throat. Two more of Barabbas's men fought Roman soldiers. One Roman soldier blocked his strike with his shield and countered by stabbing him with a thrust to the body. Another of Barabbas's men charged and crashed into a Roman soldier's shield. He then slashed his neck with a side strike. The remaining archer killed another Roman soldier.

The fray alerted Centurion Magnus. He galloped in with Optio Flavius and six soldiers. Barabbas's archer shot an arrow at the Centurion. He blocked it with his shield and countered with a Javelin throw. Direct hit! The archer keeled over the parapet, his blood dripping onto the pavement. Barabbas then attacked the Centurion. Magnus blocked his sicae strike with his shield, knocking it from his grasp.

Before Magnus could strike him with his sword, Barabbas pulled his harev dagger from his outer garment and stabbed his horse. The animal turned his head and neighed in pain before falling and pinning the Centurion's left leg to the pavement. Barabbas leaped on the Centurian and thrust his blade at his throat. Magnus grabbed his wrist, pinched his median nerve, and twisted. Barabbas dropped his dagger. He punched Magnus in the face with his free hand, stunning the Centurion. Barabbas throttled him. Magnus could smell the rage in his acrid breath and see the veins in his crimson-flushed eyes. His uneven beard underscored his hatred. Magnus tucked his chin into his chest, elbowed Barabbas's temple, and kneed his groin. Magnus extracted his left foot from his thrashing horse and twisted Barabbas's arm behind him. Optio Flavius came over and bound his wrists. The other soldiers subdued the two surviving Sacarii insurgents.

"Take them to the Antonia Fortress jail." Magnus pointed to the bound and restrained captives. "They'll soon wish they died here in battle."

Optio Flavious punched his chest and saluted with a stiff right arm. "Hail Caesar."

Centurion Magnus returned the salute. "Hail Caesar."

Chapter 2

Rivka gazed into her mirror. Set an eye-width apart, her almond-shaped, olive-green eyes reflected sadness and longing. Each stroke of her comb brought lament as well as pride.

"My hair is the color of honey...so long and beautiful." She pushed her tress over her left shoulder.

"Thick and wavy like a cloak made from a lamb's fleece. Why must I cover it?"

She then dipped her fingertips into a mixture of crushed berries and oil. Delicately stroking her lips, she thought, *'What profit lips as cherry silk yarn if no brave man can kiss them.'* She kissed the air. After cleaning her fingertips with a sudarion cloth, she dipped them in oil and rubbed them into her florid cheeks and olive-toned skin. Next, a gentle pat from a camel-haired brush perfected her longish, oval face. She smiled and took a deep breath before a thought broke her fleeting reverie, *'How can I flee this drudgery and remain loyal to my God? Will I forever be a potter's daughter? Dare I hope to rise and serve God like Ruth and Sarah?'*

Rivka then picked up a lyre from her table, strummed it, and sang, "Oh, how beautiful to be, but no love sees me. I dream of hills beyond while here I sit and long. If I dare go, what will I find? Death or a love divine? For here I must stay, with only my lyre's chime."

She stood and dared to spread her tunic, admiring her reflection. *'I am a woman now. Would Solomon sing that they're like two fawns, twins of a gazelle.'* As usual, she struggled to secure her tunic and stola. *'I am brave and strong but treated like chattel. Dare I dream of a man to love and respect me like Father Abraham did Sarah.'* She then covered her hair with a black and white patterned veil.

Rivka exited her bedroom and entered the courtyard.

"Rivka!" Her father shouted. "Get in here at once."

Rivka entered the kitchen. Her father, Jacob of Capernaum, grabbed her arms and dug his fingers into her skin. "Late again, I see," He glowered, "wasting our time by painting yourself. You're my daughter, not my harlot. Now help prepare the table. My guest will soon arrive."

Rivka blanched at the stench of wine on his breath and dropped her head.

"Look at me, daughter!" He slapped her face. "You're hiding something from me."

They restored eye contact.

His eyes were glazed. He said no more and staggered away.

She trudged to a storage cabinet, gathered clay plates and drinking vessels, and placed them on a low, wooden table. Next, she put cushions under each table place. Two servants then placed an array of ceramic dishes of flatbread, olives, dates, and figs, and two large plates of fish, caught in the nearby Sea of Galilee, on the table. The servants also included a jug of fresh water and two containers of wine.

***

Jacob lay on his left side at the table head. His wife, Hannah, reclined at the table side. Hanna was taller than her husband, as were her daughter Rivka and son Samuel. Rivka had no seat as her duty was to wait on the guests. Their chatter, combined with the clanging of plates and utensils, dribbled in her ears. After dinner, the female guests adjourned to a separate room.

***

"Sit with us, Rivka." An older woman beckoned her. "Although you are young, you are now a woman. Let me see your hands." The women took Rivka's hand and perused it. "So soft and lovely. How long will that last if your father continues to treat you as a servant? Why can't he save your delicate hands for putting the final touch on the pottery? He has the money to hire more help."

Rivka blushed and dropped her head.

"Don't answer. I know it's forbidden." The woman smiled. "And you keep what I say a secret. What is no secret, no matter how much our traditions hide it, is that you are beautiful, Rivka. In a different time and place, you would inspire psalms, songs, and sculpture."

Rivka sat at the table. "Thank you, Mirriam."

Mirriam poured a goblet of wine and handed it to her.

"I thank you," Rivka took the goblet and sipped. "I appreciate your respect."

"Nonsense." Miriam finished her goblet of wine and then poured another. "You are one of us. Someday, I know you will be a woman among women. I'm no soothsayer, as that is forbidden, but my intuition can't be denied."

Rivka lowered her head.

"Rivka," Miriam gulped her wine. "It's not just the wine making me speak out of place. I know I'm a guest here and enjoyed a hearty meal." She took Rivka's hand. "I also know I should not have said what I said without your mother Hannah's presence." Her eyes moistened as she gazed into Rivka's eyes. "Tomorrow, you and your brother Samuel are taking pottery to the market in Chorazin. Word has reached our village that the rabbi everyone speaks of, the one who can make the lame walk and the blind see, will speak on a hill overlooking the road."

6

"You must mean Yeshua of Nazareth." Rivka squeezed Miriam's hand. "Rabbi Nicodemus calls him a blasphemer. My father hates him. He would punish me if I stopped and gave him my ear."

"Rivka. You must go and see him. Never did I realize that God loves us. Yeshua preaches that God loves us and loves everyone equally, from the lowest slave to the wealthiest noble. He is the first rabbi to treat women with respect and dignity." Miriam placed her wine goblet on the table. "Listen to Yeshua. Take him into your heart. Then you will know of your exalted spiritual worth that I speak."

***

Jacob of Capernaum remained at the table head.

His neighbor, James, scratched his beard, "Your meal was a delight. Thank you. We are pleased to share in the success of your trade. I salute you." He held up his wine goblet. "L'chaim!"

The other guest raised their goblets. "L'chaim."

Jacob then stood and walked over to the two windows. He secured the shutters. He sat and looked furtively at each guest. "I would be doing much better if the Romans weren't stealing what I make. May God smite the Romans. May he damn them and their tax collectors to Gehenna."

"Amen! Amen!" The gathering concurred.

"This new rabbi." James placed his goblet on the table. "Yeshua of Nazareth. He claims he's the Messiah." He folded his hands. "They say he heals the sick. I heard he even walked on water."

"I refute that!" Jacob stood up and prodded. "All right, James. What if he can heal the sick or even walk on water? You tell me." Jacob prodded. "What good are his miracles to me? Of what benefit to our people? Until he can smite the

Romans and free us like Moses freed our ancestors from Egypt, I refuse to believe that he is anything other than a magician, a heretic, and a blasphemer."

"Maybe we should grant him patience." James placed his hand on his goblet. "He quoted Isiah in the synagogue, saying that Yahweh had anointed him to preach to the poor and free the oppressed." James stood and raised his hands. "He made a known blind man see before an entire synagogue of witnesses."

"You ask me to be patient?" Jacob banged the table. "Rome robs the fruit of my labor and arrests and even kills any of us that dare object. Until this prophet of yours smites the Romans," He stood and prodded, "he remains a heretic and blasphemer."

"Well, Jacob," James sipped wine. "Word is that Yeshua dines with prostitutes and tax collectors." He returned his goblet to the table. "I, for one, am glad that you did not suffer to have a Roman or tax collector sit at your table. The meal was a delight." James drank the rest of his wine and then scanned the Room. "Word is that the Romans arrested Barabbas."

"Yes. Barabbas." Jacob stood. "He had the guts to do something about our oppression, not just talk about it. So, this so-called Messiah Yeshua claims he's the Son of God? If so, why didn't he smite the Romans for daring to erect a statue of Jupiter on temple grounds? It took a man like Barabbas to put a stop to it. And now he faces crucifixion for his bravery. Give me a choice between Barabbas and a so-called prophet who not only refuses to liberate us from Rome but brings dissension to the synagogue. "Jacob gulped more wine. "I'm choosing Barabbas."

"Amen!" The guests raised their wine goblets. "L'chaim"

"As much as your meal was a delight." James quaffed more wine and leered at Jacob. "An even bigger delight was your daughter, Rivka. She is lovely as a sunrise through a garden mist. Someday soon, a wealthy man will give you a generous dowry for her hand in marriage."

"What good is she to me? A generous dowry for my daughter? Huh! The Romans can tax a king's ransom into a pauper's seleh."

***

After the guests left, Rivka helped the hired servants clear the table. Jacob lurched in, grabbed her arm, and turned her to him. He slapped her.

Rivka placed her hand over her cheek and winced in pain.

"What kind of harlot are you?" He grabbed the scruff of her stola and shook her. "Because you went and painted yourself, the men leered at you and then talked about you with lust." He released his grip and prodded. "Never again will you leave this premises lest your reputation cost me a suitable dowry."

Rivka's brother, Samuel, ran into the room. "Father. Stop." Samuel stood a head taller than his father. His body was lean from physical labor. He wore a short beard over his square-jawed face. "Rivka did nothing to bring you shame." He stood between his father and Rivka. "If it may honor and please you, I will go with my sister whenever she leaves the household. Tomorrow, I need her help in taking our pottery to the market in Chorazin."

Jacob started to feel dizzy. His head whirled from too much wine. Samuel braced his arm under his shoulder and helped him to his bed.

Chapter 3

The Roman military castrum fortresses Aelia Capitolina and the Antonia sat near the Second Jewish Temple in Jerusalem. Defensive walls and watchtowers surrounded the Aelia Capitolina. Inside the compound, Roman miles soldiers and Optio sergeants trained close combat sword and shield tactics. Their barracks were placed by the south wall in a grid pattern. The headquarters building was positioned in the facility's center. Here, Centurions Magnus, Longinus, and Camillus sat at a large marble table with carvings of Eagles and laurel wreaths. Jasper, onyx, and carnelian jewels lined the table rim. A Statue of the Roman God Mars, six smaller sculptures of Roman warriors, and a bust of Ceasar Tiberius lined the walls.

The Centurions snapped to attention, punched their chests, and extended their right arms. "Hail!"

Two facial sword scars enhanced the warrior aura of the Legatus Legionis, the legion commander, Octavio. Although his body was battle-worn, his demeanor commanded respect. He stood at the table head for four seconds before motioning for the Centurions, Longinus, Camillus, and Magnus to sit. He then sat and began his briefing. "Excellent work, Magnus, for ending Barabbas's uprising. I commend you for capturing him alive. We will make an example of him as a reminder of the cost and futility of opposing Rome. What we do to Barabbas will make Judaeans think twice before daring to defy Roman rule." The Lagatus placed his hand on his bronze helmet. "We did, however, lose five good soldiers and a civilian artisan. They killed two slaves and we had to use resources to re-capture four others. We also lost an expensive statue. We must keep order." Octavio banged the table. "We must also not provoke an uprising. The less negative reports that reach Rome and Caesar Tiberius, the better for Pontius Pilate, me, and the three of you." Legatus Octavio stood and held his helmet by the crest. "A man named Yeshua of Nazareth is calling himself the son of God. We have reports that he is mesmerizing his followers with miracles. Herod Antipas personally told Pontius Pilate that he is an agitator and that his following grows. I want both of you to deploy your centuries to keep an eye on the situation. Keep me informed. A greedy yet reliable Jewish quisling reports that this Yeshua is speaking by the road to Capernaum and Chorazin. Magnus, take Opio Flavius and ten miles ranked soldiers with you. For now, we'll let them have their foolish beliefs and even let them make wild claims. But any defiance of Roman rule must be met swiftly and severely." Legatus Octavio extended his right arm. "Hail Ceasar!"

Centurions Magnus, Longinus, and Camillus raised their right arms. "Hail Ceasar!"

***

The morning breeze wafted through an olive garden to the Jacob family compound. Hannah stood tall and slender. The lines on her face added character to her natural beauty. Her long hair, hidden under a green and white striped veil, had gray streaks. She started the morning by supervising their hired help in loading pottery onto two donkeys. She placed a breakfast of the previous night's leftover fish and flatbread on the table. "Samuel. Take Rivka with you to the Chorazin market." Rivka entered the room. "Shalom Rivka. I want you to go with Samuel. The donkeys are packed and ready. Eat quickly and go now." She waved at the door. "Before your father awakens." Rivka stuffed a piece of fish between slices of flatbread, thanked her, and left with her brother.

***

Magnus and his soldiers rode down the center of the road to Capernaum. The civilians quickly made way for them. As the roadway became more crowded, Magnus knew he drew closer to where this so-called Prophet named Yeshua would speak. Soon they arrived. Centurion Magnus and his second in command, Optio Flavius, watched a large gathering at the foot of a berm. Magnus stationed soldiers at various points around the crowd.

"How can he claim to be the Son of God?" Flavius pointed to the man speaking from the hilltop. "Look at him, Centurion. He looks like an ordinary man. He's not handsome like Apollo, nor is he muscular like Mars."

"In my briefing with Lagatus Octavio, I was told that Herod Antipas alerted Pontius Pilate that he was an agitator. Our orders are to listen and report." Centurion Magnus sat tall in the saddle. He wore a segmented steel breastplate. His arms, muscular from military training and a Centurion's diet, held a gladius short sword at his side. His clean-shaven face featured a strong jaw and high cheekbones. "If he says anything inciteful or in defiance of Rome or if the crowd gets unruly, they are to be dealt with swiftly and severely."

The man on the hill addressed the crowd with deft and authority. "Blessed are the poor in spirit, for theirs is the kingdom of Heaven. Blessed are those who mourn, for they will be comforted. Blessed are the meek, for they shall inherit the Earth."

"That doesn't sound too subversive." Flavius laughed. "Meekness will never defeat mighty Rome." Flavius was shorter than Magnus and had a rounder, plumper, and difficult-to-shave face.

"I looked directly into the eyes of Barabbas." Magnus clutched his sword. "I saw a spirit of fire, rage, and murder. Nothing about his spirit was weak. This man," he pointed to Yeshua, "is nothing like him. Yet I feel this man's spirit bears a truer and much greater power."

***

Rivka and Samuel tied their pottery-laden donkeys to a tree and stood by to hear Yeshua speak.

The speaker raised his open hands, "Blessed are those who hunger and thirst for righteousness, for they will be filled. Blessed are the merciful, for they shall be shown mercy. Blessed are the pure of heart, for they will see God."

Samuel stared straight ahead. Rivka closed her eyes and lowered her head.

***

"Blessed are the peacemakers, for they will be called sons of God."

***

Octio Flavius smirked. "Blessed are the peacemakers? It doesn't sound like we'll get to fight. It looks like our battle with Barabbas and his forces was as good as it gets here in Judaea."

"We are professional soldiers. That is why they fear us." Magnus lowered his shield. "Our army is mighty and well-trained. Yet, we must never underestimate the enemy. What they lack in men and weapons they compensate in cunning and guile," Magnus moved closer to Yeshua, "the

Sicarii are as deadly as anyone in the empire. And lest we forget that Barabbas and his men killed five Roman soldiers."

***

"Blessed are you when people insult you, persecute you, and bear false witness against you because of me. Rejoice and be glad because great is your reward in Heaven."

***

"I will watch the donkeys and our goods." Samuel turned to Rivka. "I see that you want to move closer."

"Yes. Samuel. I do. Thank you. His words have touched my heart."

"Now I understand why father hates him so." Samuel jerked his arms.

"I wish he were here." Rivka kept her gaze fixed on Yeshua. "This man speaks of love. Love that can defeat hatred, bitterness, and anger."

***

"For I tell you that unless your righteousness exceeds that of the Pharisees and teachers of the law, you will not enter the kingdom of Heaven. For you heard do not murder, but I tell you that anyone angry at his brother has committed murder."

***

"Now I know why Rabbi Nicodemus of the Pharisees also despises him." Samual placed his hand on his donkey's reigns. "The words of this Yeshua have power. He has convicted the Pharisees."

"Yet this Yeshua is showing us love and the way to forgiveness. His words not only speak of righteousness but of love and forgiveness. He puts love in my heart and gives me peace of mind." Rivka worked her way through the crowd but could not get as close as she wanted.

***

"If someone strikes you on the right cheek, turn to him the other one also."

***

"Let one of them strike my cheek." Optio Flavius laughed. "He tells them that if your right-hand causes you to sin, cut it off." Flavius guffawed and wielded his gladius sword. "Let one of them strike my cheek, and I'll cut off his hand all right." Flavius kept laughing. "Like the man said, better to go into Heaven lame than go to Hell able-bodied." Flavious guffawed. "And telling them to walk a second mile for us? I wonder if he secretly works for Rome."

"No Optio." Magnus shook his head. "In our briefing, Legatus Octavio made it clear that he is not a Jewish quisling or a Roman agent. We are ordered to keep a close and wary eye on him. Besides, I detect nothing political in his speech. I do not doubt that he is a spiritual leader. What spirit owns him I do not know. He never once raised his voice, yet he speaks with a power and authority that I have never seen or heard. While he does bear watching, I do wish all of Judaea would take his words to heart." Centurion Magnus turned to Flavius. "It would make our job easier. Submissive, obedient Judaeans, please Rome." Magnus looked directly at him.

"Remember that if you want to rise to Centurion. "Never do what pleases you; do what pleases Rome."

***

After Yeshua finished speaking, the crowd followed him and his disciples. Rivka stood still, too amazed to move. One of Yeshua's inner circle, a woman, approached her.

"Rivka." The woman was shorter and thinner than Rivka. She wore a green veil over her hair. She had a round face with a button nose. Her brown eyes conveyed both strength and softness. "I am sorry, but because of the crowd, he can't speak with you, so he sent me."

"How did you know my name?"

"His father knows the number of hairs on your head. Even if we must cover it." The woman chuckled. "So, of course, he knows your name." She smiled. "I am Mary of Magdalene. He spotted you in the crowd. Remember what he said? *'Broad is the path to destruction, but narrow is the way to salvation.'* You are blessed among women, Rivka. Do you choose to follow that narrow path and receive him and follow him as your Lord and Savior?

Rivka looked deep into her eyes and saw a vision of Yeshua. She bowed her head. "Yes. Mary. I do."

Mary of Magdalene then laid her hands on Rivka's shoulders, closed her eyes, and bowed. "Rivka, do you take Yeshua into your heart, and will you believe in him and follow him as your Lord and Savior?"

"Yes." Rivka lowered her head. "I will. I believe with all my heart." Rivka felt a burst of light. She felt the peace that had always eluded her. Rivka then looked back at Mary of Magdalene. Tears flowed from Rivka's eyes.

"The comfort of the Holy Spirit has descended upon you." Mary of Magdalene then braced Rivka's shoulders.

"This is only the beginning. Your commitment will require great sacrifice, even up to the pain of death."

"Before now, I sometimes felt like I was dead. Now, I have found love and peace. I feel it deep inside me. I never knew that it existed before."

'Yes, Rivka. His spirit shines inside you; now, your outer self may radiate his love and peace to others."

"But Mary, you say, living for him may bring about my death." A tear again welled in Rivka's eyes. She then dropped her head. "I understand now. Many hate him and hate those who love him. I love him. I am willing to pay that price."

"Rivka, I can tell that your spirit has truly received him. Our Lord teaches us that "he who loves his life shall lose it, but he who hates his life in this world will keep it and find eternal life." Our Lord loves us so much that one day soon, he will willingly pay the ultimate price to grant us eternal life. Rivka, I love you as he loves you and as our brothers and sisters in him love you." Mary Magdalene then braced Rivka's shoulders and kissed Rivka's cheek before embracing her. Rivka returned her embrace and kissed her cheek. "Tomorrow, Rivka, John the Baptist will be in Galilee. Go with your brother to the fish market. On the way, John will baptize you in the name of the Father, the Son, and the Holy Spirit." Mary of Magdalene again braced Rivka's shoulders. "Go now, take your wares to the Chorazin market. Your Earthly father, Jacob of Capernaum, wants you to sell all to Batoum. He has lost respect for your Earthly father. Batoum will try to cheat you. You now have the strength to resist him. Sell your wares to individuals. You have a new confidence. God will bless your business. Trust and obey." Mary of Magdalene braced Rivka's shoulders and kissed her forehead.

As Rivka walked back to her brother and their donkeys, she glanced at the Centurion observer. The Centurion looked back at her. They made eye contact. Rivka was taught to fear Roman soldiers, especially a Roman officer commanding the rank of centurion. Yet somehow, for an unknown reason, she couldn't look away. She held her gaze.

Unknown thoughts rushed through Magnus. From the age of eight, Magnus's parents sent him to Rome's most elite military academy. He briefly recalled his experiences. Here, he was sequestered from all females. *'I know nothing of this thing they call love. My only love is loyalty and duty to Rome. Yes, I have fond memories of the academy. I won awards for horsemanship, and I could beat everyone in the class at hand-to-hand combat.'* Magnus smiled at a memory. The other cadets and teachers cheered and shouted as he pinned an older, more advanced cadet to the ground and was declared the victor. *'I also earned top grades in the language arts, Roman history, and military tactics. But what of this woman? What is this oddity that threatens to overcome me?'* Magnus looked away from her and watched the dispersing crowd.

It took a split second for Rivka to note that the centurion was a handsome and strong man. *'His eyes are even-set, brown, rich and bold. No. No. Look away. Look away. I was warned to keep a low profile with the Romans. But he is so different.'* Rivka got a flashback of her father, Jacob of Capernaum. *'"Fail to be a virgin on the day that I give you into marriage, and I will cast the first stone to put you to death."'* Rivka turned her head and joined her brother Samuel. The holy spirit had filled her with the love of God and his son Yeshua. She understood the sororal love of his close follower and disciple, Mary of Magdalene. *'But what of this forbidden mystery? This mystery of love is still greater than the mystery of death.'*

***

Centurion Magnus returned to his home. As a high-ranking officer, he had earned a sturdy brick home. It featured Doric columns and an arch entrance to a central courtyard, topped with a decorative keystone. He had three servants with whom he seldom spoke. A guard opened a wrought iron gate of spiked bars. After entering, he stood in his courtyard and felt a strange loneliness. *'Legatus Octavio had briefed me that as a Centurion on the rise, political and social dealings with the high command and the Roman administration would prove as valuable as battlefield conquest. He told me a wife who could serve and entertain the higher-ups would prove invaluable. He then pictured Rivka. 'That young woman had such beautiful, intriguing eyes. I could see through them to her inner beauty and strength. But for a centurion to take a Jewish girl of ordinary status as a wife? That would not go well with the high command.'* He forced her image out of his mind. *'I must prepare my briefing for the Legatus. What of this man, Yeshua? Do I report that he is just a teacher? Yet something about his lessons went beyond just teaching. Optio Flavius thought he taught submission to Roman rule. I will report that to Legatus Octavio. Yet I sense something far deeper than that. I just can't put it in words.'*

***

The Chorazin market featured merchant stalls with technicolor fabric canopies. Depending on the wind direction, one could smell various spices and cooked meat or the sweat and manure of livestock. The bleating of sheep and goats competed with the merchants hawking their wares. A crowd had gathered around a stall belonging to a tall, blonde-haired man from the North selling beer. Others gathered around a black-skinned merchant from the South selling garments made of wildlife skins. Batoum had a drawn face and sunken eyes. He turned to his assistant and pointed, "Here comes Rivka and Samuel of Capernaum. They once made the finest pottery in Judaea. Now that their patriarch is a drunkard, their quality has declined. Jacob used to bargain with us directly. Now, he stays home, imbibes wine, and sends his son and daughter. Their wares are still high quality." Batoum smirked. "Watch me undercut them."

Samuel pointed. "There's Batoum. Father wants us to sell everything to him."

"Let's have faith and trust." Rivka turned to him. "We can do better selling individually than everything to that mammon."

"I don't like Batoum either. But father has dealt with him for years."

"We'll give him a chance." Rivka nodded. "But I am going to trust my spirit of discernment."

"Shalom Batoum." Samuel greeted the dealer. "Here are our wares. The quality is as fine as ever. Yet I will sell at the same price of ten denarii."

"The quality of your pottery has fallen, Samuel." Batoum grabbed a vase and held it up. "So plain and basic. What happened to the artistry? I will give you five denarii."

Samuel blanched.

Rivka stepped forward. "Our deal is ten-denarii."

"Our deal?" Batoum laughed. "You show me a written contract. We had no bargain. Ten-denarii is the usual price, not the agreed-on price." Batoum frowned. "Now I will only pay Five-denarii. Take it or leave it." He shoved Rivka by the arm.

"You will neither touch me again nor get any of our wares." Rivka prodded.

"Such a gorgeous young lady. Jacob will one day get a big dowry for you." Batoum leered at her. "He better act soon before his foolish little girl squanders her virtue and his money. That's assuming he doesn't drink it away first."

Rivka squared her shoulders and cocked her hand to slap him. She then recalled Yeshua's words, *"Blessed are you when people insult you, persecute you, and bear false witness against you because of me. Rejoice and be glad because great is your reward in Heaven."* Rivka grabbed Samuel by the arm and led him away.

"Now what, Rivka?" Samuel raised his palms. "We can't go home empty-handed."

"Have faith and trust, Samuel. I will take one donkey to the stand of those blond men. Their draught has put the people in a festive mood. I will sell them there."

"I will sell the other donkey load by Ethiopians." Samuel nodded to Rivka. "Their exotic garments are attracting much attention."

***

Samuel and Rivka arrived at their home. They lead the donkeys into their stalls before going inside the atrium. Jacob lay on his side with a jug of wine. "Did you get me my ten-denarii?"

Rivka then handed him twenty denarii. "Are you pleased, father?"

"You smug, insolent young woman." Jacob sat up. "How dare you show me up?"

Samuel stood in front of her.

Jacob secured the Roman coins and then gulped more wine. He slept.

**

Rivka gazed into her mirror. Her olive eyes gleamed back at her. She shook her head. Long, thick, honey-colored hair cascaded about. She smiled at her reflection. *'What a blessing to have straight, white teeth.'* She grabbed her lyre, strummed it, and sang the Hallel of Psalms 113-118. Suddenly, she felt a light shine on her. She closed her eyes and let its radiance of love fill her. She then got a vivid flashback of Mary of Magdelene telling her that *'Yeshua would willingly pay the ultimate price for us to gain eternal life.'* Rivka then sang Isaiah 53:5 to the melody of the Hallel. "He was pierced for our transgressions; he was crushed for our iniquities; upon him was the chastisement that brought us peace, and with his wounds, we are healed."

Chapter 4

Rivka placed her fingers on a clay lump spinning on a foot-operated wheel. Each of her precise kneads shaped what was once a lump into a vase boasting elegant curves. She already planned its ornamental finishes.

"Rivka. That looks wonderful! Your artistry is why we live well." Hannah then handed Rivka three silver coins. "But today is market day in Galilee. I know that you can do as well buying fish and bread as you did selling our pottery. You and Samuel can take one of the donkeys.

***

The road from Capernaum to Galilee was made of compacted soil and gravel. Each of their donkey's steps raised a cloud of dust. After an hour-long trek, Rivka and Samuel reached the top of a berm. The wind wafted in the scent of fresh water. "Look down there at the sea." Samuel pointed down the road. "A commotion."

Rivka beamed. "That must be him! John the Baptist."

As Rivka approached the gathering, she felt trepidation. *'He looks like a wild man. His scruffy beard and wild eyes scare me. But Mary of Magdelene sent me to him. I will trust her.'*

"Repent!" John the Baptist yelled as he dunked a young man in the Sea of Galilee. "I baptize you with water for repentance. The one more powerful than I has arrived. I am not worthy to carry his sandals. He is here to baptize you with the Holy Spirit and fire. I baptize with water." John the Baptist walked onto the shore. "You! Woman!"

23

Rivka stood among a crowd of over a hundred people. Her nerves jittered. She slumped and pointed to herself, silently mouthing, "Me?"

"Yes! You! Rivka! Mary of Magdelene had sent you to me. You have received the one far greater than me. Come. You are blest among women."

Rivka raised her head and pushed her shoulders back as she marched to the river. *'His wild eyes now reflect a strange serenity. The man has true faith and awe for the son.'* Rivka walked into the water and stood next to him.

John placed his hand on Rivka's forehead and back. "I baptize you in water. Rivka. Do you repent and believe in the only one who can forgive and cleanse you of sin?"

"Yes."

John the Baptist then dunked her into the Sea of Galilee and then quickly lifted her.

The water felt cool and cleansing.

"Bother Samuel. Do you repent and believe?"

Samuel stood still for five seconds. He then approached John the Baptist.

"Your sister will face danger. Protect her." John the Baptist then baptized Samuel in the Sea of Galilee.

Rivka and Samuel embraced. "We are baptized." Samuel then looked into her eyes. "As your older brother, I will fulfill his command to look after you."

"You have always been a good brother and you have always protected me." Rivka smiled and nodded.

"I am afraid that father is falling deeper into drunkenness and anger." Samuel placed his hands on his hips. "We must always pray for him. Yet may God forgive me for saying this. He is becoming a danger to you and Mother."

Rivka pursed her lips. "He gets crueler and more erratic by the day." She embraced Samuel. "You are not just my brother by birth. You are now my brother in the Messiah."

Rivka and Samuel stood next to each other and watched John baptize many others.

***

The market at Galilee featured a variety of big and small freshwater fish. Small, colorful boats were moored in the shallow water or dragged up on the beach. The aroma of warm, freshly baked bread mingled with fish preserved in salt or spiced with coriander, cumin, dill, and mint. Rivka and Samuel walked through the rowdy crowd and negotiated the best prices for bread and salted and dill-spiced fish. They then loaded them into the donkey's panniers and headed for Capernaum.

After about an hour into their return journey, the traffic of pedestrians and domestic animals briskly moved aside. Optio Flavius rode on horseback with six miles-ranked soldiers on foot. "You two." He pointed his pilum spear at Rivka and Samuel. "Don't you know to move aside for a Roman patrol?"

Rivka and Samuel stopped and looked at him with blank expressions.

"Just so you remember next time. You two can carry their loads." He then looked at their donkey's saddle bags. "Give me a piece of that bread and a salted fish."

Rivka handed Him a loaf of bread and salted coriander and spiced mint-spiced fish.

Optio Flavius and one of his foot soldiers then handed Rivka and Samuel their personal items. Rivka had to stoop over to carry the burden. Dust and road grit clung to her sweat. The entire time, she sang hymns and praises. Samuel had to balance the items on his shoulders and secure them with his left hand as he led their donkey with his free hand.

"All right. The mile is up." Optio Flavius again pointed his pilum at them. "Put the load down and continue. Next time, make way for a Roman patrol.

"No Optio." Rivka looked up at him. "Let me bear your burden for another mile. Take another loaf of bread from our donkey."

Optio Flavio's jaw dropped, and his lips circled. "So, you're a follower of that Rabbi from Nazareth. Very well then. Carry it another mile, and I will take another piece of fish along with that loaf of bread.

Centurian Magnus galloped on his horse to the scene.

"Attention!" Optio Flavius shouted. The miles-ranked soldiers came to attention, punched their chests, and raised their right arms.

"Optio Flavius." Centurion Magnus looked at him sternly. "What's this all about?"

"These two were too slow to make way for our patrol." Optio Flavius sat at attention in his saddle. "It's our law that they must carry our loads for a mile if we so demand."

"I know Roman law. What I want you to tell me is why you, as a trained and conditioned Roman Optio, must have a woman bear your burden."

Optio Flavius did not respond.

"You." Magnus pointed to the Optio. "Get off your horse. This woman shall ride it the rest of the way to her home."

"But Centurion."

"Are you challenging my orders?"

"No Centurion Magnus." Optio Flavius vaulted from his horse. "Never." He punched his chest and raised his right arm.

Magnus and Rivka's eyes met. "Let me help you onto the Optio's horse." He then took her hand. He only used a custodial touch to help her mount the horse. Yet, never had he appreciated the sensation of something so soft and so delicate yet with just the right firmness. "

"No Centurion." She pulled her hand away and began to dismount the horse. "I can walk."

"The horse can walk better. I can see that my men exhausted you."

Rivka looked at him. *'His brown eyes look soft, nothing like a battle-hardened Centurion.'* She allowed the Centurion to boost her onto the sella saddle.

Magnus rode next to her, holding the reigns of the Optio Flavius's horse.

Rivka relaxed. *'What is this feeling that's come over me? I don't fear this man. I feel safe and secure.'*

Magnus looked at Rivka. *'What is this strange feeling?'* Ultra-masculinity marked his entire life. *'I have known women before. Why does this one make me feel complete? I must protect her.'*

Rivka felt drawn to him like an incoming tide of the Great Sea to the sand. She looked to her right. *'His jaw is so rugged. His Roman nose is so well centered.'* His galea helmet with an ornate, red-dyed horsehair crest enhanced his features. She jerked her head forward. *'What can I say to him? Do I tell him of Yeshua and his message of grace and salvation? Something good about Rome such as aqueducts and well-constructed roads, or that the Roman patrols kept the robbers at bay. Yes, the soldiers were often bullies, but they're far better than the highway robbers.'*

Magnus glanced at Rivka. Her wet garment clinging to her body didn't escape his notice. He saw the grandeur of her honey-colored hair at the edges of her veil. *'I am a Roman Centurian, not a miles-soldier. What can I say to this young Jewish woman that befits my rank?'* Magnus closed his eyes and spoke. "I am Centurion Magnus. What is your name?"

Rivka's voice felt more like a squeak. "Rivka." She took a deep breath. "Why so kind to me?"

"I am a Centurion. I am to uphold the dignity and professionalism of my rank. What my Optio did was legal but unbecoming." He turned to her. "I saw you at the gathering by the hill. What do you make of that man?"

Rivka closed her eyes. Rather than darkness, she saw light. "He is truly the son of God. He brings us spiritual salvation."

"You never heard him challenge the authority of Rome?"

Rivka smiled. "He speaks of an authority higher than anything on Earth."

"I will try to understand. He is gathering quite a following. Yet he doesn't speak of sedition." Magnus smiled at Rivka. "I saw you with pottery. Did you make them?"

"Yes." Rivka blushed and lowered her head.

"I am more than a killing machine, Rivka." Magnus chuckled. "As a centurion, I am also trained in the art, music, and culture of Rome. I noticed the craft and refinement of your wares."

"Thank you." Rivka blushed.

'I want to say it. I shouldn't. Be professional.' Magnus felt like he was outside of his body. He seemed to see and listen to himself from above. "You are not Roman, yet you're more beautiful than anything our mighty empire can boast. Even more beautiful than the statue of Venus de Milo."

Rivka blushed, dropped her head, and looked away.

"As a high-ranking officer in the Roman legion, I apologize to you."

Rivka raised her head, looked in his eyes, and smiled. "No. Not at all. It's just that, well, nobody has ever said anything so kind to me." She then lowered her head and frowned. "No one has ever even noticed me before."

"Surely you've noticed yourself."

Rivka saw a vision of herself looking in her bedroom mirror. "Yes." She looked away.

"Then you know that you are beautiful."

Rivka blushed. Magnus and Rivka spoke no further in voice until reaching Capernaum. "What is your brother's name, Rivka?"

"Samuel"

"Samuel. Help your sister from my Optio's horse."

After Samuel helped her down, Rivka and Magnus looked into each other's eyes. She then turned away, grabbed her brother's arm, and walked home. Her feet felt like dove feathers. *'I felt such a divine love after my baptism. But what of this Centurion? Magnus? Am I allowed these feelings? No. Father would have my death by stoning. But rather death than never feeling alive.'*

"I wish every Roman was as professional as that Centurion." Samuel led their donkey by its reigns. "Then Father and our neighbors wouldn't hate them so much. Unfortunately, scores of them earn our ire."

Rivka sensed that his actions were not just professionalism.

Centurion Magnus waited before following them just long enough to see where she lived.

***

29

Samuel unloaded the donkey and took the bread and fish to the kitchen. Hannah greeted him. "You're back." She smiled. "You and your sister did well with our money." She and Samuel put the fish and bread on the table. "I will put this away. You need to rest, Samuel. Tomorrow, go north of the Sea of Galilee and get ten shekels worth of clay."

"Shall I take Rivka?"

"No. We need Rivka's gift of craftsmanship. She shall stay here and finish making wares with our remaining clay."

***

Rivka tied the donkey to the hitching post. Jacob imbibed wine from a leather bota. He spotted Rivka in the stable and staggered toward her. "What is going on here? You're soaking wet!" He dug in his fingernails as he clutched her arm. "Look how your mantle clings to your body. You look like a harlot on display." His bloodshot eyes flared. His breath was wet with wine.

Rivka pleaded. "No, Father!" Her body and head shuddered. "I found the Messiah. John baptized me in the Sea of Galilee. I am cleansed of all sin and reborn in the Son of God." Tears streamed from her eyes. "Please listen to him. He is about love. And once you understand his message of love, mercy, and forgiveness, you will realize that not all Romans are bad."

"Not all Romans are bad? How dare you say that under my roof. You're a madwoman! And I have heard enough about that blasphemer from Nazareth." Jacob clenched his fists. "Now his heresy has spread to my own family?" He slapped her. "And how dare you let that wild man touch you? He's insane. He lives in the wilderness and eats locusts. You want cleansing of sin? I will now cleanse you of that blasphemer and his madman." Jacob clutched Rivka's hair

at the back of her head. "I hope this cleanses your madness."
He then dunked her head into the Donkey's water manger
and held her underwater.

Unlike the Sea of Galilee of John's baptism, the water
felt foul and fetid.

Jacob kept holding her head underwater.

Her shock devolved into terror. Her terror turned to
torture. Her lungs screamed for air. She flailed her arms to
no avail. Once the agony passed, she saw a gentle light. She
felt the blessed assurance of where she was going.

***

Magnus rode back to Jerusalem with Optio Flavius and
eight miles-ranked foot soldiers. Flavius trembled with each
glance at Magnus. He remained silent. Never looking to the
left or the right, Flavius thought, *'His expression is unusual.
He doesn't look angry. That's a good thing. He can have me
beaten or reduced in rank. But he looks wistful. After all, how
serious was my offense? It's a Roman soldier's right to have
a subject carry our load for a mile.'*

Magnus firmly gripped his spear and looked straight
ahead. He paid no attention to the timing of the civilians
getting out of their way. *'Rivka. Rivka. What is coming over
me? What is this feeling, Rivka? Do I fear you? Yes, I want
a son—someone to continue the glory of the Roman Army in
my name. But I see so much more Rivka. You're so healthy
and so beautiful. Yet your delicateness? I am just starting to
understand?'* Magnus tried to pay attention to his
surroundings. The danger of sniper arrows and Sicarii
ambushes were real. He breathed through his nose.
Remembering the scent of coriander and mint made him
again think of Rivka. He pictured her smooth, rich olive skin,
her light-olive eyes, and her luxuriant honey-colored hair. *'I*

have ventured to foreign lands and fearlessly fought Rome's
enemies. This is more powerful than any enemy or danger.'
"Optio. I leave the patrol in your hands. I am riding ahead.
"Hah." He prodded his horse with a light kick and galloped
ahead.

***

Samuel walked over to the stable to check on the
donkeys for the next day's journey. It took three seconds for
his mind to register what his eyes saw. "Father! Stop at
once!" Samuel ran into the stable, pulled his arm from
Rivka's head, and twisted it behind his back.

Rivka yanked her head from the water. She fell into a
small puddle on the dusty stable floor. Her world was a
twirling blur. Each gasp for air tasted ambrosial. "Thank you,
Yeshua. Thank you, Yeshua." The shouting between Samuel
and Jacob in the background sounded distorted. Rivka
managed to climb to her hands and knees. Still gasping, she
stood. Her garments and face were covered in mud and dust.
Her veil had fallen from her hair. Clumps of mud were caked
in her long tress.

Samuel restrained Jacob by twisting his arm behind his
back. Jacob yelled threats of stoning both him and Rivka.
"Rivka!" Samuel shouted. "Go to your room and move your
table in front of the door!"

Rivka sprinted to her room, slammed the door, and slid
a table across it. She looked at a reflection of the dirt, mud,
and moisture covering her clothes and face. Falling on her
bed face first, she bawled.

"Don't cry, my blessed and lovely one."

Rivka looked up. The sight stunned her. A woman with
wings of shocking white feathers and a matching white gown
stood before her. The gown's cut enriched the beauty of her

large, shapely breasts. She smelled better than a mythic flower garden. Rivka was taller than most women of Judaea, including Roman women. Yet this woman was even taller. Her shoulders were full, one-and-a-half times as wide as her hips. She wore no veil over her thick bounty of hair, blacker than a moonless midnight and flowing like a mountain stream weaving over smooth stones, coming to a textured end just above her heart-shaped buttocks. The width of her forehead was identical to her jaw before it angled to a chin curved to match her lower lip's vertical line. Her upper and lower lips of exact thickness were full and red as a blossoming azalea. A mid-sized celestial nose centered cheekbones that looked like cabochon cut gems placed under her blemish-free ivory white skin. Her raven hair eyebrows were as wide as her cheekbones and just high enough above her most striking feature. Set with an eye-width gap between them, her large almond-shaped eyes glowed blue like the sea on a mid-summer day. "Rivka, I am Isolde Maria. I am your guardian angel. Heaven sent me to watch over you and care for you." Isolde Maria extended her arm and offered her hand to Rivka.

Rivka couldn't help but feel soothing relief from her soft yet firm hand. She admired the perfect tone of her arm and the glisten of the gold band around her upper arm. "Isolde Maria? Such a strange name. I have never heard anything like it."

"I am from a place more splendid than your grandest imagination." Isolde Maria guided Rivka to her feet. "God has sent his son to pay the price for you to one day spend an eternity there with us. Our Father Yahweh gave me my name. An angel is created a step above a human. Yet your thick honey hair is the envy of even the angels."

"No! No! I look terrible." Rivka covered her face and cried.

Isolde Maria chuckled. "We're not going to let a little mud and dirt rob your beauty." Isolde Maria then showed her a gold comb embedded with a row of diamonds. She combed Rivka's hair.

Rivka at last breathed through her nose. Her nostrils were cleared of the vile manger water, mud, and dust. She inhaled deeply to imbibe every molecule of Isolde Maria's aroma, a fragrance unmatched even by a lavish garden of roses, lilies, and hyacinths.

Each delicate stroke dried and cleaned her hair. "There we go." Isolde Maria grasped Rivka's shoulders and turned her toward the mirror. "Have a look."

"Huh?" Rivka's hair was dry and clean. Her thick, honey-colored hair was fluffed like a lion's mane and glowed like heated bronze.

"We need not let a little grit and tears hinder your lovely face." Isolde Maria touched her fingertips to her tongue; she softly bent her wrist, and like an artist putting the final touch on her masterpiece, she caressed the contours of Rivka's face.

Rivka could not help but hold the Angel's wrist and nibble and kiss her fingers.

"Look in your mirror, my blessed Rivka."

Rivka beamed as her skin now glowed like fresh olives in the midday sun.

"And you should wear something pretty." Isolde Maria's fingertips next kneaded Rivka's dress. "Look Rivka."

"Huh?" Rivka beamed. She folded her hands and raised them to her face. "My clothes. So clean, dry, and colorful," She grinned and turned to Isolde Maria. "You've made me look so beautiful."

"That didn't take much work." Isolde Maria chuckled. "Our Father in Heaven has already gifted you with beauty."

"Why are you doing this for me?"

"The one who sent me teaches us wonderful things. Yeshua taught a parable of talents. One servant was given ten denarii; another servant was given five denarii, and the other just one. The wise servants double their master's money. The one whom one was given just one denarius hid it. When his master returned, he only had only one denarius. The master took his one and gave it to the servant with ten." Isolde Maria took Rivka's hands, "Rivka, our Father in Heaven gave you great talent. Your gifts far exceed what's given to most mortals. You were given much. Much is expected. I will look after you and help you achieve his will on Earth as it is in Heaven."

"I still don't understand." Rivka squeezed Isolde Maria's upper arms. Rivka's droopy eyes had formed tears. She gazed into Isolde Maria's eyes.

"You are new to the faith." Isolde Maria held Rivka's shoulders and returned her gaze. "Your savior Yeshua taught that new faith is like a mustard seed. The seed that falls in fertile soil grows many times larger. Other seeds fall in rocky soil and bear little fruit. Others have birds snatch away their mustard seed of faith and bear nothing." Isolde Maria smiled and nodded her head. "Heaven wants to do everything possible for your faith to blossom and bear a harvest of fruit."

"But my father, Jacob, has treated me so harshly."

"Your new battle is not against flesh and blood but against powers and principalities. Heaven has opposition.

Did you think Satan won't do everything possible to prevent the great works for which you are destined?"

"But my father?" Rivka raised her palms. "He is always drunk and can be so cruel."

"Not everyone is destined to know our Lord. Some harden their hearts and refuse to see. Our Lord is a God of free will. I will do everything possible to help you and to protect you. Ultimately, the final decision to serve and obey our Lord is yours. You will influence many people. They will have to decide on their own whether to accept your message. Besides, Rivka, Yeshua said these words, "I did not come to bring peace on Earth. I did not come to bring peace, but a sword, for I have come to turn a man against his father, a daughter against her mother, a daughter-in-law against her mother-in-law. A man's enemies will be members of his household."

"My brother Samuel." Rivka smiled. "He received him and was baptized. I have already seen his growth. He is now standing up to my father Jacob's drunken abuse. If not for him, I may have drowned."

"Yes, Rivka." Isolde Maria pointed upwards. "Samuel's name is now written in the Lamb's Book of Life."

Rivka shrugged.

"Don't worry." Isolde Maria chuckled. "That will be revealed to you at a later time." She again held Rivka's shoulders and gazed into her eyes. "In the meantime, know that I am your Angel, and I love you with all of the power given to me from above." Isolda Maria then pointed to Rivka's berry and oil mixture on her table. "I think we can better that.

"But your lips are so perfect and beautiful." Rivka smiled and raised her hands. "And redder than fine rubies." Rivka placed her hands on Isolde Maria's shoulder. Their arms entwined. "I need berries and oil." Rivka smiled and shook her head. "How do you do you make your lips so lovely?"

Isolde Maria chuckled and smiled. "I am an Angel. Yahweh created my lips this way. Would you like lips like mine?"

Rivka blushed. "What girl wouldn't? They're gorgeous, Isolde Maria."

Isolde Maria embraced Rivka. Rivka returned her embrace. Isolde Maria then planted a long, closed-mouth kiss on Rivka's lips. "How red and lovely your lips." She pointed to the mirror.

Rivka beamed at the sight of her lips, now red as dahlias.

"We can move this table from the door. The excess wine made your father unconscious. He is not called. Your mother, Hannah, wants to visit." Isolde Maria looked at the table. Suddenly, it moved away by itself. "Your mother may want to hear what you have learned." Isolde Maria winked. "Goodbye, for now, my precious Rivka." Isolde Maria and Rivka exchanged and final embrace and kiss. "Always know that I am with you and looking out for you." Isolde Maria then vanished.

Rivka sat by her table. Although never moving from her chair, she felt herself rise. She said to herself, *'I feel like a dove feather floating in the wind but under God's guidance and direction.'* She again admired her reflection in the mirror, but rather than vain pride, she felt gifted and chosen. She knelt and braced her elbows on her bed. *'Much is expected of me. I accept, dear Lord.'*

Rivka then heard a knocking on the door. "It's me, Rivka."

"Come in, Mother,"

Hannah gasped at the sight of Rivka. "Samuel told me what happened. I expected you to be filthy and messy. But you are clean and dry and more beautiful than I have ever seen you. But I see more than just physical beauty. You radiate. You look like you were kissed by an angel."

Rivka chuckled. "Yes, Mother. The Messiah is truly here, and he can send angels to protect us, guide us, and bless us. An angel did visit me, and she kissed me."

"Rivka. I want what you have. How can I come to believe in Yeshua of Nazareth?"

"Take my hands, Mother." Rivka reached out to Hannah. They held hands. "Mother, will you take Yeshua into your heart and be born anew in his spirit."

Hannah squeezed Rivka's hands and looked into her eyes. "I do."

"Do you repent of your sins and accept the cleansing and forgiveness of Yeshua?"

"I do." Hannah squeezed her daughter's hands. Rivka glowed. Hannah then felt herself rise. It was not just her daughter but a powerful spirit swathing them both.

"Please stay with me, mother." Rivka pecked Hannah's lips. "I love you. Let's grow in him together."

"Rivka, you are the apple of my eye. You have been the apple of my eye since long before your birth. Now, I see you as God sees you. I am overwhelmed. I can't protect you like the angels can protect you. But just as Moses's mother had to give up her son to save him by floating him away in a basket. Rivka." Hannah closed her eyes and wept. "Your father, Jacob, has terrible things planned for you. You must soon leave. Run from here. I know that you have nowhere to go, and Judaea is a dangerous place for women alone." She hugged Rivka. "You will need our savior's hand and guidance now more than ever."

Rivka then squeezed her mother's hands. "Yeshua taught us this prayer. Let us pray together." Rivka and Hannah both went on their knees and faced each other. "Our Father, in Heaven, hallowed be your name. Your kingdom come, your will be done, on Earth as it is in Heaven. Give us this day our daily bread. Forgive our debts, as we have forgiven our debtors. And lead us not in temptation but deliver us from the evil one."

Hannah again embraced her daughter. "Thank you, Rivka, and thanks be to God in Heaven. I can see part of his vision for you. Rivka, for the first time in years,' Hannah beamed. "I feel good about the future."

Chapter 5

Rivka worked behind her potter's wheel. As the clay spun, her fingers put the finishing touches on her prize vase. Its curves and contours made it a refined craft rather than a utensil. Next, she sculpted two heart-shaped arms and attached them to its sides. Skilled needle and tweezer work added artistry and ornamentation. She sat back and admired her vase. *'Even Father would have to say something good about this. I wish I could keep it. But it will make us good money at the market.'*

Jacob glanced at the workshop to ensure that Rivka and the hired help were working. He had rationalized the worst of what he had done to his daughter the day prior. *'She looks strangely at peace, and her work habits are better than ever. It looks like my baptism cleansed her of the evil influence of the blasphemer and his mad baptizer.'*

Rivka spotted her father peering into the workshop. She gasped and turned pale. Suddenly she saw an image of her angel, Isolde Maria, replete with warm smile and soft blue eyes. *'I am here Rivka. I will always protect you.'* Jacob then left. Rivka sighed. The Holy Spirit comforted Rivka. She focused on her vase, using incisions to add an intricate floral design to it.

***

Optio Flavius met with tax collector Manchon. "Manchon. Do you have my list of delinquencies?"

"Yes. Here are my records. Only minor violations."

"I see that the potter, Jacob of Capernaum, has shorted Rome." Optio Flavius tapped the scroll. "We must also pay Joseph the baker and Isaac the butcher a visit." Flavius then turned his focus to Manchon. "Don't worry, Manchon. You will get your share. Inside information that advances the interests of Rome is always rewarded."

Manchon then smirked. "This Jacob of Capernaum, the potter, he brings guests into his home and rails to them against Roman taxes."

"If I were to arrest every Jew who rails against Roman taxes, we would fill the Antonia Fortress ten times over." Flavius placed the butt of his spear into the ground and leaned on it. "Are people listening to him?"

"He's not wealthy, but he's better off than most in Capernaum." Manchon nodded his head, "So, he does wield influence in the community."

"We'll be back, Manchon." Flavius raised his spear to port arms. "We will give you your share.

***

Optio Flavius rode on a tan horse with a white blaze on his muzzle and forehead. Six miles-ranked foot soldiers joined him. A foot soldier kicked open the gate to Jacob's compound. Jacob ran from the main dwelling.

"Jacob of Capernaum." Flavius rode up to Jacob. "You have underpaid your obligation to Rome. I am here to collect what you owe."

"But I have no more money to give you."

"That doesn't surprise me." Flavius dismounted his horse. "By the smell of your breath and the glaze in your eyes, I can tell that you spent all your money on wine. It's not medius dies and you're drunk already." Flavius then put his armored chest to Jacob's chest. "Did you think you can drown out your obligation to Rome with drink?" Flavius made sure that Jacob could smell the garlic on his breath. "You're a well-known potter. Take me to your workshop.

41

Perhaps you can pay what you owe to Rome in merchandise."

Rivka and a hired helper gasped as the soldiers entered. Samuel was away in Galilee buying clay. Hannah was in the kitchen.

"That should be sufficient." Flavius pointed to a shelf with three ceramic jugs, ten ceramic bowls, and ten ceramic plates. "Soldiers. Secure those items for Rome."

Jacob seethed as the soldiers took his wares. He narrowed his eyes and grimaced at the soldiers.

Flavius then pinned Jacob against the wall and pushed the edge of his spear shaft against his chest. "I can see by your expression that you don't like paying your fair share to Rome." Flavius scowled at him. "Do you care to say it out loud to me?" He sprayed spittle in Jacob's face.

"No dominus."

"So, what you're saying is that you decided to love Rome?"

"Yes, dominus." Jacob squeaked and dropped his head.

"I can't hear you!" Flavius jammed his spear shaft deeper into his chest. "And look at me when I speak to you!" He scowled. "And when you speak to me!"

Jacob spoke up. "Yes, dominus." He looked directly at the Octio.

"Yes, what?

"Yes, dominus. I love Rome."

You choose wisely Jacob of Capernaum." Flavius then shoved him to the ground. "Always remember," Flavius prodded, "that the walls have eyes and ears. Change your mind about your feelings for Rome, and I will be back. And next time, it will prove even more unpleasant."

As they left, something on Rivka's table sparked a miles-ranked soldier's interest. He snatched Rivka's prize vase and put it in his personal bag.

Five minutes later, after he ensured that the soldiers were long gone, Jacob screamed, "Romans! Yahweh, if you exist, smite them all!" He flipped over a table and threw a chair against the wall.

Hannah entered. Jacob could feel her scanning his disheveled clothes and dirty face. He looked at her. *'She's looking at me as less than a man. A nabal.'* His humiliation turned to anger. "And you, woman!" He prodded, "Stop looking at me that way. And what are you doing here anyway?" He waved his arms. "Go back to where you belong." He then lurched over and struck her with an overhead punch to her back. Hannah fell to her knees. Jacob stomped on her shoulder blades, forcing her face into the dust. He then stormed from the room.

"Mother!" Rivka ran to her. She dropped to her knees and cradled and hugged her mother. They cried together.

***

Centurian Magnus started his day in his private gymnasium. His routine began with lifting boulders over his head and swinging sandbags. He topped it off with various push-ups and chinning movements. His dedication to fitness helped advance him in the ranks of the Roman army. His physique surpassed that of the sculpted musculature of his breastplate. Often, he would wrestle and defeat the best wrestlers in his legion. After his workout, one of his servants prepared him a breakfast of lamb, bread, goat's milk cheese, and nuts. Magnus then rode his white horse to the Aelia Capitolina fortress compound. His first order of the day was to inspect the barracks of his legion.

"Attention!" Optio Flavius shouted before punching his chest and extending his right arm.

Magnus returned the salute.

The soldiers in the barracks stood at rapt attention in front of their living areas. "Hail!" They yelled in unison as they punched their chests and extended a stiff right arm.

Magnus said little as he walked the floor until something caught his eye. A miles-ranked soldier had something hidden in his footlocker. "You!" Magnus pointed at the soldier. "Show me that item." The soldier's hand jittered as he handed an ornamental vase to the centurion.

Magnus examined it. "Where and how did you get this? Your answer will decide the severity of your punishment."

"I got it from Capernaum." The soldier clenched his teeth.

"From the workshop of Jacob, I take it."

"Dominus," Flavius interjected. "Jacob of Capernaum was delinquent in his taxes. We took his wares as payment."

"I am well aware of our tax collecting procedures, Flavius." Magnus turned to the soldier. "Miles, how did this get in your personal effects?"

The pallid soldier remained silent; only his jaw chattered.

"You didn't just steal this item from a subject. You, in effect, stole it from Rome." Magnus hunched his shoulders and craned his head toward the soldier. "Do you have something to say for yourself?"

"I'm sorry, Centurion Magnus. I was wrong."

"What you did is often done. That doesn't make it right and I will not tolerate bringing down the glory of Rome by common theft."

The soldier squeezed his urethra to no avail.

"One of our horses died yesterday. It's already on a cart. You," He prodded at the soldier, "get a shovel from the storeroom, take the horse outside of the compound, and bury it."

***

Centurian Magnus took four soldiers as a security detail and rode to Capernaum.

Jacob first spotted the Centurion enter his compound. Jug of wine in hand, he ran to his bedroom and hid in a closet.

"Oh my!" Hannah put her hands over her face. "It's not just soldiers. A Centurion is here."

Rivka's face illuminated. Her eyes opened wide as spiral galaxies. She ran to the window. *'It's him! It's him!'* The thought made her smile wider than her eyes.

Magnus dismounted his horse and entered the workshop. "Shalom aleichem. Fear not. I am here to restore the honor of Rome. One of my legionnaires stole this from you." Magnus pulled Rivka's vase from his sarcina bag and handed it to Rivka.

Rivka smiled; her teeth flashed like sunbeams. "Thank you." She took the vase from him and placed it on the shelf. She then turned to look at him. Her hand accidentally brushed against his arm. Her first thought was to grab his arm and hold it, to feel the ripples and contours of his muscles. She rather stood with her arms to her side and gazed into his eyes.

Magnus returned her gaze. *'She's even more beautiful than last I saw her. No. No.'* He forced his arms to his side, fighting the urge to embrace her.

Hannah placed her hand on her chin, noticing how her daughter and the Centurion looked at each other. *'This can't happen. Her father would have her stoned. But what if he loves her? A centurion wields more power than any Jew. In that case, Jacob would not dare do anything against her. But a gentile? No. Not my daughter.'* Hannah then closed her eyes and prayed. *'Yeshua. This is my first prayer to you. Give me understanding.'* Hannah felt a floating sensation. *'You have spoken. The Messiah is here. He has come to save all of mankind. We are no longer Jew or Gentile but one in Messiah Yeshua.'*

Rivka and Magnus simultaneously reached out and touched hands for a brief and fleeting second before a hasty retraction.

Hannah smiled. "Centurion. Won't you stay for lunch?"

Magnus looked at Hannah. He could sense her sincerity. He turned to Rivka. Her eyes looked brighter than polished emeralds. "Yes. Adonit. I accept your offer of kindness and hospitality." He then returned his gaze to Rivka. "That vase is true artistry. Please don't sell it in the market. I would like to proudly display it in my home. Would you accept my offer of ten denarii?"

Rivka and Hannah beamed at each other.

Rivka's arm quivered. *'Should I take his hand and lead him to our dining room.'* Rivka nodded her head toward the door. "Let me show you to our dining room."

Hannah dropped her jaw. *'A Centurion is to be feared. How is this all possible?'*

Rivka, Hannah, and Magnus lounged by their low dining table. A servant served them a meal of lamb, hummus, figs, and barley bread.

"Adonit."

Hannah held up her palm and outstretched arm. "Please call me Hannah."

The centurion chuckled. "And you can call me Magnus. The meal is delicious. I thank you."

"It's humble. After all, as a Centurion, you get to enjoy the best food in the land."

"In that, you are correct." Magnus smiled at Hannah. "Do lions on the savannah savor their food? Or is it just an act of instinct and survival? You have prepared a meal with love and care. You made it something far more satisfying than just food."

Hannah blushed. "Each moment I am around you, I realize that you are more than just a brute Roman soldier."

"Mother. Magnus is educated in the highest of Roman art, music, literature, and culture." Rivka beamed. "I am sure that he can appreciate the refinement of your cooking."

'Have they talked before?' Hannah wondered.

"Rivka, Hannah, this afternoon was like no other in my life." Magnus stood. "A Roman centurion, the Roman Army in general, is to be feared and to inspire fear among the civilians. My lower-ranking soldiers fear me and must address me with the utmost reverence. When everyone fears you, one tends to lose their humanity. That sense of elevated ego and self-esteem turns to isolation and loneliness. Your inner strength, presence, and, how do I say it? Your Love? Humanity? I am hardened from battle and have killed men without mercy."

Rivka and Hannah blanched.

"What is this notion of compassion?" Magnus lowered his shoulders and eased his arms. He felt his voice lower; it even seemed to stumble, although he did not stutter so much as a syllable. "What you have shown me has touched me in a way that I cannot fathom. I hope soon to understand."

Rivka looked at her mother and then to Magnus. "We understand that you are a brave soldier and leader of men.

What you must do in battle is not you." Rivka walked over and looked into Magnus's eyes. "My mother and I understand. We have come to know the true living God. Our hearts and minds are opened to love, compassion, and forgiveness as never before."

"I have heard him. What he teaches is not what our Roman Gods stand for. We are taught vengeance, boldness, and ferocity. You have only one God; he is starting to make sense to me." Magnus then snapped his posture rigid and straight, put his helmet on, and then tipped it to Hannah and Rivka. "I must go now."

After Magnus mounted his horse and galloped away, Rivka ran to the window. She watched him until he faded from sight. She then turned to her mother. Hannah looked softer and gentler than she ever remembered, even as a child.

Hannah saw a gleam in her daughter's eyes that she had never seen.

Mother and daughter looked at each other for the longest three seconds of their nearly two decades together. They ran into each other's arms and embraced.

***

Jacob sat in the corner of his closet. He had finished the jug of wine, placed the empty vessel between his legs, and slept.

***

That night, Rivka took a parchment she had saved for two years. She had a brush made from animal hair. Using charcoal in a dish, she drew a portrait of the Centurion. She held it up to her eyes and stared. She kissed the portrait before hiding it.

Centurion Magnus stood alone in the main room of his house. Here, eight trophies for wrestling and athletics, as well as ten campaign medals and six crowns for valor and bravery, were on display. He shoved his two highest awards aside. He held Rivka's prize vase in front of him. His imagination transformed the vase into Rivka's face of perfect balance, thick honey hair, and alluring olive eyes. He kissed the vase before putting it on the shelf between his Corona Civica crowns.

***

Hannah opened her bedroom closet. She gasped. Her husband sat unconscious in the corner of the closet. She closed her eyes and recited Proverbs 26:17 "For it is written, like one who grabs a stray dog by the ears is someone who rushes into a quarrel not their own." Hannah slowly and cautiously took the empty wine jug from Jacob's hands. She took it to the kitchen and filled it with wine. She then held her breath, put it beside him, and slowly closed the closet door.

Chapter 6

Centurions Magnus, Longinus, and Camillus stood by the marble table in the Fortress Aelia Capitolina war room. "Hail!" The Centurions shouted and extended their right arms as the Leganus Legionus Octavio entered the room. He stood in front of the table for four seconds before motioning for the Centurions to sit. "Centurion Longinus, our Prefect, Pontius Pilate, is going to personally reward you. Our frumentari gave you effective information on the location of the Sicarii cell. It was your command and personal valor that killed two of them and arrested two others. Those two will be publicly crucified on the hill at Golgatha alongside Barabbas. They will serve Rome as an example and warning to anyone who sympathizes with their subversion and murder. You have done well, Longinus. You have again courageously and faithfully upheld order and furthered our mission to acquire riches and resources for Rome." Octavio slid his gold helmet topped with a crest of purple horsehair aside. "The Jewish Sanhedrin and Herod Antipas have the Prefect Pilate's ear, and, of course, Pilate reports directly to Ceasar. The Frumentari reports that this self-proclaimed Messiah is gaining more followers by the day. Magnus, your patrols have monitored his gatherings. What can you tell me?"

Magnus placed his hands on his helmet. "I can confirm your reports that, in appearance, he is an ordinary man. But to encounter him." Magnus raised his palms. "Leganus Legionus, there is nothing ordinary about him. He has a strength that goes well beyond physical might. His message is of an eternal kingdom, not of this world. He preaches peace, submission, and forgiveness. Yet, I can feel a unique presence. He commands the strength and authority of a powerful leader." Magnus raised his arms. "I wish I could tell you more, dominus. It surpasses my understanding. As a Centurion loyal to Rome and who places no other above Ceasar, I can report that his gatherings are peaceful. I have yet to hear him speak a word against Rome." Magnus relaxed his posture and kept eye contact with Octavio. "In my evaluation, Yeshua of Nazareth is no threat to Rome." Magnus nodded. "But I will watch him closely and keep you informed."

"I applaud the honesty and the depth of your report. Yes. I want you to learn more about this man and report what you learn to me. We must give Pilate an informed briefing. He needs to know the Roman outlook beyond the opinion of Pharisees." Octavio pointed at Magnus. "You are as strong and loyal a warrior as I have ever had the honor of commanding. I will trust the integrity and aptitude of your take on this Yeshua of Nazareth. If he does not speak against Roman authority, let him be. Keep the peace and order. The moment he talks subversion, rebellion, or uprising, arrest him immediately. Am I understood?"

"Yes, dominus!" Magnus punched his chest and extended his arm.

"Hail Ceasar!" Centurions Longinus and Camillus punched their chests and raised their arms.

"Our Frumentari informs me that he will speak in Galilee on the ninth hour. Magnus take Optio Flavius and a contubrium of eight miles ranked soldiers and monitor the situation. As a great crowd is expected, Centurion Camillus, I am having you join him. Take Optio Claudius and a contubrium of your choosing with you. Leave now. Time is short." Octavio stood. The Centurions then stood and remained at attention until he left the war room.

Hannah and a servant prepared a breakfast of fish, dates, cheese, and almonds. "Rivka. I got word that Yeshua is speaking in Galilee today. I want to go and see him with you."

"Yes!" Rivka beamed. "Thank you, mother! I wrote a song for him. Would you like to hear it?"

Oh, my beautiful daughter." Hannah walked over and placed her hand on Rivka's shoulder. "I would love to hear it. But don't you think our Lord and Savior Yeshua should hear it first?"

"What if he doesn't like it?" Her tenor then dropped. "But what about father? He hates him, and we have no reason to leave."

"He won't awaken anytime soon." Hannah chuckled. "Just in case, Samuel, I know that you also want to go with us. But I think it better you stay behind and deal with Father when he comes to."

"I understand, Mother." Samuel ate a piece of fish. "I will think of something. My new faith is helping me to better deal with him. I know how important this is to both of you. Leave now. It's a long walk."

As Rivka and Hannah were leaving, Samuel ran outside and grabbed Rivka's arm, pulled her aside, and spoke to her softly and with minimal lip movement. "It will be dark by the time you get back. I am concerned that the road after dark is not safe for two women." Samuel furtively scanned the surroundings. "Perhaps you can ask that kind Centurion to have some soldiers ensure your safety."

Rivka beamed before kissing her brother's cheek.

***

Word had spread throughout Judaea that Yeshua would appear in Galilee. The roads were jammed with pedestrians, donkeys, horses, and oxen carts. Goat herders and wagons loaded with live poultry added to the clamor. Ravens cawed and squawked as they jockeyed and swooped for discarded pickings. People brought their lame on wagons and led their blind in the hope that Yeshua would perform a healing miracle. "Move aside!" A horse-mounted Roman legionnaire brandished his riding crop as he pushed through the crowd. "Move aside!" A goat bleated his objection.

Rivka and Hannah did their best to trek on. At last, they saw what looked like thousands of people gathered beneath a hill. They moved through the crowd and ascended the bank. Rivka spotted Disciples Mathew, Phillip, and James. She could not find Yeshua. Mary Magdeline made eye contact with her and gestured for her. Rivka smiled and walked to her. Mary Magdeline hugged Rivka and then kissed her cheeks. "I am so glad to see you, Rivka. Our Lord is praying with Simon, Peter, and Andrew. He tells me that you wrote a song for him."

Rivka's mouth and eyes opened wide.

"Why are you surprised? Did I not tell you that he knows the number of hairs on your head." Mary smiled and stroked Rivka's hair. "In your case, that's a miracle in itself." She chuckled. "Our abacuses don't have enough beads to count that high." Mary Magdelene then held Rivka's shoulders. "There's at least 5,000 people here. They are growing restless. Won't you treat them to your song before our Lord speaks?"

Rivka blanched. "I don't know if my song is any good. No one has seen the words or heard it."

"He has seen it, and he has heard you sing it."

"But I've only sung it to myself, locked in my room."

Mary Magdeline chuckled. "The Son of Man sees and hears all." She nodded and blinked her eyes. "He wants you to sing it."

"Now. In front of all these people?" Rivka stepped backward.

"Yes, Rivka." Mary Magdeline beamed.

"I can't." Rivka fidgeted. Her hands trembled. "I'm not a singer. I only sing to myself or sometimes to my mother. I've never even spoken to a group of people, much less sang before so many people." Rivka shook her head. "No. Mary. I can't."

Hannah smiled and walked over to her. "You can."

Yeshua then appeared. He looked directly at Rivka and smiled.

Rivka felt her knees wobble. Within seconds, she felt her spirit strengthen. She stood tall and beamed at Yeshua.

Yeshua approached her and put his right hand on her shoulder. "Sing my song for me and my followers."

Disciple Andrew then handed her a lyre.

Mary Magdeline nodded to Yeshua, put her arm on Rivka's back, and directed her to face the crowd.

***

Centurions Magnus and Camillus strategically placed their soldiers around the parameter of the crowd. Optio Flavius sat on his horse next to Magnus. "This crowd is huge. There must be at least five thousand. They're growing restless. What if this Yeshua agitates them?"

"We have dealt with crowds this size before. We will deal with this one as well." Magnus pulled back the reins on his horse. "Do nothing until I command. For now, stand down. This Yeshua has yet to cause trouble for Rome."

"If he does," Flavius raised his dagger, "we know what to do."

"You are a well-trained and experienced soldier Optio. You know how to follow orders, and you know how to lead lower-ranking soldiers." Centurion Magnus looked directly at Flavius. "Stay alert."

***

Rivka breathed deeply. She stood still with her lyre as the throngs settled. She looked back at Yeshua, Mary Magdalene, and her mother.

***

"Dominus." Flavius pointed to the hill crest. "That tall woman with the lyre." He turned to Magnus. "Isn't that the woman that you let ride my horse?"

Magnus gasped. He stared at Rivka. He felt as if he and his horse could fly like Pegasus.

"Centurion…" Optio Flavius chose to remain silent. He stayed beside Magnus.

***

Rivka faced the crowd. She strummed the introductory notes on her lyre. Her audience quieted. She sang.

"Come and follow him."
"Open your eyes to a World of seeing."
"Come and follow him."
"He'll show you a whole new meaning."

"Hear what he has to say, let him show you the way."

"Trust in him and obey, and he will wash your sins away."

"See Heaven through the son, living waters soft and sweet."

"You will find eternal life, believe, and he will set you free."

"His love flows upon the shores of time, From oceans deep to mountains high."

"He'll lift your spirit far and wide; for his love is true and divine."

"The seed that he plants today, Tomorrow will grow into a tree."

"See Heaven through the son, living waters soft and sweet."

"You will find eternal life, Believe, and he will set you free."

"His love flows upon the shores of time, From oceans deep to mountains high."

"He'll lift your spirit far and wide; for his love is true and divine."

Rivka stood still before the silent crowd. Suddenly, they applauded and cheered with vigor and enthusiasm. Rivka smiled and nodded. She turned. Yeshua was in front of her. He touched her shoulders, smiled, and nodded. "Thank you, my child."

Rivka walked back to Mary Magdalene and her mother Hannah. She hugged her daughter. "How blessed you are, Rivka. You've been kissed by an angel and touched by the hand of God."

The crowd remained silent as Yesua stood alone on the hill to speak to them.

***

Rivka's singing made Magnus smile wider than when he received a medal for winning his military academy wrestling tournament.

"Centurion!"

Optio Flavius snapped him out of his reverie. His broad smile now embarrassed him. He felt guilty for not staying vigilant.

"Yeshua is about to speak."

"Listen to his words carefully, Flavius. Leganus Octio wants a full report on this man and this event."

***

The crowd silenced as Yeshua appeared to them on the hill crest. "I am the way, the truth, and the light. No one comes to the Father but by me…"

***

Optio Flavius turned to Magnus. "Did you hear what that man just said? Is he deluded or mad?" '*I am the truth, the way, and the light?*' Flavius raised his hands. "Are these people taking such a claim seriously?"

"That is irrelevant." Magnus turned to Flavius. "We must listen to him only to ensure that he is not instigating against Rome."

***

"for I speak to you the truth. The man who does not enter the sheep pen by the gate but climbs in another way is a thief and a robber. The man who enters by the gate is the shepherd of his sheep. The watchman opens the gate for him, and the sheep listen to his voice. He calls his sheep by name and leads them out. When he has brought out all his own, he goes ahead of them, and his sheep follow him because they know his voice. But they will never follow a stranger; in fact, they will run from him because they do not recognize a stranger's voice." Yeshua paused to give the crowd a moment to reflect and ponder his words. "Verily, I am the gate. All who ever came before me were thieves and robbers, but the sheep did not listen to them. I am the only gate; whoever enters through me will be saved." The crowd sat silent and in awe. "I am the good shepherd. The good shepherd lays down his life for his flock. The hired hand is not the shepherd who owns the sheep. When he sees the wolf coming, he abandons the sheep and runs away because he is only a hired hand and cares nothing for the sheep. I am the good shepherd; I know my sheep, and my sheep know me. And I know the Father- and I will lay my life down for my flock. I have other sheep in the pen. I must bring them also. They, too, will listen to my voice, and there shall be one flock and one shepherd. The reason my father loves me is that I lay down my life- only to take it up again."

***

"You heard him!" Optio Flavius turned to Magnus. "The wolves are Rome!" Optio Flavius raised his sword. "He's referring to the wolf that nursed Romulus and Remus, rescuing them to later find Rome and for Romulus to become our first king. The flock that he talks about are the Jews, and he's saying that if they don't rise, the wolf of Rome will devour them."

"Optio. A man who says to love your enemies, give your assailant your other cheek to strike, and carry a Roman soldier's load an extra mile is not talking uprising. Have you forgotten that young woman? The one who sang so fair and lovely? She offered to carry a load, heavy only for a fit soldier, an extra mile. Has that young woman not convinced you that this man and his followers are not agitating against Rome?" Magnus looked at Flavius with a focused gaze. "He speaks in parables and metaphors so all will listen and understand. He is talking spiritual matters and not political." Magnus pointed at Flavius. "How long have you been stationed in Judea?"

"Three years, dominus."

"Have you not learned by now that the Jews always quarrel among themselves over their scriptures? Yeshua is telling them that only he knows the true God."

"But Jupiter is the highest God, and we answer to Ceasar alone."

"Again, Flavius. Let the Jews and others believe what they want to believe as long as they obey the decrees of Ceasar and pay their taxes to Rome. Our duty to Rome is to keep the peace, not instigate rebellion." Magnus pursed his lips and set his eyes on Flavius. "You are a good soldier, Flavius. You have risen to the rank of Optio. Heed my words, and your military career will continue to rise."

***

"No one can take my life from me; I will freely give you my life. My Father has given me the power to lay down my life and to take it up again."

***

Three spectators stood. One of them raised his hands and shouted, "He's mad! He's insane!"

The other added, "He's demon-possessed! What sane man claims that he can rise from the dead?"

The third pointed to Yeshua, "He's a blasphemer. Someone silence this Heretic!"

"Shut your mouths!" A follower confronted them. "I saw this man give a blind man sight." He prodded the chest of a skeptic. "I had known that blind man. He had been blind since birth. Yeshua gave him sight."

Another follower remained seated but shouted, "I was at the pool of Bethesda. I saw this man make a lame and twisted paralytic person walk. Yeshua truly is the Son of God."

The three skeptics then marched over to Magnus and Flavius. "You heard him! He is mad. Arrest this demon-possessed heretic before he incites a riot."

Magnus dismounted his horse and confronted the skeptic. "Are you telling a centurion how to conduct his duty?"

The Skeptic blanched.

"The only unruly people in this crowd are you three." Magnus prodded. "I will, therefore, give you three choices. You can sit down and shut your mouths. You can silently walk away. Or you can continue to agitate, and I then take you to the Antonia Fortress jail in chains."

The three men slumped and said nothing.

"Wise choice." Magnus addressed them as they turned and trudged away.

***

Yeshua raised his open hands. "If the good shepherd has a hundred sheep, and one gets lost, would he not leave the ninety-nine to go and find the one that is lost? And when he finds his lost lamb, would he not carry it home on his shoulders and rejoice that he found it?

Rivka looked over and spotted Magnus on his horse. She bowed her head in prayer. "Oh Lord Yeshua, in the name of Father Yahweh, find this brave and noble Centurion, and like the lost lamb, bring him into your flock.

***

I tell you that in the same way that the good shepherd rejoiced, Heaven will rejoice more over one sinner who repents than over ninety-nine righteous people who do not need to repent. For I am as a vine; you are its branches. If a man remains in me and I in him, he will bear much fruit; apart from me, you can do nothing. If anyone does not remain in me, he is like a branch that is thrown away and withers; such branches are picked up and thrown into the fire and burned. If you remain in me and my words remain in you, ask, and you shall receive. For I am the bread of life. He who comes to me will never go hungry."

***

Disciple Thomas turned to Disciple Phillip, "We understand that he's talking about spiritual nourishment." Thomas raised his arms. "But this crowd, there must be 5,000 people; they are getting hungry. I wonder how many of them believe that our Lord will feed them actual bread? What if they get restless? I see two centurions and their soldiers. You know their tactics and how they will act to restore order."

Yeshua turned to them, "Where shall we buy bread for these people to eat?" He grinned and slowly shook his head.

"That will cost Eight Months wages!" Phillip shrugged his shoulders and raised his open hands. "Even eight months wages would not buy enough bread for everyone to even get one bite!"

"Look." Andrew, Simon Peter's brother, pointed. "Here is a boy with five small barley loaves and two small fish." He shrugged his shoulders. "How far will that go among all of these people?"

***

Centurion Camillus alerted his soldiers. "Be watchful. Don't do anything without my orders. The crowd is growing restless as they are hungry. This Yeshua promised them bread. If he doesn't deliver, we could have trouble."

***

"Optio Flavius. Put our miles-soldiers on alert. I will move closer to Yeshua and his disciples. Do nothing without my signal." Magnus then flashed the sun from his shield to Camillus. Camillus signaled back likewise.

***

"Have the people sit." Yeshua gestured to his disciples, Mary Magdalene, Rivka, and Hannah.

The disciples, Mary Magdalene, Rivka, and Hannah had the people sit on the soft grass in groups of fifty and a hundred.

"Bring me the five loaves and two fish." Yeshua closed his eyes and held the bread and fish aloft. He prayed. Next, he broke the bread and handed a piece to his disciples, Mary Magdalene, Hannah, and Rivka. "Feed my flock."

Each time the disciples, Mary Magdalene, Rivka, and Hannah handed out bread and fish, another serving appeared. Hannah and Rivka never felt more elated.

At the end, they picked up a dozen basketfuls of broken pieces of bread and fish.

Yeshua then left them, heading out alone to the mountains.

***

Centurion Camillus road up to Centurion Magnus. "I am astonished. I am still trying to fathom what I just saw. This man, Yeshua. He is the Son of God."

Magnus turned to him. "You mean like Hercules?"

"Yes and no. Hercules was born of Jupiter and the mortal woman Alcmena. Yeshua's father is Yahweh, and his mother is a virgin human. Yeshua is real. Do we have any proof that Hercules ever existed? Even Jupiter. Has anyone seen them? I now know that it's only myth and legend. Our Roman Gods go from prosaic to monstrous. No man can invent Yeshua. He is real and has performed a miracle before our eyes. Does Jupiter love us? Mars? Neptune? Has Venus ever appeared to us, or is she just a fantasy? I will continue to serve the Roman army as a Centurion. Nevertheless, I have found my true God." Camillus signaled to Optio Claudius and his other soldiers. They rode away.

Magnus scanned the peaceful and orderly crowd as they dispersed. He found who he was looking for. He spotted Rivka, walking with her mother and Mary Magdalene.

He rode up to Rivka and dismounted his horse. He saw that her eyes were open like stars. Her smile seemed affixed. "Rivka?"

"Magnus. You only saw a miracle? I didn't just see it; I participated in it. He is the Son of God, Magnus."

"Rivka." He braced her shoulders. "I saw it all, and I do not doubt that he performed a miracle. I can't yet figure out exactly what I just saw or what it means. I am a Roman and a Centurion. I am not yet ready to renounce our traditional Gods." He gazed into her eyes. "I do now see evidence of a loving, creating God. I see something fairer than even my Roman God of Love, Venus. Venus may or may not be a figment of Roman imagination. But like the miracle that I just saw Yeshua perform, one more lovely than Venus stands before me."

Both Magnus and Rivka stared into each other's eyes.

Magnus realized that people had noticed them. "Rivka, we can't talk here. Too many eyes and ears. Can you leave your house tomorrow at Midnight? Meet me outside the rear wall of your compound."

Rivka gasped. She blushed and lowered her head. She then raised her head and looked into his eyes. Her voice felt detached from her body. "Yes."

Magnus nodded and boarded his horse.

Mary Magdelene and Hannah had watched her and Magnus. Rivka walked over to them. The three of them embraced.

Magnus and Flavius then rode over to them. "Rivka, Hannah, it grows dark. The highway is no longer safe for women. Flavius. Accompany these two back to Capernaum. And this time Flavius, "you," He pointed at him, "can carry your own load." Magnus smiled. Rivka, Hannah, and Mary Magdelene laughed. Flavius pursed his lips and looked straight ahead.

***

Yeshua later joined his twelve apostles and Mary Magdelene. They walked together on the road to

Capernaum. Centurian Camillus rode up to Yeshua on his horse. He dismounted and confronted him. The apostles gasped and froze in place. Yeshua hand gestured to them to fear not.

"Yeshua, I have heard your words, and I have seen your miracles." Centurion Camillus opened his hands. "I renounce the Roman Gods. You are the true Son of God. I believe in you as my Lord." Camillus raised his right hand, palm facing forward. "I am often away on campaign. My maidservant is like a second mother to my children. My wife adores her. She now lies at home, suffering and paralyzed. I fear for her life."

Yeshua nodded to him. "I will go and heal her."

"Lord," Centurion Camillus replied. "I am unworthy to host you in my house. But just say the word, and my servant will be healed, for I am myself a man under authority, with soldiers under me. I tell this one, 'Go,' and he goes; and that one, 'Come,' and he comes. I say to a servant, 'Do this.' And he does it."

Yeshua opened his eyes wide and slightly dropped his jaw. He turned to his disciples and Mary of Magdalene, "I tell all of you the truth. I have not found anyone in Israel of such great faith." He then faced the Centurion. "Go! It will be done for you as you believed it would."

Centurion Camillus then galloped home to Capernaum. The sights and sounds of the road were fuzzy and blurry. He neglected to consider a Sicarii ambush. Briefly, the image of his maidservant dying and his wife and children crying beset him. He pictured Yashua and vanished the thought. At last, he arrived home. His wife greeted him with a broad smile. The sky seemed to have descended upon his home, casting an azure backdrop. His maidservant stood next to her; a gleam shined from her garment. She was holding hands with his son and his daughter, smiling and laughing.

Chapter 7

Herod Antipas, Roman tetrarch of Galilee and Perea, rode in his carriage next to his wife, Herodias. His two advisors, Calimthum and Phylinthius, sat across from him. Constructed of fine cedar, the carriage's exterior was adorned with silver motifs. The interior walls were purple velvet, while purple silk covered its padded seats. A team of four horses with ornamental harnesses pulled the carriage. Six miles-ranked Roman soldiers escorted the carriage.

"What is that commotion?" Herod pointed out of the window. "It looks like at least two, maybe three hundred people are gathered by the Jordan River."

Calimthum, a gaunt man with a thin beard and receding hairline, peered out of the window. "It's that wild man, John, known by the followers of Yeshua as John the Baptist."

"Yes." Herod clenched his fist. "I know of this man. I heard stories that he had risen from the dead and that he has miraculous powers."

Phylinthius added, "Some say he is Elijah or another prophet from long ago."

"I want to meet this man for myself." Herod opened a window and shouted to the coachman. "Pull over to that crowd."

"Repent!" John the Baptist yelled as he dunked a young man into the Jordan River and just as quickly pulled him back up.

Herod Antipas and Herodias approached John the Baptist.

"Repent!" John pointed at Herod and Herodias. "Now!"

"Repent?" Herod skewed his head at John the Baptist. "By whose authority? Do you know who I am?" He pointed to himself with both hands, "Don't you know that I answer only to Pilate and Ceasar"?

"Repent of your sins in the name of Yeshua, the Son of God, whose sandals I am unfit to tie." John prodded. "He knows who you are and can count the number of hairs on your head. He knows of your every sin and abomination. I am not the light, but I was sent to bear witness to the light, and what you have done in darkness, he shall bring to light."

"Sin and abomination?" Herod Antipas looked around. The crowd had closed in on him; he signaled for his soldiers to circle him. "I am the Tetrarch of Galilee and Perea. Upholding the interests and policies of Rome is what is right in the eyes of mighty Jupiter and the Roman Gods."

"Sin covers you like a pig caked in mud." John pointed to Herod. "You divorced your legal wife to take your brother's wife." John pointed at Herodias. "You both live in sin and adultery. Repent!"

Some of the crowd gasped. Scattered laughter could be heard.

The laughter reverberated and amplified in Herod's skull.

Herodias blanched and clutched her chest. "How dare you insult me!" She prodded at John. "You savage stultus!" She spat on him and then turned to Herod, crossing her eyes and glaring at him.

Herod looked away from her, turning back to John.

John remained stolid before them, ignoring the spit. His eyes drilled into Herod.

"I should put you to death right now." Herod stepped back and prodded. His finger jittered." The crowd inched closer. '*I can't have an uprising.*' He touched the bridge of his nose. *'That would bring the disapproval of both Pilate and Ceasar.'*

"I fear not the man that can take my life from me in this World." John pointed at Herod. "I only fear the one who has the power to condemn me to Hell for an eternity."

"Are you afraid of this man?" Herodias put her hands on her hips and glared at Herod. "You let him shame your wife? And in front of these Judaeans?' She glared and spread her arms. "And you let him dishonor Rome and your title?"

Her scorn pierced him. His head wavered between Herodias, John, and the crowd. *'But Killing him will cause a riot.'* Herod motioned to his soldiers and pointed at John. "Arrest this man!"

The soldiers then grabbed and restrained John. He didn't resist as they took him away.

***

Herod Antipas's palace had imposing high battlement-topped walls. Guard towers were positioned on each corner. Inside the palace, a soft breeze swirled through the atrium's high impluvium ceiling. Sculptures of warriors, Roman Gods, and athletes sat in front of its walls. A large fountain centered the atrium. The walls were covered in tapestries. Torchlight cast shadows on paintings of Ceasars and Roman war heroes. Tonight, Herod hosted a grand feast for Roman political dignitaries. Skilled musicians played tunes on the harp, lyre, flute, trumpet, cithara strings, and a tympanum drum. The aroma of roasted lamb, pork, beef, and poultry sifted throughout the rooms open to the atrium. Seafood was served on small plates. One could smell the freshness of the fruits and dates. Herod's guests could choose from a variety of breads and sweet pastries as well as different cheeses. Above all, wine was abundant and copiously drunk.

Herod Antipas sat next to his wife, Herodias. Yet with each quaff of wine, Herod stared more intensely at his stepdaughter, Salome. She wore a tight, silk toga-like outfit. Her legs were long and lithe, her buttocks a shapely crescent. She gently swayed her hips with each step. She wore nothing beneath her attire's silk top. As the evening progressed, she inched open her bodice, exposing more cleavage.

Herod gorged on a smoked turkey leg before rubbing grease over the part of his toga covering his ample waste. He gulped a cup of wine and then signaled for a servant to refill his glass. Two beads of sweat appeared on his right cheek as he again leered at Salome. Herodias, at first, glowered at him. She then made eye contact with her daughter and grinned.

A Roman governor strolled over and sat next to Herod. "The food, the wine, the music. You have impressed many important people with your feast and festivity." He then moved his mouth close to Herod's ear. "Nothing here is a finer morsel than that." He pointed at Salome. "If she would dance for us, your party will not only prove unforgettable, but all will remember when the time comes for recommendations for a new Praetor."

Herod looked again at Salome. He licked his lips and then wiped the sweat from his brow.

Herodias grinned and nodded to her. Salome returned her gestures.

The Roman governor adjusted the gold and ruby fibulae pinned to his toga. "I understand that you have that madman Judaeans call John the Baptist in your carcer." He braced his right hand over the diamond ring on his left ring finger.

"He disrespected Rome and my title."

"I applaud you. Judaeans need to know who rules them. It's a pity Rome lets them have their foolish beliefs. Their Gods keep getting more bizarre. I have heard stories of this man who allegedly walked on water and can raise the dead." He raised his hands. "Soon, the time will come when we put a stop to this nonsense. The Judaeans must know that Ceasar is the highest God. Any objection should be considered blasphemy and subject to swift and severe punishment."

"Concedo." Herod grinned and raised his wine vessel. "Let this John the Baptist serve as an example."

"I also applaud you for constructing the Jerusalem Aqueduct. Its proximity to the Temple may offend some of the more fanatical Jews, but Rome knows what's good for…" The governor realized that Herod was not paying attention. Beads of sweat clung to Herod's cheeks like raindrops on a window. His expression was frozen in a leer. The governor pulled on Herod's arm and chuckled. "I can't say I blame you for finding something more intriguing than Roman policy." He pointed at Salome.

Salome approached him. She flicked her tress of fiery red hair and tilted back her head, allowing her nardinum perfume to steep their nostrils. She approached Herod and put her hands on his knees briefly enough to tantalize. She batted her dark eyes and eyelashes at both Herod and the governor.

Herod panted. He looked at the governor. He was also spellbound. Herod stood. He reached out to grasp Salome. She backed away, just out of his reach. He looked back at the governor. He was also sweating. Herod asked, "Salome. Dance for us?"

Salome tilted her head to the side, smiled, and pivoted her hips toward the governor and Herod.

"Dance for us. Please dance for us." Herod then proclaimed, "Dance for us, and I will give you anything that you ask, up to half my kingdom."

Salome entwined her arms around Herod's neck. "Are you a man of your word?"

Herod surveyed the room. The guest now focused on them. "Yes! Yes! I give you my word as a Roman Tetrarch," He gasped. "Dance for us."

Solome left the atrium. Five minutes later, she returned wearing a gown of seven veils. She nodded to the musicians. Her dance started with slow, seductive movements. As the musicians upped the tempo, she danced faster and more salaciously. With each syncopated beat, Salome removed a veil and threw it toward Herod. The guests cheered and encouraged her. As the musicians played the outro, she removed the final veil. She held both ends of the veil, put it behind Herod, and rubbed his neck by moving it back and forth. The guests hackled lewdly. As the song ended, she collapsed onto Herod's lap and kissed his cheek. She then stood and walked over to Herodias, who covered her with a discarded garment.

Herod stood. "Now for your reward. Shall we go to my vault? I will give you what you choose."

"No!" Salome pointed at him. "I want John's head on a silver charger."

Herod gasped. *He has the power to curse me and my entire household.* He then spoke aloud, "I will hire the most skilled gemmarius and aurifex in the kingdom. I will spare no expense. They will shape silver, gold, diamonds, and rubies to your beck and call, to your every wish and delight. We will then go to the best vestiarius in Rome. He will make you the most elegant and gorgeous gown that the kingdom has ever seen. It will match your new jewelry." He beamed at her. "Rome will see you as a Goddess."

"I said, 'I want John the Baptist's head on a silver charger'."

Herodias cackled.

Herod made eye contact with many of his guests. He then motioned for his advisor, Calimthum. Herod inhaled deeply before saying, "Grant her wish."

Herod collapsed on his chair. He guzzled a glass of wine, signaled for more, and drank it. After another glass of wine, Herod heard gasps and groans from his guests.

A black hooded executioner entered the atrium. He displayed John the Baptist's severed head on a silver charger.

Herodias and Salome guffawed.

Herod vomited.

Chapter 8

Magnus galloped to Capernaum. He had fought battles and campaigns before. Yet, never had he felt more adrenaline-charged. A new adventure and mystery awaited. He had a lifetime of conditioning and training to suppress emotion, to lead by stern example, and to fight without forethought or afterthought. But this was no battle. This was no fight. This was not all about him, his soldiers, or a military mission. This was about someone far more important.

***

Rivka could not sleep. She alternated between pacing about the floor or nervously brushing her hair. The moments crawled closer at inchworm pace; Rivka wiped cold sweat from her brow. She stared out of her open window. *'Am I doing wrong? What if I get caught? I promised him. I want to see him.'* Rivka dropped to her knees and knelt over her bed. "Oh, dear Heavenly Father, in the name of Yeshua, am I doing the right thing? If it is right by you, give me courage." She smelled fragrant flowers before feeling a soft hand gently on her shoulder. "Isolde Maria!"

"Hush, my precious one." Isolde Maria put her finger before her lips. Rivka gazed into the samphire glow of her eyes. Isolde Maria then placed her hands on Rivka's shoulders. Rivka also put her hands on Isolde Maria's shoulders, their arms touching. "We must not awaken anyone." Isolde Maria nodded. "I love you, Rivka. I love you as only a Heavenly Angel can love you. The one who created us loves you more than you will ever know in this life. My lovely Rivka, some are called to love the Father, Son, and Holy Spirit alone. Others have hearts like a precious gem.

It's not complete unless each facet is honed and polished. Go to Magnus without fear. Heaven knows that you love Yahweh through his son Yeshua with passion and purity. He knows that you are incomplete until each facet of your heart can shine."

"I am still afraid, Isolde Maria." Rivka lowered her head. "You smell so delightful, like a lush garden of every flower in creation." She looked at Isolde Maria with a hint of a tear in her eye. "I have been sweating. I have no perfume to please my beloved."

Isolde Maria then touched her cheeks to each of Rivka's cheeks.

Rivka touched her cheek, smelled her fingers, and beamed. "Thank you, Isolde Maria."

"I have something else that you may need." Isolde Maria chuckled before planting a long, closed-mouth kiss on Rivka's lips. "Look, my darling dear." Isolde Maria took a hand mirror from her white gown and showed Rivka her reflection.

Rivka beamed at seeing her lips full and red.

"Come, Rivka." Isolde Maria led Rivka by the hand. "Your beloved has arrived." Isolde Maria disappeared through Rivka's open window. Rivka beamed and followed her through the window.

Rivka felt as if her feet were velvet slippers walking on a cloud. No doubts hindered her as she strolled behind the back wall of her compound. She first gasped and then beamed. Magnus smiled at her. He had removed his breastplate and had placed it over his horse's saddle. He had also removed his helmet. His wavy dark hair glowed in the moonlight. She saw that his pectorals surpassed the form and contours of his breastplate.

"Rivka." He smiled at her in a way that he had never smiled before. Her smile, her olive eyes, and most of all, at last, she wore no veil over her flowing, luxuriant tress of honey-colored hair. It mesmerized him.

She sauntered over to him. After ten steps, she ran into his arms.

Magnus squeezed her but not with at full strength lest he hurt her. He felt a fullness with the softness of her breasts meeting the hardness of his pectorals. Closer he held her, wanting to protect her, feeling her become that elusive missing part of him. *'What has come over me? What is this strange, powerful, wonderful feeling?'* He then stroked her hair. *'May it never end.'*

Rivka tilted her head back. She looked into his dark eyes, braced her arms under his shoulders, and pulled him closer. "For so long," she breathed deeply. "For so long, my world had been closed and empty. I longed for a love that I couldn't fathom. I felt a longing, but for what? Then Yeshua filled my heart and opened the Heavens. But you have opened the World where I stand. Now I know that I found what I was looking for."

Magnus briefly touched his nose to her nose. "I have traveled this known world. I never stopped to smell the flowers, the honey, or even the freshness of the air. I never stopped to gaze upon the beauty of the trees, the mountains, or the sea. Now I have found everything in this World that I have missed." He again touched his nose to hers. "Rome has many splendors. Our artists and craftsmen have built tremendous buildings and intricate sculptures. I once compared you to our statue of Venus. No sculpture or anything that man has ever created can ever come within a mile of you. I would walk a thousand of those miles on my knees just to be near you. A statue is chiseled out of stone.

You are soft and melt with my body. I feel your heartbeat. I can imbibe your aroma, more delightful than the Gardens of Lucullus. But a flower is cold. You are so warm."

She moved her face closer. She touched her nose to touch his without retracting it. "I have had to grow strong in mind and spirit." She embraced him firmer and rested her chin on his shoulder. "But I need your strength. You are strong in a way that no woman can ever be strong. I feel something for you that no girl, only a woman, can feel." She inhaled and then exhaled deeply. "I love you, Magnus."

"What is strength without tenderness? A bear or a lion is strong. Oxen and draught horses are strong. Now, I know that it takes more than a beast's strength to be a man. You make me complete, Rivka. I love you. Love is but a mystery that only we can solve together. I love you more than a mighty cedar loves the sun and the rain."

"I love you, Magnus. I love you beyond the number of stars in the sky. I have solved the mystery of my heart. Yet what is desire? I desire the love of my Lord with my soul; How do I answer my desire as a woman and my love for you?" She pecked his lips.

Magnus could smell her breath. Her eyes were tantalizing inches from his eyes. He felt that he could peer into her soul. He saw a beauty well beyond the divine artistry of her face and body.

She placed her hands behind his shoulders. He had entwined her torso. Noses still touching, they breathlessly gazed into each other's eyes. Their lips met. At first softly. This time their tongues connected. No delight had she ever experienced than this scintillation. Rivka felt pulses and waves echo through her being. She massaged his arm muscles and ever so slightly turned her head to deepen their kiss.

Magnus drew her closer to him. He had never tasted anything as delectable as her mouth. No fragrance was finer than her cheeks. He briefly paused in kissing her lips to kiss her cheeks. Rivka tilted back her head so that he could kiss her neck.

They looked at each other and smiled. Their lips met; their tongues entwined. The tempo of their kiss reached a rhapsody. She nibbled on his lips. They kissed in syncopated beats. She felt a euphoric rhapsody. Her mind played back a long-ago, pleasant memory of a visit to the great sea and seeing saltwater flow through two boulders. Her knees buckled. She grasped him behind the neck to prevent falling. He held her up.

Suddenly, Magnus heard an angelic voice. "I am Isolde Maria. I am Rivka's guardian angel. I love Rivka. But I love her differently than you love her. She has lost herself to you. I want you to honor her above all human beings, even Ceasar. You don't yet believe in Rivka's God or the God that sent me. I do ask that you uphold the honor of a Centurion. Don't make her dishonor her God. Don't make her later feel shame. Let her feel comforted in her love for you. Let your actions prove her dignity and worth as a woman. Besides, it's dangerous for her to be out here with you. Please, take her back now to the safety of her room."

Magnus then subtly pulled away from her. "I bought this as a gift to you." He handed Rivka a thin gold necklace with a ruby pendant.

Rivka clutched it with both hands and held it to her heart. "Thank you, Magnus." She blushed. "Thank you so much. It's beautiful. I have never owned anything near as precious."

"We will meet again three nights from now."

"I will be here for you."

"I must go now." He tipped his head. "No one is here. All is quiet. Go now and be safe."

***

Rivka had safely glided through her window. She clutched her new necklace and knelt by her bedside. "I thank you, Lord, for your love and protection. I thank you for knowing and filling my deepest heart's desire. I pray Magnus has a safe journey home. I know that you are a God of free will. I do ask that you make things happen so that Magnus will come to know you as I have come to know you." Rivka slept soundly.

Chapter 9

Centurions Magnus, Longinus, and Camillus stood by their places at the marble table inside the Aelia Capitolina war room.

"Hail!"

They snapped to attention, punched their chests, and extended their right arms as Legatus Legionis Octavio entered the room.

He stood at the table head for four seconds before motioning for them to sit. He doffed his gold helmet, placed it on the table, and sat. "One of our most dependable Jewish quislings has informed the Frumentari that a Sacarii cell is conducting a meeting in a stable just off the road, about a mile from Gadara." He folded his hands, "Delators tend to be dualistic and untrustworthy people. Greed and avarice are their credibility. This delator is expensive. Nevertheless, his information has proven dependable, and I know that he will not risk losing his income by giving Rome bad intelligence. Our stance is to despise our enemies but to respect their capabilities. The Sacarii are expert assassins and well-versed in close-quarter combat. Therefore, Magnus, as our best hand-to-hand fighter, I assign you to take an eight-soldier contubernium in addition to Optio Flavius. This is a dangerous mission. Flavius is a soldier on the rise. I am sure that he will ably serve as your right-hand man. I want them all captured or killed. They will fight you to the death as they know that death by the sword is far better than crucifixion. Leave in the afternoon to arrive at dusk. Our delator informs us that they will be there at that time." Legatus Legionis stood and donned his gold helmet with purple plumes on the crest. "Centurions. You have provided excellent intelligence on this Yeshua of Nazareth. I now know of his inner circle of twelve men and one woman. Our informant is one of them. You may know of him. He is Judas Iscariot."

***

The stable sat off the road at exactly where Judas Iscariot told the Roman Frumentari. He had demanded an added ten denarii should the mission prove a success. Magnus had tried putting thoughts of Rivka out of his mind. He had never feared battle or dying before. Yet her visage of beauty, her feeling of softness and, her delectable scent of flowers stuck in his mind, '*I must return to her. If I die tonight in battle, how can word get to her"?* As his contubrium drew near their destination and appointment with battle, he, at last, cleared his mind. He pointed his spear at the inornate stone structure with a wooden roof. He then moved his spear in a circle. Eight of Magnus's soldiers surrounded the stable. Magnus nodded to Flavius and muttered, "May Mars strengthen us and embolden us with his ferocity." Magnus crept closer to the stable door. Suddenly, he kicked the door in. Magnus charged in first; Flavius followed. Six Sacarii insurgents were gathered around a table. "Keep your hands on the table." The other eight Roman soldiers stormed in. "Resistance is futile." Magnus instinctively felt an unseen danger.

Sacarii insurgent hiding behind a rafter leaped with feline stealth, landing on Magnus's back. It buckled him and dislodged his breastplate. In one motion, the assassin swiped his sicae dagger's curved blade at the centurion's throat. He missed his throat but slashed a nasty gash across his chest. Magnus hooked his arm under the assassin's knife-side armpit and used momentum to flip him over. The assassin screamed as Magnus twisted his arm behind his back and dislocated it. The stealth attack gave the other six Sacarii an opening to grab their weapons and fight. One of them lunged at Magnus with his sword. He stepped back and hit the bell guard of the Sicarii's weapon, knocking it aside. Magnus rushed in and killed him with a counterthrust. Flavius did a feint on a Sacarii swordsman and then killed him with a lunge to his abdomen. Flavius next killed a Sacarii by stabbing him in his side as he fought a Roman soldier. Another assassin swiped his sicae at Magnus. Magnus blocked his arm and then knocked him unconscious with a punch to the jaw.

Magnus then shouted, "Close ranks!" The soldiers stood shoulder to shoulder. Touching shields, the soldiers pushed the remaining two insurgents against the wall.

One of the soldiers hit a Sacarii in the solar plexus with his shield edge, making him groan and keel over. The other Sacarii spat in Magnus's direction. "Kill me now!"

"Why should I grant you that mercy?" Magnus sheathed his weapon.

"You Roman karrar." He again spat.

Save your insults for when you're nailed to a cross." Magnus pointed at the surviving Sacarii. "Soldiers. Take them to the Antonia Fortress."

Flavius then walked over to Magnus. "That wound looks bad."

Adrenaline had deadened Magnus's pain.

Flavius moistened a rag and handed it to him. Magnus wiped the blood from his chest. "I'll be fine. I'll let the Medicus take care of it when we get back." Magnus smiled. "All in a day's work, Optio."

"Yes, Dominus," Flavius smirked. "Too bad that Judas Iscariot is the only one getting a cash bonus.

Chapter 10

Jacob had finished his jug of wine. Hannah had both worked and supervised the day's pottery operation. Hannah, Rivka, Samuel, and their hired workers were grateful for his absence. Rivka had finished for the day. She washed the clay from her hands from a cistern and wiped the sweat off her brow with a cloth. She then retired to her room to change into clean clothes and rest before dinner. Jacob waited for her to close the door before creeping toward her room. He peeped through a crack between the door and the door frame. Rivka doffed her sweat and clay-soiled outer garment and cast it aside. Jacob dropped to his knee and panted. He next saw Rivka reach under her bed cushion. She held a gold and ruby necklace in front of her and kissed it. *What is that? How did she get that? It's gold and ruby! She couldn't afford that with a lifetime of her allowances.* 'Rage met realization. *'That necklace is Roman!'*

Jacob kicked open Rivka's door, lurched at her, and snatched the necklace. "Who gave you this." He spat wine-laced spittle on her. "Tell me!" Furrowing his brows, he glowered at her.

Rivka's jaw chattered as her jittery hand reached out for the necklace.

"I know how you got this." He clenched the necklace in a tight fist and brandished it in her face. "It's bad enough that my daughter's a whore. But a whore for a Roman?" He backfisted her, drawing blood from her lip. He then threw the necklace against the wall and grabbed her arms, digging his fingernails into her flesh. He put his face close enough for her to smell his alcohol-laced breath and feel the heat from his eyes.

"No, Father!" Tears sprayed from her eyes. "It's not like that."

"Ma he zeh! Harlot! You're worthless to me if you're not a virgin. What man would pay a dowery for a woman defiled by a Roman?" He prodded. "Could I sell you for even one denarius as a concubine?"

"No, Father!" She shook her head. Tears continued to pour from her eyes. "I am a virgin. I have done nothing to shame our Father Yahweh."

"How dare you say his holy name." He clawed his fingernails deeper into her flesh and shook her. "You rejected our teachers and scribes for that heretic and blasphemer." He clenched his teeth and seethed. "Seeing that you cost me a fortune by defiling yourself with a Roman, seeing how I have fed you, clothed you, and housed you, well, like Lot, I am entitled." He released her and tore off his kethoneth. He then ripped her tunic's bodice and pinned her wrists to the bed. "Oh, yes. Lovely. Oh, King Solomon. See what I see. Yes. Two fawns, twins of a gazelle."

"No!" Rivka tried to stand.

Jacob kept pinned her to the bed. He then mounted her.

***

Samuel patted one of their donkeys. "Here you go. Dinner time." He put a scoop of feed in front of them. "B'teavon."

A mysterious, strangely accented female voice then spoke to him. '*Samuel. Run to your sister. Hurry. She's in grave danger.*'

Samuel next heard a commotion coming from Rivka's bedroom. He sprinted.

***

"No!" She spat in Jacob's face. "Samuel! Somebody! Help me!" She tried to head-butt him. She snapped her jaws three times, vainly trying to bite him.

Samuel ran into the room. "What the?" He pulled Jabob off her. Samuel scowled at him. Seeing the depravity of his expression and the evil in his eyes, Samuel slugged him in the jaw.

Jacob fell to the floor. "By the law of the teachers and scribes," he messaged his jaw. "You're to have your hand cut off!"

"In the eyes of any decent God, you are beneath the vilest criminal. Even crucifixion is too good for you." Samuel folded his arms. "You're a drunk. Nobody in Capernaum respects you. Your word is karrar."

Jacob remained seated against the wall. "This is my house! Get out! Never come back!" He prodded. "You're dead to me."

"You're worse than dead to me. You're already burning in Gehenna as far as I'm concerned." Samuel put his hands on his hips. "I'm going far away and changing my name. I want no one to know that I am related to you. But I won't leave until tomorrow. I must stay and protect my sister." Samuel lurched over, pulled Jacob to his feet, and tossed him out of the room.

Rivka was now seated. Her face was buried in her hands. She wailed.

Samuel sat beside her. "Are you alright?"

"Thank you and our Father God through his son Yeshua." She uncovered her eyes and looked at him. "You arrived and stopped him before he could defile me." She then held both of his hands. "Let's pray together. 'Yahweh, in the name of your son Yeshua, forgive Jacob, for he knew not what he did. I thank you for sending Samuel to save me from whatever evil possessed him. Amen."

"Amen." Samuel stood. "You do know that I must leave in the morning and never return. You may come with me."

"Thank you, Samuel. But now I must stay and protect our mother."

Samuel stood and left the room. "Wait here for me." He returned three minutes later. He handed her a dagger. "Keep this with you at all times. Rather you stab him with this than he…I think you understand. And always watch our mother. He is cruel to her too." Samuel smiled. "Oh, I think you dropped this." He picked it up from the floor and then handed Rivka Magnus's gold and ruby necklace.

Rivka took the necklace, squeezed it, and beamed.

Chapter 11

Hiren was the wealthiest man in Capernaum. The merchant had established a trade network that reached the far corners of the known civilized world. He later expanded into finance and lending. He had an attendant bring Jacob of Capernaum to his home in a horse-drawn carriage. Hiren's bodyguards, one an Ethiopian, stood as tall as a draught horse and the other a thick bearded Hebrew with a gut and chest like an ox. Hiren had them escort Jacob to his atrium and seated him at a large cedar table. Torchlight cast shadows on tapestries adorning the wall. Hiren chomped into a leg of lamb, spilling bits onto his wiry, gray-specked black beard. He washed it down with wine, dribbling it from his lips to his beard. The stench of garlic remained on his breath. Jacob sat stiffly in his chair.

"Jacob, I understand you're quite a lover of fine wine." Hiren snapped his fingers. "This comes from Hispania." His attendant, a tall, gaunt man with deep-set black eyes, filled Jacob's wine glass. "I think you will find it to your liking." Hiren sipped from his wine goblet. "Let's talk business." Hiren leered at Jabob with wide-set eyes, small in proportion to his round, beefy face. The top of his head was bald and dome-shaped, while the sides matched his beard. "You have something that I desire, and I have something that you need." Hiren paused for effect. "What you need is money and lots of it."

Jacob nodded.

"What I desire is your daughter." He folded his hands. "You have a decent setup. You have a house, a workshop, and a stable." He wiped sweat and oil from his brow. "But for how long? We both know that the wine has gotten the best of you. You're losing your business reputation, and you spend too much of your operating budget on drink. If you lose everything, what becomes of Rivka? Look around you. Look at the luxury and comfort I can give her. In exchange, she will comfort me in my bed." He nodded to his Ethiopian bodyguard. He went to another room. Three minutes later, he reappeared with a foot-long and half-foot-deep teak chest with ornamental gold bands and placed it on the table. Hiren opened it.

Jacob beamed. His eyes lit like torches.

The chest brimmed with solid gold coins.

"I think that you will find this a sufficient dowery for your daughter."

Jacob put two hands around the chest, pulled it close to him, and hugged it.

"Have her ready. I will come for her tomorrow." Hiren beamed. He snapped his fingers. His attendant filled their wine glasses. "But for tonight. We drink to our delight."

Jacob drank his goblet of Liberian wine in one gulp. Hiren's attendant refilled it.

Chapter 12

Rivka knelt by her bed. "Please, Lord, be with me. Let my meeting with Magnus be your will, and may you be with us." Excitement had supplanted fear. After what had happened with her father, she didn't just want Magnus, she needed him. She gazed at the sky. At last, the time had come. She slipped through her window and ran to the outer wall. Her smile radiated above the moon, the stars, and the planets above. He stood waiting for her. She ran into his arms and buried her face in his chest. Her tears soaked his tunica.

Magnus held her close. He felt her distress. The battle-hardened centurion felt a strange sensitivity. He did not question it. "Rivka!" He held her close. "My happiness in being with you cannot match your sorrow. What is wrong?"

"It's my father. Jacob. Each day, he falls deeper into drunkenness. Evil has overcome him." She squeezed him tighter and cried.

"Talk to me, Rivka."

"He tried to, he tried to, it was terrible. If not for Samuel, he would've," She bawled.

Magnus understood. "I can have him arrested, or I can kill him myself."

"No. No." Rivka loosened her embrace. Her teary eyes met Magnus's eyes. "Don't do that. Samuel is gone. He is cruel to Mother, but her home and the pottery business are all she knows."

"I love you, Rivka. Before you, I never understood that thing they call love. Now I know. Marry me, Rivka."

"Before Yeshua, I obeyed our traditions. I would never marry a Roman. Now all, whether Roman, Ethiopian, Egyptian, Greek, or Jew, are one in him."

"Rivka, I have heard him speak. The first time I heard him, Optio Flavius mocked him. My only concern was how his words affected Rome. I have lived a hard military life. Within our ranks, we enforce a creed of fearless vengeance, and we do so with harsh discipline. Yet Yeshua backed up his message of love and compassion with inner strength and conviction. He performed miracles before my eyes. Yet the greatest miracle of all is in my arms. It took holding you close to me and feeling the love in your heartbeat to make me understand. I still am unsure if he is the true Son of God. What I am sure of is my love for you, Rivka." Magnus smiled. "Marriage between a centurion and a Jewish woman is also frowned upon in some Roman circles. Yet my commander, the Legatus Octavio, has encouraged me to take a wife. I can think of no woman on Earth whom I would be prouder to have by my side than you."

Rivka then felt a strange comfort fill her being. She received a vision of Isolde Maria smiling at her. Then she saw Yeshua open his arms to her. He smiled at her and nodded. "He is the Son of God. Through him, all blessings flow. All that is good. All that is kind. All that is just and merciful. Would he have sent you to me if that were not so? I love you, Magnus. Yes, I will be your partner. I will be your wife."

"Leave with me now, Rivka. I have a wonderful home waiting for you."

"I can't just now." A tear welled in Rivka's eye. "I have to prepare my mother for this."

"Surely she will approve."

"It's not that Magnus."

"Then what is it? Bring her with you."

"I wish it were so easy. Our laws and traditions make it almost impossible for a woman to divorce a man." Rivka pursed her lips and looked directly into his eyes. "My father wasn't always like this. Only in the last three years or so did his bitterness against Rome overwhelm him, and his turning to drink corrupt his spirit."

"I am starting to doubt the existence of my Roman Gods." Magnus moved his hands to Rivka's shoulders. "Yet we don't have a deity as evil as what your father tried to do to you."

"Yeshua and our Father Yahweh who sent him are real. Satan, his adversary, is also all too real. He is beyond the evil of any pagan god." Rivka lowered her head, breaking eye contact with Magnus. "After John Baptized me, my father got so angry that he dunked me in our donkey manger. I don't know what would have happened had my brother not intervened. Even though he beats Mother, she would never just up and leave." Two teardrops fell from her right eye. "This means that I will never see her again. My father's hatred of Rome has turned his blood to viper venom. If I leave with you, I can never return."

"Can't your mother come and visit us?"

"Father would never permit it, and he would punish her severely if she tried."

***

"Jacob got so drunk that he forgot our contract." Hiren handed a parchment to his attendant. "Take this to him. We'll claim my bride in the morning."

***

Magnus embraced Rivka. She returned his embrace.

"Magnus." She briefly kissed his lips. "Give me time with my mother. Let me prepare her. I will miss her horribly.

But…" She gazed into his eyes. "Yeshua taught that one leaves their parents for their spouse." She kissed him and held it for three seconds. "I am a woman now. I am ready to be your wife."

Magnus and Rivka held each other tight and kissed passionately and hungrily.

Hiren's attendant arrived at the Jacobs compound with the contract. He gasped at the sight of Rivka and Magnus. He turned and beelined back to Hiren.

Chapter 13

Mangus had mounted his horse. Optio Flavius rode beside him. Six miles-ranked foot-soldiers followed. They conducted a routine patrol of Lower City Jerusalem. Magnus looked up and squinted at the morning sun's glare. Suddenly, intense gold light seared his eyes, cloaking the azure sky. Shining even brighter than the sun, she appeared. Never had Magnus imagined a more breathtaking woman. Prismatic colors sheened like light from a pearl upon her flowing, long black hair. Her eyes shined like polished sapphires. Her gown and wing feathers were whiter than imported Merino wool. "Magnus."

Magnus squinted. "That voice. Your strange accent. Yes, I remember from …"

"Yes, when you were first alone with Rivka. I am Isolde Maria. I am her guardian angel. No time for small talk. Rivka is in grave danger. Hurry. Follow me!" Isolde Maria then flew away.

"Optio. I have another mission. Take command." Magnus followed the angel at full gallop.

***

"A carriage dropped him off last night." Hannah poured Rivka a cup of herbal tea. "He could barely stagger through the door. He won't awaken anytime soon."

"Mother." Rivka sipped her herbal tea. "Seeing that we have a few hours, I want us to go to town. Let's pray together at the synagogue. Then I wish to share something with you."

Hannah glanced at Jacob's bedroom. "We can do that. Let's go!"

***

Jacob stumbled out of his bed. His head felt like a mason was banging the inside of his skull with a hammer and chisel. Suddenly, he heard a loud banging. It took three seconds for him to realize that someone had kicked in the front door. He lurched into the atrium. Flanked by his two bodyguards, Hiren stood stiff and straight. Shoulders hunched, arms flared, and fists clenched, he glowered at Jacob. He then snapped his fingers. His bodyguards seized Jacob, twisting his arms behind his back. "My money!" He flared his nostrils and narrowed his eyes. "Get me my money." He prodded. "Now!"

"It's in my bedroom." Jacob's voice screeched with pain. "I'll go get it."

"Oh no, you won't. Essau," Hiren pointed to his stout Hebrew bodyguard. "Hold him." Hiren motioned to the giant Ethiopian, "Abede, go to his bedroom and get my money."

Essau continued twisting Jacob's arm. He could only wince and dart his head back and forth as he heard the crashing and shattering of his bedroom getting torn apart.

Abede returned and placed the chest of gold coins on the table. Hiren opened the chest and inspected the coins. "I would have given you more for your daughter if you weren't so drunk and greedy. If you held out, I might have doubled this. That's what she's worth to me as a virgin and a wife. As a harlot, I might give you this," Hiren held up one coin, "to add her as a concubine. As a Goy's whore, she's worthless to me. But a whore to a Roman soldier,' he prodded, "and a Centurion at that, she should be dumped alive in the Valley of Hinnom. Lucky for you, you didn't spend any of my money. Nevertheless, you held my money overnight. You owe me interest. Abede, take his interest payment." Abede slugged Jabob in the gut. Jacob groaned. Essau released him.

He fell on the floor, gasping for breath. The three left with the chest of gold coins.

***

Faster and faster, Magnus galloped, keeping pace with the angel's flight.

***

Jacob stormed toward the Capernaum town square.

***

The Capernaum town square bustled with activity. The cacophony of voices and the sights and smells of colorful canopies over merchant stalls selling food, spices, and clothing created a festive vibe. After the service and prayer, Rivka and Hannah walked between the synagogue's stone columns and descended its eight steps. They stood in the shade of the synagogue's twenty-degree roof pitch. They faced each other and held both hands.

"Mother, I can't hold this back from you any longer."

"Don't say anything, Rivka. I know what you are going to tell me." Hannah had a soft glow in her eyes. "You are in love with the Centurion, and you want to marry him."

Rivka's jaw dropped. Her lips formed a circle. "How did you know?"

"I am your mother. When a mother loves her daughter as much as I love you, I can feel the love in your heart. I don't fully understand this thing called love, but I have a sense of it and how it affects you. My marriage to your father was arranged by our parents. Love didn't matter. It was my duty to serve as a wife and not ask questions."

"I have only seen him take you for granted and act with cruelty. I feel that we both are his chattel and no better than livestock to him." Rivka squeezed Hannah's hand. "Magnus is different. He has not yet taken Yeshua in his heart, but he understands his message. He has treated me with respect and honor. I love him, and he loves me."

"If you had told me this just a couple of months ago, I would have torn my garment and considered you dead. Traditions are tried and true principles and customs give a people and a community purpose and cohesion. Yeshua is not asking that we abandon our traditions. Yet he puts love, fellowship, and unity among his followers first. Therefore," Hannah smiled, "you have my blessings to marry Magnus."

Tears streamed from Rivka's eyes. "Mother." Rivka cried. "This means that I must leave. Father would kill me before allowing me to marry a Roman." Rivka lowered her head. "I may never see you again." She raised her head. "You may also never again see your son, and now you are alone with," she sniffled, "him."

"Rivka. My new faith will see me through. I have no more to do. You and Samuel are adults now. I will pray that both you and Samuel fulfill God's purpose for your lives. You must both go your own way and make me proud." Hannah put her hands on her shoulder. "God will look after me."

Rivka and Hannah both cried and embraced.

***

Isolde Maria flew ahead. Magnus galloped through the gates of Capernaum.

***

Jacob stormed onto the Capernaum town square. He spotted Rivka, pointed at her, and shouted, "Harlot! Whore!" He lurched at her, grabbed her by the hair, and dragged her.

Rivka screamed. Each hair follicle was a tentacle of agony, causing her to fecklessly thrash her limbs.

"Stop!" Hannah grabbed Jacob's arm.

Jacob slugged her with his free arm. After she fell, he kicked her.

The commotion drew a crowd. Rabbi Nicodemus ran from the synagogue to see what was happening.

"This woman is a whore" Jacob pointed at Rivka while facing Nicodemus. "She is not just any whore. She is a whore to Roman soldiers. By our laws and traditions, she must be put to death by stoning."

"No!" Hannah scrambled over and lay on top of her daughter.

Jacob kicked her in the ribs, causing her to roll from Rivka. "As her father." He reached down and grabbed an egg-shaped, smooth stone from the ground. "I shall cast the first stone." He cocked his arm and threw the stone at his daughter.

Magnus had dismounted his horse and ran to Rivka. He caught the stone and hurled it back at Jacob. It struck Jacob in the forehead, crushing his skull. He collapsed dead on the ground. Magnus then grabbed his shield. "I am going to suspend Roman law. You have my permission to try to kill me by stoning. I, in turn, will both defend myself and take the offensive."

The men of Capernaum dropped their stones.

"Wise decision. Roman law is back in effect. Is there a physician here?"

An elderly man wearing a white robe raised his hand.

Magnus knelt and helped Hannah to sit. "Care for this woman. Here. This should cover your fee." Magnus reached into his pera and threw five coins to the doctor. "If anyone harms this woman, even if by word, I shall return and personally nail him to the cross."

Rivka wailed. Her hair and body were blanketed in dirt. Magnus helped her to her feet and boosted her onto his horse. The townspeople waited until he and Rivka galloped out of sight. They then hurled stones in his direction and yelled curses to Rome.

***

Rivka squeezed Magnus and pressed her crying eyes into his back, and they galloped away from Capernaum. He stopped and dismounted. He then helped her off the horse. They faced each other. He looked into her terrified eyes. He warmly embraced her. She kissed his neck and trapezoids. They again faced each other. They kissed, their tongues darting rapturously. "It will be all right, Rivka. You have nothing to fear."

Rivka sniffled. "Where are we going, Magnus? I do fear my God, and I want to obey his commands."

Magnus smiled at her. This morning, during a patrol of Lower City Jerusalem, I saw some of Yeshua's disciples. Even before we clean you up, I have a plan that will put you at ease." He kissed her again before taking her hand and helping her back onto his horse.

Magnus spotted Simon Peter, Andrew, James, and Mary Magdalen gathered under the shade of a fig tree. The Centurion rode over to them. Mary Magdelene greeted them first. "Rivka! What happened to you." She walked over, embraced her, and kissed each of her cheeks. "Let me at least try to clean you up some." Mary Magdelene dipped a cloth in a water bowl and wiped the worst of the dirt from Rivka's face. She then looked at Magnus. "Welcome to our gathering. Yeshua is away in private prayer. I know that you love my sister in Christ and that you will protect her and treat her with love and respect. Come. I am sure you know who they are." She turned her head to the three male disciples."

"Yes. I have watched you closely. You have nothing to fear from me. I know that you are not in opposition to Rome."

"What can we possibly do for you?" Simon Peter took three steps toward him. "You are a Roman Centurion. I was but a humble fisherman until Yeshua made me a fisher of men."

"I would like for you to unite Rivka and me in Holy matrimony."

"But you are a Roman and not just any Roman; you're a Centurion, and she is a Jew. You are not yet a believer in Christ Yeshua." Peter crossed his arms. "You may have the authority and ability to strike me dead, but I refuse."

Andrew and James remained quiet and still.

"How do you feel about a woman marrying you?" Mary asked, "It's seldom done, but it's not forbidden in my culture for a woman to conduct a wedding."

"I have heard Yeshua's teachings. I have seen his miracles. My heart has softened. But I am afraid that I am not yet ready to believe that he is the son of the one God. Nevertheless, his example of dignity for all is not lost on me. A woman conducting a Roman wedding is also seldom done, but I would be honored if you would unite Rivka and me in matrimony."

Rivka beamed at Mary Magdelene. She then took Magnus by the arm and led him to her.

"Magnus." Mary Magdeline beamed. "With God as our witness, do you take Rivka as your wife, to honor and to protect, in sickness and in health, for richer or poorer, to forsake all others, until death do you part?"

Magnus peered into Rivka's olive-green eyes. "I do."

"Rivka. With God as our witness, do you take Magnus as your husband, to love and to trust, to honor and to obey, in sickness and in health, for richer or poorer, to forsake all others, until death do you part?"

Rivka beamed at Magnus. "I do."

"I pronounce you man and wife." Mary Magdelene smiled. "You may kiss the bride."

As Magnus and Rivka kissed, James, Andrew, and even Simon Peter cheered.

Chapter 14

Rivka sat on Magnus's horse. Magnus held his horse's reins and walked them into his compound. Rivka's eyes widened and brightened as a guard opened the gate for them to enter under an arch supported by Doric columns. Three servants, two females, and one male, stood juxtaposed in the courtyard to greet them. "At Ease," Magnus addressed the servants. He then helped Rivka from the horse, held her hand, and took her to the servants. "Claudius, Floria, and Deanza." Magnus beamed. "Introducing my new wife and your new Domina, Rivka."

The servants bowed to her.

"I know what you're thinking, Floria." Magnus chuckled. "I can always read your mind." He took Rivka's hand and led her to Floria. "Please take her to the bathhouse and help her. She's had an eventful day, to say the least."

Floria stood two inches shorter than Rivka and was thinner. She wore a white linen uniform of a tunic and a blue apron. "Here, Domina," she extended her hand.

Rivka looked back at Magnus. He nodded to her.

Rivka took Floria's hand. She led her to the bathhouse.

***

Rivka and Floria entered the dining room. Rivka wore an elegant purple robe with gold embroidered fringes. A meal of roast lamb with flatbread, zucchini, and peppers, spiced with mint, cumin, and sumac, awaited them. Claudius poured Magnus and Rivka a goblet of wine.

"Ohhh." Rivka covered her beaming smile with her hands. "It looks and smells sumptuous."

"Floria, Claudius, Deanza, pour yourselves some wine and join us in a toast." Magnus held his wine goblet aloft. "Lo Saturnalia."

The five touched glasses and repeated, "Lo Saturnia."

Rivka kept her goblet aloft, "L'chaim!"

Their five glasses touched as they said, "L'chaim."

They all laughed together.

***

Magnus set up a pulvinar in what is now their bedroom. He had gone to the bathhouse to clean up. Rivka's hand jittered as she brushed her hair and looked at her pallid face in the mirror. She suddenly gasped. "Isolde Maria!"

Isolde Maria appeared. She kissed both of Rivka's cheeks, took her brush, and combed Rivka's hair. With each stroke of the angel's long, toned arm, Rivka's hair grew thicker and glossier.

Rivka stood and warmly embraced her.

Isolde Maria held her tight. "Rivka." Isolde Maria pulled her head back so her blue eyes could glow into Rivka's eyes. "I love you. I love you with a love from Heaven. Have no fear, my dearest one. Heaven has chosen Magnus for you. He is an outstanding man. He has not yet received the son into his heart. Don't worry; Heaven has unlimited patience. We would not have chosen him for you if that wasn't so."

"I am scared." Rivka put her hands on the angel's shoulders. "I have never been with a man. Magnus is the only man that I have ever even hugged or kissed."

"You are a married woman now. We have watched you grow from a little girl to a young lady to a woman." Isolde Maria also put her hands on Rivka's shoulders, their arms touched. "Fear not Rivka. You have faithfully waited.

Embrace the moment as I want you to embrace your husband." Isolde Maria smiled at her. "You may feel a little pain at first. But you will gain a lifetime of joy."

"Will you be with me?"

"Don't you want privacy?" Isolde Maria chuckled. "I am an angel. I can't help you with that. An angel can't marry or be given in marriage. The sacred act of marriage is a gift to humans. That is for you and Magnus to enjoy together."

Rivka blushed. "I thank you, Isolde Maria. I am no longer afraid." She grinned. "Please, Isolde Maria. Can you help me again?"

"Of course, my sweet darling Rivka." Isolde Maria hugged Rivka and touched her cheeks to each of Rivka's cheeks, transferring her floral fragrance to Rivka. They then gazed into each other's eyes for six seconds before sharing a long, closed-mouth kiss on the lips. "Goodbye Rivka." Isolde Maria beamed. "Tonight is your special night." They again embraced at full strength. Five seconds later, Rivka held only air.

Rivka looked in the mirror and saw that her cheeks were flush, and her lips were florid. She also had the fragrance of a flower garden.

Magnus then entered the room wearing only a white toga.

***

"You look so sad?" Floria served Rivka a lunch of fish, flatbread, and dates.

"It's nothing." Rivka wiped a tear from her eye.

"I may only be your servant and you my Domina, but if I may be so bold, Domina," Floria bowed her head. "There's something soft and lovely about you. If something is bothering you, well, I think you can also count me as your friend." Floria winked at Rivka. "Anything that you say will be our secret."

"Thank you, Floria." Rivka nodded. "Of course we're friends. You may work in a Centurion's house as a maidservant, but we're not in the Centurion's legion. There's no rank and file in my mind." Rivka smiled at her. "From now on, you can call me Rivka."

"Thank you, Rivka." Rivka and Floria hugged.

Deanza then entered the room. "Domina, when Magnus returns, tell him that I have prepared the extra bedroom as he asked."

"I will." Rivka half-smiled. "You can both rest." Rivka half-smiled. "Floria will fill you in on how to address me." Rivka winked at Floria. "I will wait for him alone."

Rivka sat alone and started to wail. Magnus arrived home and walked into the room.

"I'm sorry." Rivka wiped her eyes with a cloth but couldn't stop crying. "I didn't expect you home so early."

Magnus scratched his chin. He felt puzzled at his reaction. He had never seen a Roman soldier cry. If one did cry, he may face harsh discipline. He always considered crying for women only; even then, a woman's tears annoyed him. Yet this was different. He had heard Yeshua teach and had seen some of his miracles. *'Are these feelings a result?'* He looked at her in silence. *'Rivka. My wife. I never dared dream...'* "Rivka?" He sat next to her and put his arm around her shoulders. "Talk to me. What's wrong?"

"Magnus. I know that Yeshua taught that a woman leaves her mother for her husband." She looked at him with blurry vision. "But I hurt for her. Can you understand?" She shook her fists. "I am not blaming you. You saved my life by doing what had to be done." Rivka clutched his arms. "Jacob drove my brother out of the household never to return. My mother is now a widow and all alone. And how long can she run the pottery business by herself? What then?"

"Anything else, my lovely Rivka?"

"Yes." Rivka, perturbed, pursed her lips. "Deanza asked me to tell you that she prepared the spare bedroom as you wanted."

"Did she tell you why?"

"No." She continued to cry. "Why do you ask?"

"I have seen Yeshua perform miracles. I wouldn't call what I have done a divine miracle. Nevertheless, it will dry your tears just the same." Magnus beamed.

Rivka raised her palms. "I don't understand."

"Ahh." Magnus pointed to the courtyard. "Do you hear those horse hooves?" He smiled wider. "I think it best you perform your duties as the house Domina and greet our guests."

"Of course, Magnus." She looked away. "I am your wife, and I have pledged to obey you."

Rivka walked to the courtyard. The carriage stopped. She stood by for ten seconds.

The coachman opened the carriage door.

"Mother!" As soon as Hannah stepped out of the carriage. Rivka ran up to her and hugged her. Both cried tears of joy.

Magnus, Floria, Claudius, and Deanza all met Hannah.

"Thank you, Magnus!" Hannah shook his hand. "Thank you so much. Just three months ago, if I said that I would live in the home of a Roman Centurion, I would have been regarded as demon possessed. What God spoke to the Prophet Isaiah is true, 'My thoughts are not your thoughts, neither are your ways my ways.'"

"Come, Hannah." Magnus beamed. "Let us show you to your room."

Rivka smiled from ear to ear as she entwined arms with her mother and followed them to her new quarters.

Chapter 15

The post-wedding party featured lamb on a spit over an open flame. The delectable scent wafted through the banquet hall's courtyard. Tables of spices and dips, as well as breads, cheeses, dates, and fruits, surrounded the table. Musicians alternated between Roman and Jewish tunes. Wine flowed like river rapids through a valley. Magnus had rented a large banquet hall in Cana for the festivities. Close to Capernaum, Magnus had hoped that Rivka's friends and close relatives would attend. The stoning incident and slaying of Rivka's father, Jacob, had made Rivka's marriage celebration to a Roman the equivalent of an influenza breeding stage to her Jewish friends and relatives. Yet some very important Jews did attend.

"Mary!" Rivka ran up and hugged Mary Magdelene as she entered the courtyard.

"Yours was the first, and it will probably be the last wedding that I get to conduct." She chuckled and gripped Rivka's upper arms. "So, how could I miss the celebration? Let me introduce you to my friend. Her name is also Mary. But she's a far more important Mary than me, Rivka." Mary Magdalene took the other Mary by the hand. Let me introduce you to Mary, Yeshua's mother."

"Huh," Rivka gasped and turned pale. "I am so honored to meet you."

"Why, it's an honor to meet you too." Mary smiled at Rivka. "I have heard so much about you. You're even more beautiful than I was told. I can tell that you have a beautiful heart. And I also heard about your voice. I do hope that later you will sing us your song."

"Centurion Camillus is here with his family and the maidservant that your son saved from the brink of death." Rivka pointed to Centurion Camillus. "He has witnessed your son's miracles and has come to believe."

Magnus walked over to his wife, Mary of Magdelene, and Mary, Mother of Yeshua.

"Magnus. Of course, you know Mary of Magdelene." Rivka pointed to Mary, Mother of Yeshua. "I am honored to introduce you to another Mary. She is Yeshua's Mother."

"Forgive me for my skepticism." Magnus opened his hands. "But as a Roman. We find the concept of a virgin giving birth hard to believe. And how on Earth did your betrothed come to accept it?"

Rivka scowled at her husband.

"It's all right, Rivka. Give him a chance. I'll help him understand." Mary then turned back to Magnus. "An angel appeared to me…"

Magnus looked at Rivka and then Mary. "I am starting to get an idea. An angel named Isolde Maria, such a strange name, appeared to me. She is of unsurpassed beauty. She is Rivka's guardian angel. If not for her, Rivka would be dead in the dust and dirt of the Capernaum town square."

"If not for your faith to obey that Angel, your wife would be dead. I am sure that this angel, Isolde Maria, was beautiful beyond compare. The angels were created a step above us humans. A male angel named Gabriel appeared to me. He told me that I was blessed among women and that God had chosen me to give birth to the savior of mankind." Mary nodded at Magnus. "The Angel Gabriel further told me that I was selected to fulfill the prophecy given to Isaiah that a virgin would give birth."

"Your husband-to-be, Joseph, must have been skeptical." Magnus raised his hands. "I know I would be."

"Yes, he was." Mary touched Magnus's hand. "But he was a good man. He could have had me put to death by stoning. Instead, he was going to quietly put me away. But an angel appeared to him also and assured him that I had not known a man but that the Holy Spirit had conceived the child." Mary winked. "You believed Isolde Maria, and because of your belief, you saved Rivka's life. Likewise, Joseph believed the Angel. And just as the angel Isolde Maria warned you that Rivka was in great danger, an angel appeared to Joseph to warn him that our child, Yeshua, was in grave danger and that we must flee to Egypt." She held his hand. "I know that as a Centurion, you are trained to be hard and unforgiving. Yet I can tell that your love for Rivka is soft and understanding. I can also tell that my son has planted a mustard seed of faith in you." She released Magnus's hand and took Rivka's hand. "It's your wedding party. What do you say the four of us share a goblet of wine?"

"Here! Here!" Mary of Magdelene put her arm around Rivka and led her and Magnus to the wine cask.

"I know that you fear the Frumentari and for good reason" Magnus smiled. "Yet this time I used them for the good. They found someone for me. He should arrive by chariot soon."

Five minutes later, a chariot arrived in the courtyard. Rivka at once recognized the tall, lean passenger with a well-trimmed beard. "Samuel!" Rivka ran up and greeted her brother with a hug.

Hannah dropped her plate of food and goblet of wine to run to her son.

Rivka led them to Magnus. "Well, Samuel, now you know that I married this Roman."

"Much has happened over the last three months and in so many ways. I am happy for you Rivka." He shook Magnus's hand. "And I am happy for you too."

"Magnus has ways of telling me that he loves me." Rivka smiled at both her brother and husband. "He has even better ways of showing me."

"I sold our home in Capernaum, Samuel. I am now living with Rivka and Magnus."

"I borrowed money at a good rate, Mother. I invested in a small shop near the Temple Mount. I am making and selling pottery on my own. I have a bed in the back room of the shop. It's not much, but it is mine, and it's a start."

"I am proud of you, Samuel." Hannah took his hand. "I knew that you could stand on your own two feet. I am proud of how you grew in strength as a man, and I thank you for protecting us from Jacob." She winced. "In the end, wine, anger, and evil consumed him."

The wedding party guests quieted. All turned to see the twelve new guests.

"It's Yeshua's disciples." Rivka's jaw dropped as she pointed to them.

Mary, Mother of Yeshua, turned to Rivka. "The surprises have just begun. A very special guest is also on his way."

Peter broke from the disciples and scowled at Optio Flavius. The Optio stiffened and glared back. Both remembered an incident from a year ago when Optio Flavius shook down Peter for a Roman tax payment.

Andrew grabbed Peter's arm. "Our master and savior asked us to attend the party and enjoy ourselves. You know that he would disapprove of your fighting."

Peter and Flavius broke eye contact. Centurion Camillus walked over to the disciples. Mathew addressed him. "We are honored by your presence. Our Lord has praised your faith."

"My faith is but a fraction of his glory."

"Then why do you still serve Rome?" Peter prodded Centurion Camillus.

"If our Lord were to instruct me to resign my position, I would do so at once. What he has done is to instruct me and my men to conduct our duties with honor, to be content with our pay, never extort money, and to not accuse people falsely. That I have done and that I will continue to do."

"Yeah, well, why don't you tell that to the gentile dog standing over there?" Peter pointed to Octio Flavius.

Flavius hunched his shoulders, spread his arms, and scowled at Peter.

"He is now under Centurion Magnus's command and he's a leader in his century. Centurion Magnus does not tolerate misconduct toward Judaeans." Centurion Camillus raised his palms. "I don't expect you to share a glass of wine with the Optio." He smiled at Peter. "You can have a glass of wine and a meal with me and my family as, for all our cultural differences, we are brothers in Christ."

Peter, at last, smiled. "Yes. It is what our lord would want." Peter followed Camillus to the food and wine buffet.

A carriage with an armed contubrium escort entered the compound. The Judaeans attending moved toward a wall. Legatus Octavio exited the Carriage. He wore full Legion commander regalia. The Romans at the party stood straight. Punched, their chests, and extended their right arms. "Hail."

Thomas turned to Simon, "You see! I told you this was a setup, a trap! Now we're all going to get arrested and hauled off to the Antonia Fortress."

"What has possessed you?" Simon skewed his eyes. "Our Lord asked us to attend this wedding party. Are you telling me that he would betray us to the Romans?"

Peter then confronted Octavio. "There was a time that the mere sound of your steps would make me tremble. Now, I do not fear you. I have no fear of anyone who can take my life on this world; I fear the one who can condemn me to Hell for an eternity in the next world." He put his hands on his hips. "Why did you need a contubrium of soldiers to attend a wedding party? Arrest us now and get it over with."

"Did you think that Pontius Pilate would need a Legion Commander to arrest unarmed or, in your case, lightly armed Judaeans? I did not come to arrest you. I came to celebrate with my Centurion his marriage to a most worthy Judaean lady."

"Then why did you bring a contubrium of heavily armed soldiers?"

"As the highest-ranking Roman soldier in Judaea, there are many who would wish me dead." He prodded. "I do not doubt that you are one of them."

Peter relaxed his posture. "At one time, you would be correct. Since I found the king of kings and the prince of peace, I no longer hold rancor toward you."

"This king of yours?" Octavio tilted his head. "Where and what is his kingdom?"

"His kingdom is not of this Earth. His adversary, Satan, is the ruler of Earth."

"If your King, Yeshua, rules a Heavenly, spiritual kingdom, then he is no threat to Rome. Additionally, we do not have an adversarial spirit toward our Gods. With the help of our Gods, Rome rules this World."

"The Holy Spirit led Yeshua to fast for forty days and nights in the wilderness, and . . ."

Leganus Octavio raised his hands. "Forty days without eating? I have led many foreign campaigns when rations fell short, but forty days? I find that hard to believe."

"Yeshua is more than just a man." Peter grinned. "The Holy Spirit called on him to fast for forty days in the wilderness so that he would confront Satan in his territory. Satan tempted him with all the Kingdoms of the World if he would worship him. Satan had to own them for it to be a temptation, right?"

"You can believe that all you want. I don't believe in this Satan." Octavius put his hands on his hips. "Moreover, I don't care about any of your foolish beliefs. My only concern is Rome. For now, I know that Yeshua, you, and his followers do not yet pose a threat to me or Roman rule. I will be watching, however."

"I'm sure you will," Peter smirked.

"You say this King, Yeshua, is the Prince of Peace?"

"Yes." Peter nodded his head.

"Then let's call it a truce and enjoy the festivities." Octavio opened his hands. "Let us all celebrate a marriage between one of mine and one of yours."

Peter saw a vision of Yeshua smiling and nodding to him. "Truce for today. Let it be. L'chaim."

Yeshua entered the courtyard unnoticed. He walked up to the bride. "Rivka. I bless your new marriage." He smiled at her. "Magnus. I bless you too. You have not yet come to believe in me. I knock at your door. It is up to you to answer. I patiently await."

"Yeshua!" It's, it's," Rivka's finger jittered. "You."

"I hope that you're not too nervous to sing for me.

"Why no, she blushed."

Centurion Camillus and his family ran over to Yeshua. "Thank you, master, thank you!" Camillus clasped Yeshua's forearm. "Thank you."

A petite woman in a white uniform then dropped to her knees and started kissing Yeshua's feet. She looked up. "I am Minji. I am Camillus's maidservant. I was paralyzed and at death's door. You healed me." She again kissed his feet.

"You are blessed, Minji. Go now. Enjoy the festivities." Yeshua smiled. "Rivka, please your song for me."

Rivka went to the musicians and taught them the song's music.

Yeshua handed Judas Iscariot a Denarius coin. "Put this on the musician's plate."

Judas walked over to the musicians. After ensuring that no one was looking, he pretended to place the coin on their plate while taking three coins from it. He pocketed the booty.

Rivka stood in front of the musicians with a lyre. After strumming three chords, she sang,

"Come and follow him.
Open your eyes to a World of seeing.
Come and follow him.
He'll show you a whole new meaning.
Hear what he has to say,
let him show you the way.
Trust in him and obey,
and he will wash your sins away.
See Heaven through the Son,
living waters soft and sweet.
You will find eternal life,
believe, and he will set you free.
His love flows upon the shores of time,
from oceans deep to mountains high.

He'll lift your spirit far and wide;
for his love is true and divine.
The seed that he plants today,
tomorrow will grow into a tree.
See Heaven through the son,
living waters soft and sweet.
You will find eternal life,
believe, and he will set you free.
His love flows upon the shores of time,
from oceans deep to mountains high.
He'll lift your spirit far and wide;
for his love is true and divine."

The wedding party cheered. Rivka smiled and bowed to them. Yeshua gently embraced her. "Thank you, my child."

Leganus Octavio clapped and smiled. He walked over to praise Rivka. He met Yeshua first. "The high priests of your people fear you. They have Pilate's ear. I see nothing to fear in you."

"Fear of God is the beginning of all understanding. I did not come to condemn. I came to save. I came to save all of mankind, and that includes you."

Although Yeshua did not raise his voice and looked at him gently, Octavius stepped back.

"It is my duty as the highest-ranking Roman soldier in Judaea to see and hear everything. I will take your every word and action into consideration, for both the good and bad for Rome."

"Leganus Octavio, all have sinned and fallen short of God's glory. No one is righteous, no not one. You are a man of great understanding. Heed my words. Call on me and you will be saved."

'He has no fear of me.' Octavio touched his chin. *'He respects me but in a way that I have never experienced. What do I make of this man.'*

Mary, Mother of Yeshua, interrupted. "Yeshua, we are out of wine."

"Woman," he spoke in a reverent tone of voice, "what do I have to do with it? My hour has not yet come." He then nodded to Mary.

Mary smiled. She gathered the servants and brought them to her son. "Whatever he asks, do it."

Yeshua pointed to six waterpots. "Fill them to the brim with water."

The servants complied.

"Leganus Octavio, I grant you the honors. Have the first cup."

A servant handed Octavio a cup of the liquid. He tasted it. He almost dropped it in shock. "Yeshua, I don't know by what magic or intervention you did this. I have campaigned over the entire empire. Never have I tasted a finer wine."

Yeshua addressed the gathering, "Every man at the beginning drinks the good wine. Then when the good wine is drunk, they turn to the bad wine. I have saved the best wine for now."

The gathering knew that Yeshua's words bore greater meaning than just the wine.

The party then drank to their heart's delight.

Magnus and Rivka entwined arms and drank wine together. They then shared a long kiss. The entire party, Romans and Judaeans alike, cheered.

Isolde Maria hovered overhead and applauded.

End of Part I

Part II

Chapter 1

Centurions Magnus, Longinus, and Camillus stood, punched their chests, and yelled, "Hail" as Leganus Octavius entered the war room.

Octavius motioned for them to sit. "The Jewish Feast of Tabernacle is over. Now, the Passover is almost upon us. The Passover is a charged time during the most mundane times. Yeshua is attracting a huge following. Thousands of people have come to worship him, just as many hate him. The Frumentari has reported that the Jewish Sanhedrin wants him dead. One of his followers, Judas Iscariot, has informed a Frumentari operative that Yeshua and his inner circle will attend Passover in Jerusalem. I expect a leader and man of Yeshua's stature to arrive riding on a white stallion. That will only add to his prestige and stir the passions of the crowd. Again, I stress, the Sanhedrin and the Jewish high priest, Caiaphas, have Pontius Pilate's ear. In addition to the furor that surrounds Yeshua, the Temple money changers are always trouble. They are cutthroats of the worst order. Some of them are Sicarii. The ones that aren't Sicarii donate to them." Octavio raised his hands. "Have your soldiers watch them closely and warn them to never turn their backs to them."

"May I have your permission to speak, Dominus?"

"Yes, Magnus. It's Centurions such as yourself that accomplish our mission and elevate my command in the eyes of Pilate and Ceasar."

"You have met Yeshua and have eye-witnessed him performing a miracle. We have determined that he is no threat to Rome."

Leganus Octavius placed his helmet on the table and folded his hands. "He is not a direct threat to Rome. As you know, I met him at your wedding party. Never has a man more impressed me. I have met emperors, philosophers, and great military commanders. Something about this Yeshua impressed me above them all."

Centurion Camillus next spoke, "Dominus, he has performed many miracles. They are verified beyond what is credited to any Roman God."

"Camillus, I am a military commander, not a Pontifex Maximus." Octavius touched his fingertips in a steeple. "You may speak freely. I want as much information as possible to further our mission and our duty to Rome."

"He raised a man named Lazareth from the dead. You met my maidservant Minji. My children love her as a second mother. My wife and I love her as a daughter. She lay in her bed paralyzed." Centurion Camillus lowered his eyebrows and looked at his commander. "She was at death's door. Yeshua healed her with just a word."

"That comes as no surprise to me." He pointed at Camillus. "When I attended Magnus's wedding party with you, I saw him turn six waterpots of rainwater into wine. It was more exquisite than any wine that I have ever tasted." He folded his hands. "That wine was fit for Ceasar." Octavius stood. "I am not a religious man. I am a soldier. My duty is to Rome and our mission. I now know that Yeshua is more than a man. Whether or not he is the actual Son of God is irrelevant to me. His presence does threaten the peace. Many Judaeans want him dead. If they succeed in murdering him, a full-scale riot is the best-case scenario; an outright civil war among the Judaeans is the worst case," Octavius paused for effect, "and fully possible. If the three of you value your military careers," he pointed to all three. "You will do everything to enforce the peace during Passover and prevent those possible scenarios." He stood and picked up his helmet. "I have full confidence that you three can lead your soldiers to achieve our mission during this heated time. Again, I am not a religious man. I am a soldier. My first and last loyalty is not to a God or Gods but to Ceasar and Rome. Magnus, I know that your lovely new wife is a believer in Yeshua. Camillus, I know that you are now a believer. That does not matter to me. I expect each of you to make Ceasar and Rome your first and last priority and loyalty." He donned his helmet. "Am I understood?"

Magnus, Longinus, and Camillus punched their chests and extended their right arms. "Hail!"

Octavius exited the war room.

Chapter 2

Magnus and Rivka held hands and lay together on a mat placed on the flat part of their house's roof. The full moon, thousands of stars, and five planets were visible in the cloudless sky.

"We believe that the stars tell a story." Magnus squeezed Rivka's hand. "Our military commanders will even consult an expert astrologus to help us with our battle strategy."

"What are the stars and planets telling you right now?" Rivka raised his hand to her lips.

"It's telling me what I already know." He turned his head and kissed her lips. "That even our Goddesses envy your beauty and grace." He kissed her again. "What the stars and planet don't need to tell me is that I love you more than I can ever hope to understand in this lifetime or any lifetime to come."

"I look at the sky and see the handiwork of God." She rested the back of her head on his chest. "I can not only admire the structure and beauty of God's creation," She pointed upward, "but I feel like I can peer into eternity."

"Do the movements and positions of the stars have meaning in your faith?"

Rivka rolled over, placed her chin on his chest, and reached up to stroke his cheek with her fingertips. "When it's our Lord's will, yes. After Yeshua was born in a manger, Father Yahweh used a giant star to show the kings and Wisemen where to find and worship the newborn savior."

"Our beliefs in the positions of the stars, moon, and planets are more than just magic and myth." Magnus stroked her hair. "Our Mathematicus scholars have studied the movements of the moon, stars, and planets and have determined the length of our day, the phases of the moon, and the length of our year."

"Our Jewish mathematicians have done likewise, but in service to God. We can use the positions of the stars and planets to determine the time for planting and harvesting of our crops and the right time for our religious festivals." She tilted her head and softly sighed in approval as he continued to stroke her hair. "Can't you see that the exquisiteness, movements, and structure of the Heavens is evidence of one all-mighty, creating God?" She tilted her head to look into his eyes.

"You have opened my eyes to many things. I have seen Yeshua make the crippled walk and the blind see. I have tasted the wine that he created from water. And you, Rivka," He kissed the top of her head, "have healed my blindness to matters of the heart."

"Your commander, who has seen parts of the world that I do not yet know exist, tells us that Yeshua turned the water into the finest wine he had ever tasted. But I cannot fathom any taste more delectable than your kiss. I could smell a rosebud sprinkled with frankincense, but its fragrance would fall short of your breath. If only I could count every star in the sky. Even so, my count would still fall short of the ways that I love you. Even my mother is happier now than I have ever seen her. When I received Yeshua into my heart, I experienced a total rebirth." Rivka kissed his lips. "I can't believe that just a matter of weeks ago, I was a sad and lonely little girl, living in terror of an abusive father. Now that I am yours and you are mine, I no longer feel like that lowly caterpillar." She kissed him again. "I am now transformed into a brilliant butterfly."

"Now, having you in my arms and feeling your heartbeat, I can assure you that you are more beautiful and graceful than the fluttering of the most vivid gossamer wings." They kissed with open mouths and fluttering tongues.

After their long kiss, Rivka rested the side of her head on his chest.

"I am no expert Roman astrologus or mathematicus." He again held her tightly and stroked her hair. "But as I look upon the planets Venus and Mars, I can picture our future son and daughter."

"Just laying here and looking at those planets won't make our future son and daughter a reality." Rivka looked up at him, arched her eyebrows, and winked; then, she gave him her most passionate kiss of their evening. "I'd like to see the stars while we conceive our first child. Even better is seeing your face kissing me." Rivka twined her fingers into his hair as they kissed.

Chapter 3

Sephegus had taken Barabbas's place as Sicarii leader. He sat in a secret, subterranean chamber, sharpening his sicae dagger. Its blade reflected light flashes from a single torch. Water seeping through the stone walls both chilled and cast a mineral odor. Two of his deputies sat next to him.

Above, Judas Iscariot entered the deserted stone mason shop. A sentry appeared from behind a pillar. He pinned Judas against a wall and put the blade of his sicae dagger to his throat. "Who goes?"

"Judas Iscariot." He kept his body still. "Sephegus is expecting me."

The sentry took the dagger from his throat and nodded toward a narrow entrance.

Judas sidled through the opening and descended ten steps to the underground chamber. "Sephegus." He put his hand to his throat. "I have served you well. Why did your lookout have to put a dagger to my throat."

"Considering that capture means crucifixion for us all, you got off easy." Sephegus continued to sharpen his blade. "What is this one going to cost us."

"Twenty-five denarii."

"Twenty-five denarii? Ha! Ha! Ha! This one better be good." He pointed his dagger at Judas.

Judas broke out in a cold sweat. "I know that you want to exact revenge against Centurion Magnus."

"You know, huh?" He prodded with his dagger. "Why do I need the likes of you to tell me that? He arrested Barabbas and recently wiped out our Gadara cell. He has killed or arrested some of my best men."

"My information will help you exact the ultimate revenge on him."

"You don't think that if I could kill him, I would?" Sephegus placed his Sicae dagger on the flat boulder that served as a table. "Not only is he a formidable foe in his own right, but he is almost always surrounded by heavily armed and shielded soldiers. Any attempt on him will result in death, or worse, capture and crucifixion."

"I have some information and a way for you to punish him worse than death. What I can tell you and what I can do for you will make crucifixion feel like less than a bee sting compared to the agony that you can inflict on him."

"You have my attention." Sephegus crossed his arms. "Let's hear it."

Judas smirked at him and raised an open palm.

"Twenty-five denarii based on what?"

"Make it fifteen now and ten after the deed."

Sephegus turned his head to his deputies. The one to his right nodded. "This better be worth fifteen denarii." His other deputy handed Judas fifteen coins. "I think you know that we have unpleasant ways of taking our money back."

Judas squeezed the coins. "Magnus has taken a wife. She is lovelier than any Goddess the Romans can conjure or that our Tanakh can describe. I never thought that a Gentile Dog like Magnus could love a woman as much as David in Psalm forty-five or Solomon in the Song of Songs. I know that when Yeshua enters Jerusalem for the Passover, she will be there." Judas put the coins in a pouch. "One of Yeshua's inner circle, a woman, Mary Magdelene, loves her like a younger sister. I will walk next to Mary Magdelene. Magnus's new wife is named Rivka. I will look for her in the crowd. When I spot her, I will point her out to Mary Magdelene. She will no doubt greet and identify Rivka for you with a kiss. An unarmed woman with no self-defense training will make an easy target, wouldn't you agree?

Sephegus nodded.

Cut her throat," Judas made a knife edge with his hand and ran it across his throat, "and you will cut the very heart and soul out of our despised Centurion."

"Well, Judas, thus far, your information is worth fifteen denarii." Sephegus stood. He picked up his sicae dagger, sheathed it, and hid it beneath his tunic. "You get the other ten denarii after we kill the Gentile Dog's traitorous wife."

Chapter 4

News of Yeshua raising Lazareth from the dead dominated talk during the Feast of the Tabernacle. Multitudes gathered by the streets of Jerusalem in anticipation of his entry. That night, Yeshua stayed in the house of Mary, Martha, and Lazarus in the slums of Bethany on the eastern slope of the Mount of Olives. Yeshua faced two of his disciples. "Go to the village of Bethphage. There, you will find a donkey with her colt. Loosen them and bring them to me. The owner will ask you why you are taking his donkey and colt." Yeshua smiled. "Tell him that the Lord needs them. He will not object."

Yeshua's disciples returned with the Donkey and her colt. They cast their garments on the colt. Yeshua then sat upon the colt and rode it down the road from the Mount of Olives toward Jerusalem. His disciples followed on foot.

***

Magnus's duties as a Centurion in the critical time of the Feast of Tabernacle and the Passover had kept him away from home. Rivka and Hannah ate a hearty breakfast of fish, nuts, and dates. They packed the leftovers in a small bag and began their walk toward the gates of Jerusalem to greet their Lord and Savior.

***

Magnus and Optio Flavius observed from a strategic perch above the street.

Optio Flavius pointed. "That's him! But he rides on a donkey? What kind of a king enters on a donkey."

Magnus replied, "Leganus Octavio told us to expect a man of his stature to ride on a white stallion."

"I met him at your wedding party and drank the wine that he made from rainwater. I saw him perform a miracle, but I will never understand his ways."

"Even though I am married to a Judaean, I don't fully understand their culture and customs. That man over there," Magnus pointed to a well-dressed, older man with a well-trimmed gray beard. "He looks like he can help us." Magnus rode his horse over to the man. "Don't be afraid of me. I only want to ask you a question so that I may better understand your ways."

The older man stopped and looked at Magnus. At first, he was fearful. Magnus's tone of voice and relaxed posture quelled his anxiety.

"I see Yeshua arriving on a donkey." Magnus pointed to Yeshua. "Should not a man proclaiming himself the Son of God and King of Israel ride on a stallion?"

"Dominus Centurion, our prophet Zechariah wrote over five hundred years ago, 'Rejoice greatly, daughter Zion! Shout, daughter Jerusalem! See, your king comes to you, righteous and victorious, lowly and riding on a donkey, on a colt, the foal of a donkey.'"

Optio Flavius folded his arms and glowered at him. "I will never understand your strange beliefs."

Magnus held up a stiff arm to silence Optio Flavius. "Are you saying that someone predicted this five hundred years ago?"

"Yes Dominus Centurion. This was predicted over five hundred years ago." The wise old man held up his open hands. "As it was written, so now shall it be fulfilled."

***

As Yeshua entered Jerusalem, the multitudes cheered and shouted, "Hosanna! Hosanna! Blessed is he who comes in the name of the Lord! Hail the King of Israel!" They showered his path with garments, sheets, and linens, as well as palm fronds. "Hoshia Na! Hoshia Na! Save us! Save Us!" They also shouted.

Yeshua's disciples followed close behind. Judas Iscariot made a point of walking next to Mary Magdelene. "Look, Mary!" He pointed into the crowd. "Isn't that Rivka?"

"Yes! It is!" Mary Magdelene beamed. "Rivka! Come!" She beckoned her.

Rivka beamed; her spirits rose. "Siha!" She pushed some of the crowd out of her way, "Menahem!" She barged through an opening and ran to Mary Magdelene. They warmly embraced.

Mary Magdelene kissed each of Rivka's cheeks. "Walk with me, my sister."

Judas Iscariot nodded to a nondescript man standing in the first row of the throng. The man reached under his tunic and grasped his sicae dagger. He crept toward Rivka.

**

The Pharisees stood back among themselves and murmured. "We have achieved nothing. The World now worships him."

**

A group of men from Greece approached Phillip. One of them asked, "We would like to see Yeshua."

Philip and Andrew then approached Yeshua with the request. "The hour has come for the Son of man to be glorified. Most assuredly, I say to you, unless a grain of wheat falls to the ground and dies, it stays alone, but if it dies, it produces much grain. He who loves his life shall lose it, but he who hates his life in this world will find eternal life in Heaven." Jesus turned to people who had gathered around them. "If anyone serves me, let him follow me, and where I am, there my servant will be also. If anyone serves me, him my father will honor." Yeshua paused and closed his eyes, *'Isolde Maria, Rivka is in danger. Get her away.'*

***

The Sicarii assassin drew his dagger; he was now only three steps away from Rivka.

***

"Now my soul is troubled," Yeshua continued, "and what shall I say? Father, save me from this hour? But for this purpose, I came to this hour. Father, glorify your name.

A tremendous voice thundered from above. "I have both glorified it and will glorify it again."

The multitudes staggered and scattered about upon hearing the voice. Some heard the voice clearly; others only heard a thunderclap. Yet some said that an angel had spoken to him.

Yeshua now had the absolute attention of the crowd. "That voice did not come from me but for your sake. Now is the judgment of this world; now, the ruler will be cast out. And if I am lifted up from the earth, I will draw all people to myself."

One of the Greeks approached him, "We have heard from the law that the Christ remains forever; and how can you say, 'The Son of Man must be lifted up?' Who is this Son of Man?"

Jesus addressed the crowd, "A little while longer, the light is with you. Walk while you have the light, lest darkness overtake you; he who walks in darkness does not know where he is going. While you have the light, believe in the light, that you may become sons of light." Yeshua then left them.

***

The assassin had his right arm cocked and ready to slash Rivka's throat. He swung his weapon in a circular strike.

Isolde Maria appeared to her. "Rivka! Duck! Run!"

Rivka ducked.

The assassin's dagger swished through the air.

She then ran with Isolde Maria through the crowd.

A woman screamed at the sight of the dagger-wielding assassin. He tried to kill her with a forward thrust, but she was two feet out of reach. Several men surrounded him. He vainly swung his weapon at them, hoping to kill anyone his knife reached.

Magnus and Flavius responded to the commotion. Magnus spotted Rivka running and galloped over to her. Flavius confronted the assassin. "Drop your weapon." He pointed his spear from atop his horse. "You are under arrest."

"Never!" The assassin charged Flavius.

Flavius impaled the assassin with his spear. He screamed and clutched his chest before collapsing onto the street. He died in a pool of blood.

"Move on, everyone!" Flavius yelled at the crowd. "Unless you care to join him!"

"Magnus!" Rivka ran toward her husband.

"Rivka." He dismounted his horse. She ran into his arms. He held her close. They kissed. Tasting and relishing every second, their minds drifted into an ether world. He paused to breathe. "Are you alright?"

Rivka's moist eyes again met his eyes. She then pressed her head against his breastplate. His heartbeat made the bronze chime.

Magnus patted her back. He then noticed a throng of shocked on-lookers. Magnus cradled her and lifted her onto his horse.

"Mother!" Rivka spotted Hannah weaving her way through the crowd.

Magnus took Hannah's hand and led her to his horse. "Up you go." Magnus boosted her onto his horse. "Clear out! Now!" He yelled to the crowd. Some complied, others ignored him, and still others gathered around them. "Move!" He brandished his gladius. The crowd dispersed. Some screamed and ran. Others quietly walked away. Three minutes later, six Roman foot soldiers arrived. "Accompany us. I am taking these two women home." Magnus turned to the stragglers. "Anyone who follows us faces the wrath of Rome."

***

Magnus and Rivka stood in the atrium of his compound. "Magnus." She squeezed him and sobbed on his shoulder. "If not for my Angel, Isolde Maria, I would be dead. I love her so much, Magnus; she has twice saved my life."

"She has also appeared to me. I am amazed by her. Her beauty is unsurpassed, but I only see her purity and her highest love for you. I have seen many unexplained things in the past few weeks. Rivka, the greatest mystery is my love for you. If I should lose you, I lose my reason for living. For years, I thought that service to Rome and the Legion was my sole purpose in life and that ferocity in battle marked a man. Rome's greatest glory cannot match just one beat of your heart. Just the sound of your footsteps makes better music than Rome's finest orchestra. As a man, I was both admired and feared, yet I knew I was incomplete. Loving you makes me whole, Rivka. You are a part of me, Rivka, a part that I care not to live without."

"You are my strength, and you are my destiny. You have filled the final piece of my heart. Rather I die in the street from the assassin's blade than to live without you."

"Rivka, now you know that marrying me has put you in danger. It's bad enough for your people that you married a gentile."

"No longer is there Jew or Gentile. We all are one in the body of Christ."

"With each hour, I come closer to understanding Yeshua's message. I have seen several of his miracles. I can also tell you from my experience in the field and access to intelligence from the Frumentari that many hate him and even want to kill him. They hate you also because of him. Not only do some hate you for marrying a gentile, but the more radical elements want you dead for marrying a Roman Centurion. They now regard you as a collaborator." Magnus looked at her with a glint in his eyes.

"I now know of the danger, yet I feel safe in your arms."

"You are safe here. I will have soldiers guard this compound." He sharpened his gaze into her eyes. "Rivka, before you met me, you were a prisoner in your father's home. I don't want you to feel that you are a prisoner here.

Yet at least until Passover is finished and things have calmed down, you must stay here."

"In my father Jacob's home, not only did I not have love; I lived in fear of him. Now I have Christ in my heart and you in my arms. I know that I should not love my life here on Earth, but I love you, Magnus, and I love being married to you. Even if I must stay in your compound, I am free. We have so much, yet we miss one thing."

"What is that, Rivka?"

"Children." She winked. "Must you return to duty right now?"

Magnus lifted her and cradled her in his arms. She put her arms around his neck and kissed him. After he returned her to her feet, she took his hand and led him to their bedroom."

Chapter 5

Centurion Magnus briefed Optio Flavius in the Temple Court of Gentiles. The area bustled with activity. Chatter from the people and merchants, along with the cooing of caged doves, the bleating of penned goats and sheep, and the mooing of oxen, meshed into a cacophony. The hot sun swelled the stench of sweaty people and animal manure. "See those men exchanging currency and selling animals for sacrifice," Magnus pointed. "They are criminals and cutthroats. I am assigning you to lead a Contubrium of miles-ranked soldiers to keep order. I know that you can be aggressive with the Judaeans. Now is a time when we need it. Don't turn your back on those men. Some are Sacarii and value cutting a Roman soldier's throat above making money."

Magnus left. Optio Flavius positioned his soldiers in strategic parts of the Court of Gentiles. Flavius and his soldiers noted that the bustle grew to commotion. Yeshua entered with his disciples and Mary Magdelene. Yeshua lurched toward the money changers and merchants. He stood tense and tall. He flared his arms, clenched his fists, and glared at them with narrow eyes and laser focus. Suddenly, he made a whip out of chords and thrashed the money changers. He flipped over their tables, poured their coins on the pavement, and then released the doves, sheep, goats, and oxen. The marketplace erupted in chaos. People scrambled and screamed. Doves, sheep, goats, and even oxen fled in every direction. The money changers and merchants cringed in fear. The temple guards stood still as if thunderstruck. Flavius and his soldiers froze. Yeshua shouted at the money changers and merchants. "My father's house is not a marketplace or a den of thieves!" His words silenced the crowd. No one tried to recover the coins or corral the animals.

Four Pharisees stepped forward, "By what authority do you do those things?"

"Destroy this temple." Yeshua pointed at them. "In three days, I will raise it again."

A Pharisee replied, "It has taken forty-six years to build this Temple, and you will rebuild it in three days?

The disciples and Mary Magdelene murmured to each other. They knew that he had spoken something profound, although yet to be revealed.

Magnus galloped to the scene. The area looked like a mighty wind had swept through.

Flavius was pallid as a corpse. His mouth and eyes were as circles. "Yeshua did this on his own. The money changers and merchants were terrified of him. The Temple guards were like stone statues. I must report, Dominus Centurion, that before we could respond, Yeshua calmed the crowd with his words alone. It was like he had the authority of Jupiter himself."

Chapter 6

A sudden scirocco blew the dust of Jerusalem's streets into vortexes. The merchants near the Temple Mount had secured their canopies from the wind. Many people covered their mouths and noses with their headdresses to avoid breathing the dust. Yeshua entered the square and headed toward the Temple. Two hundred people braved the wind to follow him. Several Scribes and Pharisees, including Nicodemus, exited the Temple to confront him.

Suddenly, two men dragged a screaming woman to him.

"Why do you treat this woman in such a manner?" Yeshua pointed at them. "Release her."

They released her and backed away. "Depart from me." Yeshua prodded. The two men ran away. The woman lay sobbing in the dirt and dust.

"Teacher." A Pharisee approached them. "This woman was caught in the very act of adultery." Nerves hoarsened his voice. "The law of Moses commands that we must stone her to death." He pointed at him. "What do you have to say about that?"

Yeshua ignored him. He stooped down and wrote with his finger on a dust mound.

"Why do you ignore him?" A Pharisee stepped forward. "Are you that ignorant of the law of Moses?"

Yeshua stood and faced them. "Let he who is without sin cast the first stone."

The men in the crowd looked at each other. Then, one by one, they dropped their stones and left. The Scribes, Pharisees, and Nicodemus returned to the Temple steps. They murmured to themselves outside on the portico.

Yeshua was now alone with the woman. He helped her to her feet. "Woman, where are your accusers? Has no one condemned you?"

She answered, "No one, Lord."

Yeshua said to her, "Neither do I condemn you; go now and sin no more." He then turned to the people who had again gathered around them. "I am the light of the world. He who follows me shall not walk in darkness but have the light of life."

As Yeshua walked away. Three of the men who had moments earlier brandished stones ran up to him. They fell on their knees and clutched his robe. One of them said, "I am not without sin. Please, Lord, forgive me as you forgave her."

"Me also, please," one of the other men pleaded.

"Me too. Me too." The third man continued to clutch Yeshua's robe. "Forgive me, for I am also a sinner."

The Scribes, Pharisees, and Nicodemus saw this and descended the Temple steps to confront Yeshua. "You bear witness of yourself." A Pharisee prodded. "Your witness is a lie."

Yeshua turned to Scribes, Pharisees, and Nicodemus. "Even if I bear witness of myself, my witness is true, for I know where I come from and where I am going, but you do not know where I come from or where I am going." He pointed at them. "You judge according to the flesh; I judge now no one. Yet if I do judge, my judgment is true, for I am not alone, but I am with the father who sent me. It is written in your law that the testimony of two men is true. I bear witness of myself, and the Father who sent me bears witness of me."

A Scribe then stepped forward. "Then where is your Father?"

Yeshua looked directly at him. "You know neither me nor my Father. If you had known me, you would have known the Father also."

The scribes and Pharisees sneered at him before returning to the synagogue. Nicodemus remained. "Teacher Yeshua, today I have seen and heard great profundity. I wish to learn more. We need to meet in secret. Tonight, at the eighth hour, go to that garment shop." Nicodemus pointed to a stall in the nearby market. "I will be in the backroom. The shop owner will show you in."

Yeshua accepted his invitation.

***

The shop owner dropped his jaw and opened his eyes wide. His knees buckled as Yeshua peered through him. He then opened the door to the back room for Yeshua to enter.

"Have a seat." Nicodemus motioned to a chair behind a rugged wooden table.

Yeshua sat.

"You do know that the Sanhedrin hates you." Nicodemus rested his elbows on the table and folded his hands. "At first, they disregarded you as just another blasphemer and madman. Now that you have a large and growing following and word of your miracles have spread far and wide, they fear you as a threat to their authority." Nicodemus opened his hands. "But I have seen your miracles with my own eyes. I have heard you speak with both calm and authority." He placed his hands back on the table. "Today, you were set up. The Sanhedrin wanted to destroy your credibility. Those two men who dragged that woman into the town square were hired goons. Even we can't control them. Our fellow Jews fear them enough that they hope the Romans will arrest them and take them away. Yet when you confronted them, they obeyed you and fled in fear." Nicodemus shook his hands. "That only confirms what I am starting to believe. The cutthroats exchanging money in front of the Temple would kill before allowing anyone to disrupt their business. Even the Sanhedrin must tolerate them. The Temple guards won't interfere with their business. Yet you arrive, unarmed and hardly the physical stature of Goliath, and chase them from the Temple. Surely, you must have the authority of God himself. I have heard your message. You mostly speak of love and compassion. My colleagues' hearts have hardened to such matters. Although that woman was a known prostitute and the goons knew where she plied her trade, even I felt for her as she sobbed in the dust and awaited a painful death. You not only forgave her, but you convicted the hearts of those who would commit malice against her. I can tell that through you, she is a new creation. Your words and deeds have convinced me that you are a teacher from God, for no one can do these signs that you do unless God is with him."

Yeshua put his open hands on the table. "Most assuredly, my response to you is this: unless one is born again, he cannot see the kingdom of God."

Nicodemus raised his eyebrows and looked at him with a sideward glance. "How can a man be born when he is old? Can a man enter a second time into his mother's womb and be born."

Jesus held up his open hands. "Most assuredly, I say to you, unless one is born of water and spirit, he cannot enter the Kingdom of God. That which is born of the flesh is flesh, and that which is born of the spirit is spirit. Do not marvel that I said to you, 'You must be born again.' The wind blows where it wishes, and you hear it, but you cannot tell where it comes from and where it goes. So is everyone who is born of the spirit."

Nicodemus shrugged his shoulders and raised his palms. "How can these things be?"

Yeshua held eye contact with him. "Are you the teacher of Israel and do not know these things? Most assuredly, I say to you, we speak what we know and testify to what we have seen, and you don't receive our witness. If I had told you earthly things and you do not believe, how will you believe if I tell you heavenly things? No one has ascended to Heaven but he who came down from Heaven is the Son of Man who is in Heaven. And as Moses lifted the serpent in the wilderness, even so must the Son of Man be lifted, that whoever believes in him should not perish but have eternal life. For God so loved the world that he gave his only begotten son, that whoever believes in him should not perish but have everlasting life. For God did not send his son into the world to condemn the world, but that the world through him might be saved."

"All right." Nicodemus stood. "I think I am starting to understand your words. I know that during the time that Moses led our people through the desert, they were plagued by venomous serpents. If a serpent bit them and they looked up to the serpent that Moses lifted on a stick, their faith would heal them. So, you are saying that likewise, if we look to you and believe, we are saved from the poison of sin?"

"Yes." Yeshua nodded his head. "He who believes in me is not condemned, but he who does not believe is condemned already because he has not believed in the name of the only begotten Son of God. And that is the condemnation, that the light has come into the world, and men loved darkness rather than light because their deeds were evil. For everyone practicing evil hates the light and does not come to the light, lest his deeds should be exposed. But he who does the truth comes to the light, that his deeds may be seen, that they have done so in God."

Nicodemus looked at Yeshua with wide eyes and slightly parted lips. He raised his eyebrows while the rest of his face remained still. Saying nothing, he collapsed into his chair.

Yeshua quietly left.

Chapter 7

The high priest Caiaphas addressed the Sanhedrin. "Each new follower that Yeshua of Nazareth gains is a loss in our prestige and power. Look around you." Caiaphas motioned to the red damask wall tapestries enhanced by dancing torchlight shadows. "His blasphemy and heresy threaten to take everything from us. Every attempt to kill him before the Passover has failed. We tried to discredit him among the Jews with the prostitute. He not only foiled us, but his reputation and following grew.

"Saving a prostitute does not surprise me." Yitzhak, a Sanhedrin Pharisee with a salt and pepper beard and colorful tunic, folded his hands. "One of Yeshua's followers, Judas Iscariot, reported to me that he allowed a prostitute to wash his feet with her tears and hair. Judas then complained that she wasted expensive perfume to anoint his feet."

"He has also associated with tax collectors." Caiaphas pointed at Yitzhak. "And that inspired an idea. I have a plan that will not only discredit him with the Jews, but we'll also get the Romans to arrest him. I know that Optio Flavius will be patrolling the area by the court of Gentiles. He is hated among our people for his zealotry and heavy-handed tax-collection tactics. He won't tolerate anyone speaking out against paying Roman taxes." Caiaphas beamed. "I have already hired my accomplices." He grinned. "Yitzhak. I will need your help."

***

Yeshua, his disciples, and Mary Magdelene approached the Temple Mount.

A young Jewish man spotted them and ran to a contubrium of Roman soldiers captained by Centurion Magnus and Optio Flavius as second in command. "Octio Flavius. You are well known among the Judeans as a hard-driving soldier with unswerving loyalty to Ceasar. A man is by the Court of Gentiles telling the people not to pay taxes to Rome."

Optio Flavius looked at Magnus. Magnus nodded.

"Follow me." The young Judean led Magnus and Flavio to Yeshua.

Magnus and Flavius recognized Yeshua instantly. Yet they dutifully positioned themselves on the fringe of the crowd.

Yitzhak made eye contact with Optio Flavius and then spoke to Yeshua, making sure that Magnus and Flavius heard him. "We know that you speak the truth and that you speak of God's way with truth. So, tell us, teacher, is it lawful by the scribes and the prophets to give tribute to Ceasar?"

Yeshua's disciples murmured among themselves. James turned to Simon Peter, "It's a trap." Peter then looked at Optio Flavius with narrowed eyes and reached under his tunic, placing his hand on his dagger. Mary Magdeline put her fingers over her lips. Yeshua noticed Yitzhak's tight-lipped smile. Yitzhak raised his eyebrows and focused on Optio Flavius. Four Pharisees standing behind him also sported mischievous grins and shifted their eyes between Yeshua and Flavius.

"Why do you tempt me, you hypocrites." Yeshua pointed at them.

Optio Flavius gripped his gladius sword and prepared to dismount from his horse. Magnus sat taller in his saddle.

"Show me your tribute money."

Yitzhak handed Yeshua a coin.

Optio Flavius had dismounted his horse. Magnus remained on his steed but walked it over to Flavius.

Yeshua glanced at the Pharisees, turned to Magnus and Flavius, and then looked back to the Pharisees. He held the coin up to them. "Who is this image and inscription?"

A Pharisee answered, "Ceasar's." He put his hands on his hips.

"Give unto Ceasar what Ceasar's. Give unto God what is God's."

Flavius, gladius sword drawn, had walked up to Yeshua. He turned and handed Flavius the coin. He dropped it and stood too stunned to pick it up. Flavius then looked to Magnus. He gestured for him to mount his horse. Magnus led Flavius and their contubrium away.

The Pharisees were left thunderstruck. Yeshua's disciples and Mary Magdelene smiled and chatted with each other.

"He's amazing." An onlooker said to his companion.

"Yes." He raised his hands. "He truly is the Son of God."

Many in the crowd said likewise.

Chapter 8

The Day of Unleavened Bread and Sacrifice of the Passover Lamb had arrived. Yeshua said to Peter and John, "Go and prepare for us our Passover supper."

Peter raised his palms. "Where do you want us to prepare it?"

"Go into the city. A man carrying a jug of water will meet you. Follow him to his house. When you arrive, say to the owner of the house that I need a room for the Passover supper with my disciples. He will show you a large furnished room. There, you will prepare the Passover."

Peter and John walked into Jerusalem. "Look, Peter. There is a man with a jug of water. He must be the one our Lord instructed us to follow."

John walked up to the man. "Our Lord has instructed us to follow you to your house. He told us that the owner of the house will have space for him to share the Passover supper with us."

The man put his jug in front of John. "I will do so only if you have him turn this water into wine. Make it like that from Cana."

John looked at Peter and shrugged. They were both about to walk away.

The man with the jug laughed. "I jest." He tipped his head to his right. "Follow me. I have what our Lord asks."

John and Peter found that the hall had everything that Yeshua told them it would. They prepared it for the Passover supper.

***

That evening, Yeshua and his disciples reclined at the table. Yeshua then stood at the table head. "I have long desired to share this Passover supper with you before I am to suffer. I will not dine with you again until the Kingdom of God is fulfilled." He held up his cup. "Take this and share it among you. For you shall not again drink of the fruit of the vine until the Kingdom of God arrives.

Yeshua then held up a loaf of bread. He looked upwards. "Thank you, Father, for this bread." He broke it. "This is my body that I give unto you. Eat this in remembrance of me."

After they ate, He held up his cup of wine. "This cup is the new covenant in my blood. I pour it out to you. But the one who will betray me is with us. Woe to the man who betrays me."

Phillip turned to Thomas and grumbled. "You always have doubted him. It must be you."

"No! Never." Thomas turned and pointed at Simon the Zealot. "Maybe it's you. You're always so sure of everything. Perhaps that's just a cover?"

"Not a chance." Simon the Zealot tapped his chest with both hands. "I am the highest among all of you. I am the one who truly believes."

Peter stood and asked, "Lord. Who is it? Who will betray you and," he glanced at Simon the Zealot, "who among us is the highest?"

Yeshua answered. "The one who will betray me is the one who I will give this piece of bread after I dip it in the dish." Yeshua dipped it into the dish and handed it to Judas Iscariot.

Judas took the bread. Satan then possessed him.

"What you are about to do, do so quickly."

Judas ran from the room.

James turned to Mathew. "I guess he is going to buy something for the feast or give it to the poor."

"I think you're right." Mathew nodded.

After Judas had left, Yeshua spoke, "Now the Son of Man is glorified in him. If God is glorified in him, God will glorify the Son in himself and will glorify him at once. For I will be with you only a little longer. You will look for me, and just as I told the Jews, so I tell you now. Where I am going, you cannot come. I give you a great command. Love one another as I have loved you. You must love one another. By your love, all men will know that you are my disciples."

Siman Peter asked, "Lord, where are you going?"

"Where I am going, you cannot now follow, but you will follow later."

"Lord, why can't I follow you now?" Peter shook his hands. "I will lay down my life for you."

"Will you lay down your life for me?" Yeshua squinted his eyes. "I tell you the truth." He pointed at Peter. "Before the rooster crows, you will deny me three times." Yeshua then smiled at his disciples. "Do not let your hearts be troubled. Trust in God and trust in me too. In my Father's house, there are many rooms. I will prepare a place for you. I will come back and take you with me."

Thomas stood and pointed. Lord, we don't know where you are going, so how can we know the way."

"I am the way, the truth, and the life. No one comes to the Father but by me."

***

After Yeshua and his disciples left the hall. The servant that Peter and John met carrying the water jug started clearing and cleaning the table. He picked up the goblet that Yeshua used to toast his disciples and drink wine from and held it before his eyes. *'I remember buying this at the Galilee Marketplace. How can anyone forget the beauty and glow of the girl who sold it to me? She told me that she made it herself. What was her name?'* He dropped the goblet in a bin with the rest of the dirty plates, cups, and utensils. *'Now I remember. Rivka.'*

Chapter 9

Judas Iscariot sprinted to the Second Temple. He stopped in front of the Hall of Hewn. After catching his breath, he had a guard escort him into a large chamber. Judas stood before a large Ceder table.

"What is this one going to cost us." High Priest Caiaphas folded his hands and rested them on the table.

"Thirty silver coins."

"Thirty silver coins?" He placed his palms on the table. "Ha! Ha! Ha! That's insane. That's a month's wages. One can buy a slave or plot of land for that amount!"

"What I can deliver to you is worth far more. Every attempt you have made to kill or discredit Yeshua has made you look like a fool."

"You listen!" Caiaphas prodded. "Just because you claim to bring us valuable information doesn't mean that I'm going to tolerate your insolence!"

"Well, be that as it may, "Judas folded his arms and tilted his chin. "We both know that it is true."

Caiaphas glowered at him for five seconds. "All right." He placed his palms back on the table. "Let's hear it, and it better be good."

"Thirty silver coins." He held his palm upward.

"For what?"

"Yeshua has proven a significant enemy of the Sanhedrin. He has walked on water, made the crippled walk and the blind see. He has even raised the dead. His following grows by the hour. It grows as we speak. You waste time."

"We don't believe those miracles came from God," Itzhak responded.

"Does that matter? The people believe in his miracles and his teaching. Shout blasphemy and heresy all you want. People are listening, and they are believing. Each new follower of Yeshua is one less follower of the Sanhedrin. He is smarter than all of you put together. I am close to him. I can end this for you." Judas again held up an open palm. "Thirty silver coins."

"What are you going to do?" Caiaphas smirked at him. "Kill him yourself?"

"I am no assassin." Judas grinned. "But I do know that for an assassin to both succeed and not get caught, he needs perfect timing. You have one shot at this. You have Pilate's ear. It is Passover. Pilate is tense, fearing any uprising will hurt his status with Rome. Now is the time to bring him before Pilate and have him crucified." Judas beamed. "Problem solved."

"Now I am interested." Caiaphas raised his hands from the table. "What's your plan?"

"Thirty silver coins." He raised his open palm.

"You play games with us." Caiaphas scowled at him. "Tell us why we should pay you what you demand, or our guards will throw you out with some whip scars to remind you of your arrogance and insolence."

"You know that he's here in Jerusalem, and I know where. Not only will I take you to him, but I can assure you that he will only be with his disciples."

"We all admit that he is no ordinary man, yet he looks like an ordinary man." Caiaphas raised his palms. "How can we know it's him?"

"When you arrive with your armed guards, I will identify him with a kiss."

Caiaphas first looked to his father-in-law former high priest Annas and then the rest of the Sanhedrin. Yitzhak was the first to nod.

"Guard." Caiaphas stood and pointed. "Go to the treasury and bring me thirty silver coins."

The Sanhedrin members grinned with delight.

Chapter 10

"Hail!" Centurions Magnus, Longinus, and Camillus stood, punched their chests, and extended their right arms as Leganes Octavius entered the war room. Octavius motioned for them to sit. He doffed his helmet and placed it on the table. "Thus far, I commend you for your excellent work. Centurion Magnus, you have a report on an incident by the Temple court of Gentiles."

"Yes, Leganes, I had positioned my soldiers in strategic spots around the court. I gave my men special instructions to be extra vigilant of the Temple money changers. Everything was normal until Yeshua entered the scene. You had to see it with your own eyes, Dominus. I am still stunned. He made a makeshift whip and beat the money changers. He then turned over their tables and released their livestock. The money changers would have killed anyone else who committed such audacity, or at the very least, the Temple guards would have beaten and arrested him. Yet those cutthroats were paralyzed with fear. They offered zero resistance. The Temple guards did nothing. The place was chaotic. Yet before Optio Flavius and his men could act, Yeshua silenced them with his words alone. Order was restored without intervention."

"That was my briefing from Frumentari Assets. I wanted it confirmed by you. All of us at this table are aware of Yeshua's miracles and capabilities." Octavius placed his hands on his helmet. "We have discussed at length that he by himself is no threat to Rome. Nevertheless, the passions that he stirs in both his followers and foes must still be met with vigilance. Passover is a charged event. Emotional and religious passions can run rampant unless we conduct our duties with utmost diligence and professionalism. Passover has caused problems throughout Judaea. Many who could not afford a pilgrimage to Jerusalem or are not religious are causing problems. I have reports of looting and robberies. Magnus," he pointed, "I am assigning you to take a vigintivirate of twenty soldiers to the Southern territories. We must keep order." Octavius turned his head to Longinus. "No one enjoys crucifying convicts. This one is an exception. It's Barabbas. Tomorrow, we are executing by crucifixion Barabbas and two of his cohorts. Centurion Longinus, I am giving you honors. I know that Optio Flavius is in Magnus's Century. But he helped Magnus arrest Barabbas. Therefore, I am going to assign him to your crucifixion team. He fought Barabbas when he killed three of our own. I want Barabbas to see the fire in Flavius's eyes as he nails him to the cross." Leganus Octavius stood. "Do you have any questions?"

The Centurions remained silent.

"Then proceed with your assigned tasks."

"Hail Ceasar." The Centurions punched their chests and extended their right arms.

"Hail Ceasar." The Leganus replied as he punched his chest and extended his right arm.

Chapter 11

Yeshua, followed by his remaining disciples, walked to the Brook Kidron, where there was an Olive grove known as the Garden of Gethsemane. The moon glowed in the night mist. The scent of olives mingled with the greenery. An Arabian wolf howled in the distance, and a nearby owl hooted. Cicadas chirped in the garden. Yeshua said to his disciples, "Pray that you will not fall into temptation." He looked at each disciple. "Wait for me here. I am going away to pray." Yeshua took Peter, James, and John with him. "My soul is overwhelmed with sorrow to the point of death. Stay here and keep watch until I return from prayer." Yeshua walked a stone's throw away and then fell to his knees. "Father, if you are willing, take this cup from me. Yet not my will, but may your will be done."

Isolde Maria then appeared to him. "Your father hears your prayers. He has not forsaken you. He wants you to finish your mission, fulfill the words of the scriptures and prophesies, and save mankind."

Yeshua's prayers became more anguished, fervent, and earnest. He began to sweat droplets of blood.

When he finished his prayers, Yeshua returned to his disciples, only to find them sleeping. "Awaken and pray, lest you fall into temptation, for the spirit is willing, but the body is weak. The hour is near that the Son of Man is to be betrayed into the hands of sinners. Awake! Rise! Let us go! Here comes my betrayer!"

Judas Iscariot led a crowd of men dispatched by the Sanhedrin. They were armed with clubs and swords.

Judas Iscariot stepped forward. "Greetings, Rabbi." He kissed Yeshua. "Arrest that man."

The men stepped forward, seized Yeshua, and arrested him.

Peter grimaced. Seething with anger, he glided over and, in one fluid motion, drew his sicae dagger and cut off a guard's ear.

"Ahh!" The guard screamed and clutched his wound. His blood seeped through his fingers.

"Sheath your sword!" Yeshua pointed at Peter. "Those who live by the sword shall die by the sword. Do you think that I cannot call upon my father to summon twelve legions of angels to my defense? But how then would the scriptures and prophesies be fulfilled that say it must happen this way?" Yeshua then healed the wounded guard. "Am I leading a rebellion, that you have come out with swords and clubs to capture me? Every day, I sat in the Temple courts teaching, and you did not arrest me. But this is all taking place so that the writings of the prophets will be fulfilled."

As the guards took Yeshua away, his disciples fled.

Chapter 12

Dawn's early light painting an orange glow on the horizon and the chirping of morning songbirds belied the foreboding of the day. Mary Magdelene ran to the gate of Magnus's compound. "Guard. Please. Bring me the Domina. Please. No need for you to open the gate. I just need to talk with her."

The guard could tell from her rapid speech, tense body, and the downturned corners of her mouth, drooping eyelids, and furrowed brow that it was urgent. "I shall at once, woman." The guard ran to Flavia. She went into Rivka's bedroom and awakened her. Rivka spotted Mary Magdelene at the gate and ran to her. She sensed her aura and saw by her body language and facial expression that a dire situation faced them. "Open the gate! Open the gate!"

The guard complied.

Mary Magdelene and Rivka embraced and held each other tight. As they kissed each other's cheeks, Rivka could feel the wetness of her tears. They then kissed on the lips with closed mouths. "Rivka! They've arrested him."

"What?" Rivka shrieked and shook her hands. "No!" Rivka shook Mary Magdelene's arms. "But Magnus's commander, the Leganus himself, met him, witnessed him performing a miracle, and said that he was no threat to Rome."

"But he is a huge threat to the Jewish high priests. The Sanhedrin, not the Romans, have taken him. He needs you. I need you. His mother, Mary, needs you. Rivka, I have loved you as my younger sister. I now love you as an equal. You have grown and matured into a noble woman of God before my eyes. You are a woman with a strong and blessed spirit.

I shall love you until the day that I die, and I will love you after I die and enter the Kingdom of God."

Rivka hugged Mary Magdelene. "You have helped me in many wonderful ways to grow as a woman and to grow in faith in our Lord." Rivka stood back. "But what have they done to him?"

"Rivka." Mary Magdelene clutched her arms. "We will pray for the best for our Lord, but we must also pray for our spiritual strengthening so that we may be there for him if the Father's will is for the worst."

"I can't leave here. My husband has asked that I stay. The Sacarii have already tried to kill me. Many Judaeans hate me and want me dead because I married a Roman Centurion. It's too dangerous for me to leave without Magnus."

"Rivka. Please." Mary Magdelene kissed each of her cheeks. "The disciples have deserted him and fled. Peter has already denied him three times. As women, he needs us to stand strong. As women, only we can comfort him should the worst happen. Please. Come with me."

Rivka stood and stared at her for five pregnant seconds.

Suddenly, Isolde Maria appeared to her. "Rivka. You must go with her. The Son and his mother need you." The angel kissed Rivka's forehead. "Fear not, Rivka. Go!"

"Let me change into my day clothes." Rivka ran to her room, changed her clothes, and ran back to Mary Magdelene. Hand and hand, they headed for Jerusalem.

Chapter 13

Caiaphas briefed Annas, the Sanhedrin, and the elders. "I have gotten word that our guards are bringing him to us."

"It looks like the thirty silver coins were a good investment," Itzhak added. "But we need better evidence. Everything we have so far is contradictory."

"I still have more witnesses," Caiaphas put his palms on the table. "Besides, we can convict him on his words alone."

Twenty minutes later, the guards brought Yeshua before the Sanhedrin and Council of Elders.

"You are under arrest and on trial for blasphemy." Caiaphas prodded. "The penalty is death."

Yeshua said nothing.

"If that's how you want it?" Caiaphas returned his palms to the table. "I call two witnesses."

One of the witnesses, a smallish man wearing soiled, tattered clothes, stepped forward. "I heard him say that he was going to destroy the temple and rebuild it in three days."

The second witness also poorly dressed and groomed, without being asked, added, "I second that. I heard it too."

Caiaphas stood and prodded. "Well, are you going to answer? What do you have to say in response to the testimony of these two men?"

Yeshua remained silent.

"I charge you under oath of the living God!" Caiaphas continued to prod. "Tell us if you are the Christ, the Son of God."

"Yes. I am." Yeshua spoke with authority. "I say to all of you, in the future, you will see the Son of Man sitting at the right hand of the Mighty God and coming from the clouds of Heaven."

Caiaphas tore his clothes. "Blasphemy! He has spoken blasphemy! We don't need any more witnesses. You have heard his blasphemy. What is your verdict?"

"Death! He is worthy of death." The Sanhedrin and elders, save Joseph and Nicodemus, all replied.

Nicodemus and Joseph dropped their heads in shame for their silence.

They then blindfolded Yeshua, spat on him, and punched his face. Others slapped him.

"Ha! Ha! Ha!" Caiaphas guffawed. "Prophesy Christ. Ha! Ha! Ha! Who hit you?"

Itzhak grabbed Caiaphas's arm, stopping him from laughing. He whispered to him, "Yes, he is worthy of death, and we want him dead. But we all know that Roman law prohibits us from executing him. Remember, you have Pilate's ear. We must take him to Pilate so that the Romans may crucify him."

Chapter 14

Judas Iscariot secured his thirty coins in a pouch and strolled toward the center of Jerusalem.

A man accosted him. He stood slightly taller than Judas; he was not fat or thin. Judas first noticed his unusual beard. His mustache did not connect to his beard. His beard ran in a thin line from just below his earlobes, along his jawline, to a well-trimmed point on his chin. His dark, deep-set, piercing eyes both scared him and intrigued him. Judas put his hand under his tunic and braced it on his coin pouch.

"I know what you're thinking. I am no robber."

Judas's body relaxed, although he still walked briskly. "I can see by how richly you're dressed that you're not a common street thug. What do you want?"

The man wore a perfectly tailored red and black silk tunic girded at the waist with a large gold buckle. "For starters, I can tell you that you're headed in the wrong direction."

"What are you talking about?" Judas stopped walking and faced him.

"You just got thirty silver coins. I thought maybe you'd like to celebrate. The best brothel in Jerusalem is that way. You can now afford it." The man pointed in the other direction. "Just one of those coins can buy you a fantastic time of sin and debauchery."

"Just who are you?"

"Me?" The man pointed to himself. "I go by many names, and I am from many places. I am often misunderstood and wrongly blamed. I rule the World but have yet to conquer Heaven. You, my friend, have done marvels for my cause. I wish to commend you."

"Again." Judas clenched his hands in a fist. "Just who are you?"

"You can call me Drago, Dominus Judas Iscariot."

"How do you know my name?"

"Is not the one claiming to be the Son of Man famous? Does he not now have a following in the thousands? Are you not in his inner circle."

"I was." Judas chuckled.

"That's why I admire you, and I am honored by your company. You have more sense than Yeshua. If you could heal the sick, make the crippled walk, make the blind see, and even raise the dead, would you live in poverty, or would you use those powers to gain wealth beyond compare? Ha! Ha! Ha! How about walking on water? Put a pool in a circus and charge admission. People would come from far and wide to plunk down their money to see you walk across it. Ha! Ha! Ha!"

Judas grinned. "Live in poverty and humility? No more."

"Then why do you dress like a pauper?"

"It's all that I could afford."

"It's all that you can afford? Ha! Ha! Ha! You just put thirty silver coins in your pouch. Let me take you to the finest tailor in Jerusalem." Drago turned and put his hands on Judas's shoulders. "You're now free of Yeshua and his nonsensical restrictions. Let's dress you like a prince, and then you will be treated like a prince at Jerusalem's finest brothel."

Judas grinned; his eyes opened wide. He started to pant.

"And what else did Yeshua teach you? To love your enemies? You know damn well that the only way to succeed in my world is to hate your enemies and crush them underfoot. Forgiveness? You want to win? You take vengeance. Ha! Ha! Ha! I say, do unto others before they can do unto you."

"You are so right." Judas smiled at Drago. "Turn the other cheek' only benefits our Roman oppressors."

"Now you're catching on." Drago slapped Judas's arm. "I also admire your courage."

"My courage?"

"Yes, Dominus Judas. Your courage." He turned and looked directly into Judas's eyes, searing right into his soul.

Judas gasped in fear. His face went pale as the sand of Egypt's White Desert.

"What would the Sicarii do to you if they knew that you set them up with the Romans? Would they not cut you to shreds and leave you to bleed to death or live life scarred and maimed? Ha! Ha! Ha! You won't have much fun at the brothel after what they would do to you."

Judas's nerves tremored.

"Why do you fear me? No need to fear me. It's as I told you; I admire you."

Judas's half smiled.

"How about that beautiful wife of the Centurian?" Drago raised his hands. "Did you not hear her song to her Lord?"

"Yes. She does have a good voice."

"Good? I was thinking lovely and delightful. I hated her song. Yet, I wish she were in service to me. Seeing that is impossible, you did right by me in trying to have her killed."

"I don't know you. Look. I needed the money. That's it."

"Does not your scriptures in the Song of Solomon say that a wife like her is worth more than all the world's rubies?"

"Yeshua taught us many scriptures."

"I know the scriptures by heart. I was there when they were written. The Centurion's wife was not worth all the World's rubies to you, was she? You tried to sell her life for twenty-five denarii. Ha! Ha! Ha! I control the World's wealth but not Heaven. That girl, Rivka, is a threat to my kingdom, and she is worth more than all the world's rubies to Heaven. She is worth even more to me dead. She escaped but not without the Sicarii assassin getting killed by a Roman. Ha! Ha! Ha!"

"I only gave them the information they needed."

"Did you not sell to the Sicarii that killing her would give them the ultimate vengeance against Centurion Magnus? Vengeance ranks high among my most cherished values. I fully sympathize with the Sicarii and their wanting to get even with the Centurion. But what did you have against him? You attended their wedding. You feasted on his food and drank his wine. Even Peter, who never backed down from a fight, agreed to a truce with the Romans. His wife and her life for twenty-five denarii. Ha! Ha! Ha!" Drago cuffed Judas's arm. "Well done. Greed and avarice are also prime parts of my creed. You do know that Magnus is the Legion Commander's favorite Centurion? If they found out that you put a hit on his wife, you know that he would have you crucified."

Judas gasped.

"Fear? Did I detect fear? I told you that I admire your audacity and nerve. You are a man who knows what he wants in life and is bold enough to get it. What's the risk of the Sicarii knowing the truth about you? What's the risk of having an innocent woman killed? What's the risk of betraying the Romans? Crucifixion is a slow, horrible death. Nevertheless, it ends in death."

"They're not going to catch me." Judas straightened his posture and tilted his head upright.

"What do you believe about Yeshua?"

"I don't believe anything about him right now." Judas grinned. "All I care about is that I got thirty silver coins out of the deal, and, as you said, I am now free to debauch at Jerusalem's finest brothel."

"Well, I know who he is." Drago narrowed his eyes and smiled with tight lips. His grin vanished two seconds later. "He is the true Son of God. I know it, and I fear him. You sold the life of God's only begotten son for thirty silver coins. Ha! Ha! Ha! Look! There he is!"

The Sanhedrin guards had Yeshua bound and gagged. They brusquely ushered him toward the Roman Praetorium.

"They are taking him to Pilate. It's a foregone conclusion that he will be crucified. Ha! Ha! Ha! Well, I no longer need you. I've already used you for everything that you can ever do for me. Just be aware that the cost of betraying the Son of God, unlike doing it to the Sicarii or Romans, never dies. Ha! Ha! Ha!" Drago vanished.

"Drago?" Judas felt his tenor evaporate like the Dead Sea at a summer high noon. "Drago? Where are you? Don't leave me, Drago." Looking around for Drago, Judas then spotted the Temple guards twisting the bound arm of Yeshua as they forced him to walk at their pace. "No! No!" Judas ran up to the Sanhedrin guards. "Let him go! He did nothing wrong."

"Go away, you!" One of the guards threw Judas to the pavement.

Judas lay on the pavement and looked upward. "No!" He squeezed his head. He felt his skull compressing. A cracking sensation tormented his mind. He rose to his feet and ran into the Temple. "I was wrong! I betrayed an innocent man! Let him go."

"We no longer need you." Itzhak pointed at him. "Get out!"

"Here!" Judas threw thirty coins at them. "Take your damn money."

Judas ran from the Temple. *'All those people. They're looking at me. They know. Make them stop looking at me.'* He squeezed his temples. *'They know what I did, and they hate me.* He then shouted out loud to the people on the street, "Stop looking at me! You don't know me. I gave the money back. Stop looking at me like that! Stop it! No! No! No!"

"Another madman." A Judaean said to his wife. "Why can't the Romans lock them all up?" Other onlookers stopped and stared. Most ignored Judas and his raving.

Judas ran aimlessly. *'Death. Yes. I deserve death.'* He looked about and saw a discarded rope. He tied it in a noose and put it around his neck. *'Yes. Death. Death will pay the price, and it will make them stop. It will all go away.'* He stood on a boulder, reached up, and tied the other end of the rope to a tree branch. Judas shouted, "Yes. I am guilty of betraying innocent blood! Now, I will pay the price!" He leaped from the boulder. After five strangling minutes, he wished that he was never born.

***

Itzhak and Caiaphas picked up the silver coins. "It is against our law to put blood money in the treasury." They agreed to use the money to buy a field to use as burial grounds for foreigners. It is still called the field of blood. The prophecy of Jeremiah was fulfilled. 'They took the thirty silver coins, the price set on him by the people of Israel. They used it to buy a potter's field as the Lord commanded.'

Chapter 15

The procession that had detained Yeshua reached their destination. The Roman Praetorium. Caiaphas approached the guard, "Guard. Summon the Prefect. Tell him that the High Priest Caiaphas has the insurrectionist I had warned him of in our custody."

Pilate appeared. "Why do you bring this man to me?"

"He is a criminal. If he were not a criminal," Itzhak stepped forward, "we would not bring him to you."

"What crime did he commit that you can't handle yourselves?" Pilate pointed at the group. "You judge him according to your law." He started to turn away.

"No, wait, Governor." Caiaphas pointed at Pilate. "It is not lawful for us to put anyone to death." He raised his palms. "That is your authority as you rule Judaea, and we are your subjects. This man is calling himself the Son of God. We thought that only Ceasar is God. He blasphemes against our beliefs and your beliefs."

Yeshua remained silent.

"If your religious authority was so respected, this man would be no threat to you. Surely, madmen walk among your people, making wild claims. Why is he any different?" Pilate turned to Yeshua, "Are you the King of the Jews?"

"Yes," Yeshua answered Pilate. "It is as you say."

"Blasphemy! Heresy! Insurrection!" Caiaphas pointed at Pilate. "You heard him!"

Crucify him!" Many in the crowd yelled.

"Don't you hear the testimony they are bringing against you?" Pilate's attention turned from the crowd to Yeshua. *'I have heard so much about this man. Now, here he stands before me. He says nothing. He shows no fear.'* Pilate scratched his head. *'He shows no loss of dignity. Look at his accusers. Those Jews act like children complaining about a favored sibling.'* Pilate spoke, "Your nation and the chief priests have delivered you to me. Tell me. What have you done?"

"My kingdom is not of this world. If my kingdom were of this world, my servants would fight so that I should not be delivered to the Jews. But my kingdom is not of this world."

"Answer me this: are you a king?"

"You say rightly that I am a king. For this cause, I was born, and for this cause, I have come into the world that I should bear witness to the truth. Everyone who is of the truth hears my voice."

"Tell me. What is the truth?" Pilate looked deep into Yeshua's eyes. The Governor needed no verbal answer. He turned back to the crowd. "I find no fault in him."

Drago circulated among the crowd. "Crucify him!" Many of them yelled.

"He has done nothing to deserve crucifixion. As is tradition on Passover, I can release a prisoner of your choosing. Today, Barabbas is slated for execution."

Four soldiers brought out a disheveled, unkempt man in chains.

"Shall I release him?" Pilate nodded at Yeshua, "or this man?"

Drago started chanting *'Barabbas! Barrabas! Barabbas!'*

The crowd responded by yelling, "Barabbas! Barabbas! Barabbas!"

Pilate then sat on his judge's seat. An advisor then gave him a message from his wife, *'Don't have anything to do with this innocent man, for I have suffered a great deal in a dream about him.'* Pilate gasped. He had to catch his breath before speaking, "But Barabbas is a murderer. What has Yeshua done?"

"Release Barabbas!" A man yelled.

The crowd then chanted. "Crucify! Crucify! Crucify!"

Drago waved his arms up and down, egging on the crowd to yell louder. "Crucify! Crucify! Crucify!"

"I give you Barabbas as per our custom."

The soldiers unlocked the chains binding Barabbas. He raised his hands in victory and mixed into the crowd. They patted him on the back and congratulated him.

"But what has this man done." Pilate shrugged his shoulders.

A woman's voice echoed, "Crucify him!"

"Yeah! Crucify him!" responded the crowd.

Caiaphas then addressed Pilate, but loud enough for all to hear. "Did he not say he is the Son of God? Is there no God but Ceasar? If you don't crucify him, you are no friend of Ceasar."

Pilate stood up from the judgment seat and said to Yeshua, "Do you not know that I have the power to crucify you or the power to release you?"

"You have no power at all against me unless it is given to you from above. Therefore, the one who has delivered me to you has the greater sin."

'What man facing crucifixion speaks like this? What is the source of his calm and composure? What if he is who he says he is? Besides, what will Rome say if I break the law and execute a man that I know is innocent?' Pilate turned pale; his nerves jittered with fear as he looked at Yeshua. Pilate felt himself shrink. *'Even bound as a criminal, he commands a kingly presence.'* Pilate shook as he turned back to the crowd.

171

"Crucify! Crucify! Crucify!" The crowd jostled with one another. Suddenly, a fistfight broke out. They pushed closer to Pilate, his entourage, and Yeshua. "Crucify! Crucify! Crucify!"

"I have given you Barabbas. Why do you want me to shed innocent blood?" Pilate raised his outstretched palms. "This man has done no wrong."

"It's Ceasar or him!" Itzhak pointed at Yeshua.

"We will not forget your choice," Caiaphas looked directly at Pilate, "and we will make sure that Ceasar doesn't forget either!"

"Oh, very well." Pilate then held up a dish of water. "I wash my hands of this." He washed his hands in the dish. "His innocent blood is on you." Pilate then signaled to his soldiers to take Yeshua away.

Pilate's soldiers seized Yeshua. They twisted his arms as they pushed him to another part of the Praetorium. They next stretched his arms around a column, bound his wrists together, and secured them above his head.

A tall, brawny soldier stood by with a scourge, a multi-lashed whip with sharp objects embedded in the ends. His first strike tore Yeshua's skin, ripping deep, bloody grooves into his back.

Yeshua winced but didn't scream.

Drago stood next to the punisher in spirit form. *'What's the matter? Are you a cinaedus? Be a man. Hit him harder!'*

The punisher whipped Yeshua again and again, hard enough to remove body tissue.

'Hit him harder, you pathetic weakling,' Drago yelled at the punisher. *'Better. Whip him again.'* Drago clapped his hands. *'Again! Now you're getting it. Whip him again. Harder.'*

The other soldiers mocked Yeshua. After releasing his arms from the column, the soldiers tore the remainder of his clothes off and put a scarlet robe on him. Next, they twisted together a crown out of thorns and jammed it onto his head, drawing blood from his pate. They spat on him and mocked him, "Hail! Hail! The King of the Jews!"

"Here," a soldier held up a wooden rod. "A king needs his staff." The soldier then whacked Yeshua over the head with it and spat on him.

***

Pilate wrote on a plaque, '*Here is Yeshua. The King of the Jews.*' He showed it to Caiaphas, "Here, look at this. I will have this nailed to the cross above his head."

"No," Caiaphas raised his hands, "Write, 'I say I am the King of the Jews.'"

"Perhaps you have forgotten who the governor is and who is not." Pilate prodded. "It stays as I have written."

***

They then removed the robe from Yeshua and put his clothes back on him. After leading him away for crucifixion, they stopped a man from Cyrene named Simon and forced him to carry the cross to *The Place of a Skull,* also known as Golgotha.

***

Mary, mother of Yeshua, and her sister Mary, wife of Clopas, Mary Magdelene, and Rivka, sat in a circle, held hands, and prayed. The Angel Isolde Maria then appeared to them. Tears streamed down her face. "I come to bring you strength. Now, you must be as strong in your faith and as

173

strong in your spirit as the great matriarchs of our faith and scripture. Mary, the Father chose you for the greatest honor ever bestowed upon a human. You are the mother of God's son. Mary." Tears now burst from the angel's eyes. "As I speak," Isolde Maria gasped to gain composure, "the prophesies are being fulfilled."

"Do you mean?" Virgin Mary felt her heart skip a beat and then beat like the hooves of a herd of antelope.

Isolde Maria sobbed and nodded.

"No!" Mary, Mother of Yeshua, shrieked and shook uncontrollably. Mary Magdelene squeezed her hand and embraced her. Isolde Maria then extended her hand to her. The Virgin Mary took the angel's hand and stood up. Isolde Maria took her other hand as well and kissed her forehead. The angel then embraced her to prevent her from collapsing. The angel then kissed her again. "Mary, I must return to Heaven. Have faith in the prophesies. Stay strong and comfort your son in these final hours."

Rivka and the Virgin Mary's sister also started crying. The Virgin Mary walked over and touched their shoulders. She then sat with them. The four again held hands and prayed.

***

The two Sicarii prisoners captured in the Gadara raid were the first to arrive with their crosses. Four soldiers held down the first one on the cross. Optio Flavius held a hammer and spike before the prisoner and glowered at him. "Do you remember me, Sicarii scum?"

The prisoner unleashed a string of obscenities and spat at him.

"What I have for you is far worse than anything you can do or say. Now you get what's coming to you, pig."

Optio Flavius proceeded to nail him to the cross. He did likewise to the next prisoner.

"This is gruesome duty, Centurion." Optio Flavius held up three fingers to a soldier for more spikes while speaking to Centurion Longinus. "But when it's an enemy of Rome, and it's personal, I enjoy it." He pointed down the road. "Here comes Barabbas. He killed three of our own and is responsible for more." He tapped his palm with the hammer. "I'm happy to serve up the wrath of Rome."

Three minutes later, The Centurion and Optio realized that the prisoner was not Barbbas. As he got closer, they blanched. "It can't be Dominus Centurion. No."

Centurion Longinus shook his head. "I don't understand this. Even Leganes Octavius said that he was no threat to Rome."

"Centurion Magnus told me that the Jewish Chief Priests had Pilate's ear, but I never…"

"Optio, you never met Pilate. I will leave it at that." Centurion Longinus took the hammer from Octio Flavius. "I won't make you do this. The other soldiers can attend to it."

"No Dominus. Those soldiers are inexperienced and nervous. They're liable to botch it. I know how to do this without breaking a bone. No need to make him suffer more than he must."

Longinus offered Yeshua wine mixed with gall. "This tastes horrible, but it will deaden the pain."

Yeshua shook his head.

Longinus quickly wiped his eyes lest someone see a tear. He then nodded to Optio Flavius. He took the hammer and three spikes from a miles-ranked soldier and then performed his gruesome duty to Rome.

Yeshua said that he forgave him.

***

Rivka saw the ghastly spectacle through blurred vision. "Ahh! No!" She shrieked. "No! No! No!" Her head ticced. She covered her eyes. The tears leaked through her fingers as she wailed. Mary Magdelene put her arm around her and squeezed her. Rivka felt her stomach churn. She fought it but vomited. "It's all right, Rivka." Mary Magdelene handed Rivka a cloth to wipe away the puke. "It's all right. His mother is here. Imagine how she feels. Be strong for her." Rivka sniffled back her tears. She then looked Mary Magdelene in the eyes and hugged her. After a long embrace, Mary Magdelene led Rivka by the hand to Mary, mother of Yeshua, and her sister Mary, wife of Clopas. The four women sat at the foot of the hill.

***

"We must go back to Jerusalem." Centurion Longinus mounted his horse and spoke to Optio Flavius, also on horseback. "Trouble is brewing outside of the Praetorium. We first need to report to the Antonnio Fortress for further instructions. Order the miles-ranked soldiers to keep guard here."

A group of people passed by and yelled to Yeshua, 'You who are going to destroy the Temple and rebuild it in three days, save yourself. Come down from the cross if you are the Son of God!"

Caiaphas and Itzhak then arrived, accompanied by several high-ranking Pharisees. Caiaphas then addressed those people. "Yes. You people are correct. He saved others, but can he save himself? Ha! Ha! Ha! He's the king of Israel." Caiaphas said in a mocking tone as he tilted his head and pulled his face. "Let him come down from the cross, and we'll believe in him. Ha! Ha! Ha! He trusts in God?"

Caiaphas folded his arms. "Let God rescue him, for he said, 'I am the Son of God.'"

The prisoner nailed to the cross to Yeshua's left said to him, "They are right! You are a blasphemer! If you weren't, you could get us down. Some Son of God you are. You can die here as the criminal blasphemer that you are!"

The other criminal rebuked him. "Don't you fear God? You are under the same sentence. We are punished justly, for we are getting what our deeds deserve. But this man has done nothing wrong." He then turned his head, "Yeshua, remember me when you come into your kingdom."

Yeshua answered, "Today you will be with me in Paradise."

***

Mission accomplished. Magnus and his vigintivirate of twenty soldiers had restored order to Southern Judaea. Each trot of his horse brought him one step closer to home and Rivka's arms. As he approached Jerusalem, he sensed an increasingly eerie ambiance. *Something isn't right. My senses, as a highly trained soldier, feel it. The people, they seem strange. It's like they're in another world.* He then pictured Rivka, her beautiful face and alluring smile, and put it out of his mind. At last, he rode through his front gate. "Rivka!" He beamed. "I'm home!"

Rather than Rivka, her mother, Hannah, greeted him without smiling. "Magnus."

"Rivka?" He sensed her alarm and immediately felt his neurons fire. "What happened to her?"

"Nothing happened to her." Hannah clutched his sleeve. "But she's not here."

"Where is she?" He shook his hands.

"I don't know. I tried to wake her up for breakfast, but she was nowhere to be found."

Magnus called over the soldier on guard duty. "What do you know about Rivka? When did she leave? Where did she go?"

"I wasn't here. But, Dominus Centurion, the previous guard, told me that she left with a woman follower of that controversial rabbi." The guard tapped his forehead. "Yeshua."

"Where is Yeshua now."

"Centurion. You have not heard? The Jewish high priests got to Pilate. Pilate is having him crucified as we speak."

"What?" Magnus raised his eyebrows and opened his mouth.

"I tell you the truth." The soldier guard raised his palms. "I know the penalty for lying to a Centurion."

"Thank you, soldier. Carry on with your duties."

Magnus galloped out of the compound.

**

"Rivka." Mary, Mother of Yeshua's copious tears had dried, although their remanence was etched on her face. "I ask you something unusual and difficult. These people are making it worse for my son. He loved your singing. I want you to sing for him Psalm 91."

Rivka, startled, said nothing. She looked into the Virgin Mary's eyes. "I will do it." Rivka walked to the middle of the hill and stood between the crowd and Yeshua. She sang, "He that dwells in the shelter of the Most High will rest in the shadow of our Almighty God. My Lord is my refuge and my fortress. In him, I will trust. He will save you from the Fowler's snare and the deadly pestilence. He will

178

cover you with his feathers, and under his wings, you will find refuge; his faithfulness will be your shield and rampart. You will not fear the terror of night nor the arrow that flies by day."

The crowd silenced to look upon Rivka with admiration. She returned to the Virgin Mary. She hugged Rivak. Both wept on each other's shoulders."

Yeshua then said to Mary, "Dear woman, here is your son." He then said to a disciple, "Here is your mother."

The disciple then took Mary, mother of Yeshua, her sister, Mary Magdelene, and Rivka, to his home.

***

The sky suddenly blacked. The Earth shook. Magnus's horse panicked, bucked on his hind legs, and threw Magnus from his steed. Magnus's armor and helmet bore much of the impact of his landing. His horse galloped away. Magnus climbed to his feet and walked in total darkness.

***

Longinus and Flavius returned to Golgotha. Leganus Octavius, under orders from Pilate, told them to return and break the crucified criminals' legs as it violated Jewish law for bodies to remain on the cross during the Sabbath.

The soldiers mocked and derided Yeshua.

"Father," Yeshua looked upward. "Why have you forsaken me?"

As darkness had consumed the sky, the soldiers guarding the crucifixion did not see their commander approach.

"What is going on here!" Longinus startled the soldiers. "Your duty as Roman soldiers is to conduct yourself professionally. You are acting like Plebians at a circus." Longinus then pointed to Yeshua's robe. Dice were next to it. "Did you cast lots to take his garment?"

The Soldiers stood still in fear.

"All of you. Return to the Antonnio Fortress for assignment. Do it fast, and I may lessen your discipline for conduct unbecoming of Roman soldiers."

Yeshua then said to Centurion Longinus. "I thirst."

The Centurion dipped a sponge into sour wine, put it on hyssop, and raised it to Yeshua's mouth. He tasted the sour wine.

"It is finished!" he proclaimed.

He gave up his spirit.

***

Magnus staggered through the darkness. After an hour, he found his horse standing beside the road, eating weeds. He mounted him and rode toward Golgotha. '*Rivka! Rivka!*' was his only thought.

***

Centurion Longinus then said to Optio Flavius. "Fulfill our orders."

"No! No!" They spotted Flavius lurching toward them while wielding a metal rod.

'*Crack.*' Optio Flavius splintered the fibulas of the two condemned Sicarii. He stood by as they choked and suffocated to death. Next, he stepped over to Yeshua's cross. He cocked the metal rod. He looked closely at his target and then dropped the rod. Yeshua was already dead. Flavius then grabbed a spear and thrust it into his side. The spear trembled in his hands and heated up like a metal rod in a fire. He quickly retracted it. Both blood and water spouted from the wound.

With a mighty rumble, the Earth shook. Rocks split. The earthquake froze Longinus and Flavius in fear.

***

Caiaphas, his father-in-law, former high priest Annas, and Itzhak gloated over their deed. Suddenly, the Temple shook. Framed paintings fell from the wall. A bust on a podium crashed to the floor. The Temple curtain tore from top to bottom. Annas hid under the table. Itzhak ran from the room and locked himself in an adjacent chamber. Caiaphas sat still, paralyzed by fear. He stared at the torn curtain.

***

The women and the male disciple had stopped and watched the finish from a distance. The earthquake shook and crumbled a building. A huge stone fell between the disciple and the four women. They dispersed in fear. Rivka was separated from the group. She was lost in the darkness.

***

Magnus arrived at Golgatha. He could almost smell the fear from Longinus and Flavius.

"We have killed the Son of God." Centurion Longines faced Magnus. "Today, we shed innocent blood."

"I am the one who killed him." Flavius lowered his head.

Magnus craned his head forward to look at him. *'What am I looking at? Do I detect a tear? Flavius can be ruthless. He's the most hardcore, zealous soldier in my command.'*

"But he forgave me." Flavius looked up at him. "Centurion Magnus, I never even knew what forgiveness was until this moment. You know that I live by the creed of a fighting soldier. Have no mercy. Smite the enemies of Rome. But Yeshua was no enemy of Rome. I believe in him now. He was the Son of God."

"I caught my soldiers casting lots for this." Centurion Longinus then picked up Yeshua's robe. "I will discipline them later with a twenty-mile forced march on their day off for conduct unbecoming of a Roman soldier. I know that your wife is a loyal believer. Here." He handed Magnus the robe. "Give it to her. She will better know what to do with it."

Magnus took the seamless robe. "Where is Rivka? She is nowhere to be found. I must find her."

"Rivka was here. She even calmed the crowd by singing a song of praise to God." Longinus cracked a smile. "She left with several of Yeshua's female followers and a male disciple."

"When did they leave?"

"Only a short while ago. They couldn't have gone far. But I'm afraid I don't know where they went."

"Do you at least know what direction she went?"

"Yes." Optio Flavius took a step toward Magnus. "I remember. They followed that road up the hill." He pointed.

Without saying anything, Magnus galloped up the road.

***

Rivka stumbled through the darkness and earthquake debris. *'Where am I?'* "Mary! Mary! Where have you gone? Lord, lord, help me. Isolde Maria. Please. I need you now." She then bawled, "Magnus! Magnus! I love you. Please find me. Find me!" Visible specters of dead saints further terrified her. She tripped over a fallen tree branch and fell face-first into the dirt. Climbing onto her hands and knees, she cried before mustering the determination to stand and walk on.

***

Joseph of Arimathea, a Sanhedrin member but secret disciple of Yeshua, and Nicodemus, a Pharisee who became a believer after a secret meeting with Yeshua, appeared before Pilate.

"I give you Jews credit for your boldness." Pilate sat with steepled fingers. "I had your enemy crucified, and it's causing me untold problems. Here you come, asking for more? Now, state your business and leave me to more important things."

Joseph looked at Nicodemus and then at Pilate. "Dominus Prefect, we wish to honor our customs and give Yeshua a proper Jewish burial. Dominus Prefect, if it may please you, may we have his body?"

"You can take it and dump it like trash in Gehenna for all I care." Pilate prodded. "Now get out and stop bothering me with your Jewish nugae."

Joseph and Nicodemus, who bought about a hundred-pound mixture of myrrh and aloes, took Yeshua's body and bound it in strips of linen with the spices, as was the Jewish burial custom. They then took his body to a nearby garden and placed it in a new tomb cut from rock. After putting his body in the tomb, they closed it by rolling a rock over the entrance. They had also fulfilled the tenets of the Jewish Day of Preparation.

Mary Madelene and Mary Yeshua's mother sat before the tomb and prayed. They also asked for Rivka's safe return.

"Rivka! Rivka!" Magnus shouted as he galloped through post-earthquake Jerusalem. He looked over every damaged structure in fear of finding the worst. Each passerby was like the walking dead, still in shock over the daytime darkness, the earthquake, and apparitions seemingly rising from tombs. Each person that he asked about Rivka merely shrugged. Sitting on his horse, he bowed his head. '*Mighty Jupiter, Yahweh, Yeshua the Son, whoever is the true God, show yourself to me by returning my beloved wife Rivka to me.*'

***

Rivka staggered on as nightfall approached. She had found a wild fig tree for some sustenance. Yet she had no money to stay at an inn, even if she could find one open after the earthquake. She stumbled upon a small stone bridge over a dried stream. She sat under the bridge, hugged her knees to her chest, and prayed until the next morning.

***

"Governor," one of Pilate's advisors briefed him, "Three of the Jewish High Priests want to see you."

"Tell them to go away." Pilate stood. "I've had enough of their nugae."

"Dominus Prefect. Their support is critical to keeping order in Judaea. I recommend that you see them."

Pilate sighed. "Very well, send them in."

Caiaphas, Annas, and Itzhak entered Pilates court and stood before his chair. "Dominus governor," Caiaphas spoke, "Part of his blasphemy against Yahweh and Ceasar is that he claimed he would rise from the dead after three days. What if his disciples steal his body and tell the people that he rose from the dead? That deception will cause you even bigger problems."

Pilate started to sweat. "He never caused me problems," Pilate prodded, "he caused you problems. Crucifying him because of you has made him my problem. What if his claims are true? As governor of Judaea, it's my job to know about your history and culture. I've studied your scriptures, and I know your history. Your God doesn't take any nugae." He threw up his hands. "What if he rises from the dead and seeks revenge on me and my family? My wife has constant nightmares about him. So, what more do you want from me?"

Annas spoke, "I suggest that you make the tomb as secure as possible, at least until the third day."

Pilate started pacing back and forth. He then stopped and faced them, "Very well, take a guard. Go make the tomb as secure as you know how."

"Shall we put the seal of Rome on it?" Itzhak asked.

"I authorize it." Pilate sat down.

***

Rivka gained the strength to climb out of her hiding nook and walk on. She could sense that she had entered an unsavory Jerusalem neighborhood. Its poorly constructed buildings failed to withstand the Earthquake. Most of the residents had fled. Rivka had to watch each step as she navigated the ruble-strewn streets. She heard two alley cats fighting. The stench from a broken sewage sluice filled the air.

Two men hid between the remains of a stone wall and a fallen beam. "Look." A man with a weatherworn face and pendulous nose pointed at Rivka. "That woman is alone. Easy picking."

"By the looks of things…" The other man had a round face with a straggly beard. "She didn't fare well in the earthquake. What's the use? She probably has no money."

"The looks of her?" The weatherworn man beamed with an open mouth, snaggle-toothed smile. "She may look dirty and tired, but she still looks mighty fine. Underneath that soiled garment is something far more valuable than money."

"Ha! Ha! Ha! It's something money can buy, but, in her case," He grinned lecherously, "more than we'll ever afford."

Rivka sensed that something wasn't right. She looked about her surroundings but saw nothing.

"We don't want to spook her," Weatherface pointed at Rivka. "Let her walk a few more steps before we follow her. When she walks past that abandoned building, we strike."

"Yes. I'm in. If we time this right, no one will notice our taking her, and once in that building." The round-faced man pointed to the entrance. "We can have our way with her for as long as we want." He flushed red and panted.

The two men then crept behind Rivka. Their furtive steps closed the distance.

Rivka felt her nerves tingle. She glanced back, took three fast steps, and bolted. She screamed.

Weatherface lurched forward and grabbed Rivka by twisting his arm around her face, covering her mouth.

Rivka kicked his shins with the back of her foot. Roundface grabbed her flailing ankles and lifted her. Weatherface lifted her by the torso. They carried her like a log toward the vacant, earthquake-damaged building.

Weatherface muffled her shrieks. Roundface curtailed her flailing legs.

***

Magnus and his horse galloped up to a contubernium of eight Roman soldiers.

They punched their chests and extended their right arms. "Hail Centurion."

Magnus punched his chest and extended his right arm. "Hail!" He lowered his arms. "I am searching for my wife. She got lost in the Earthquake."

The contubernium Optio responded. "We have a description of her. Tall. Medium frame. Long honey-colored hair. The Leganus has every soldier in the vicinity looking for her. Octavius needs you to return to the Antonnio Fortress right now. The Passover, combined with the crucifixion of their divisive rabbi, and now the darkening and the earthquake, has created a volatile situation. Some are even claiming to have seen apparitions rise from tombs. You're needed."

"Keep an eye out for her. I will personally reward anyone who returns her safely to me."

"Hail!" The Optio punched his chest and extended his right arm.

"Hail!" Magnus returned his salute. He took a deep breath, looked around, and saw no sign of Rivka. Magnus chose to obey orders. He galloped back to the Antonnio Fortress, continually looking right and left and shouting the name of his beloved.

***

Rivka tried to bite Weatherface's gagging hand. She twisted and kicked to free herself. All in vain. She couldn't think. It was happening too fast.

The men suddenly dropped Rivka. Her replacement's beauty surpassed all imagination. Her long, wavy tress of Raven hair had an indigo sheen. It was uncovered and flowing. Her sapphire eyes, jewel-like cheeks, perfectly angled jaw and chin, and her upper and lower lips equally flush, stunned them. They leered in at her shocking white gown, the outline of her breasts captivating them. They panted like thirsty dogs. Suddenly, her eyes changed from sapphire to ruby. Their red lust turned to pallid terror. She sharpened her focus. Her face scrunched into a scowl. She launched Weatherface and Roundface like boulders from a catapult. They flew backwards. A nano-second later, they slammed into a stone wall. A fissure opened in the street. The rapists rebounded off the wall and into the crack. It resealed.

"Isolde Maria!" Rivka ran to her, dropped to her knees, and hugged her ankles. "I love you, Isolde Maria." Rivka wept and kissed the angel's feet. "You have saved my life twice, and now you have saved me from a fate worse than death."

Isolde Maria bent over, took Rivka's hands, and helped her to her feet. The angel looked into Rivka's olive eyes. She then planted a long, closed-mouth kiss on her lips before bracing Rivka's shoulders.

Rivka inhaled deeply through her nose as the angel's floral aroma blocked the area's sewage stench.

"Rivka, I am going to share revelations from Heaven. Much evil exists in this World. Our Lord will one day return as a warrior and defeat evil once and for all. That is not yet written. I can say no more. I can say that one day, you will be among the first to read God's final revelation and that you will play a crucial role in getting it to the churches. I wish I could protect every person from evildoers and harm. Our kingdom is not of this Earth. Satan has taken control. One day, the Son will wrest the world from the evil one. For now, he has opened the way to the Father. It's only through him and him alone that mankind can find salvation. Salvation cannot be bought with money and conversion can never be by the sword. Humans must make their choice between good and evil. Now you understand the power of angels and Yeshua's word when he told his disciples that he could call twelve legions of angels to rescue him from the crucifixion." Isolde Maria nodded to Rivka. "Now you know that he suffered an excruciating death out of his own free will. Now you know why man must freely choose to believe?"

Rivka hugged Isolde Maria and cried into her shoulder. "But why did he have to die like that? Why? I loved him so." She lifted her head and looked into the angel's eyes. "It was horrible beyond any nightmare." She sniffled. "I will never get over it."

Isolde Maria smiled at her. "Do you not know that all things work together for the good of those who love the Lord? Do you not know that Yeshua does more than cure the sick and cleanse the spirit; he heals emotional trauma as well?"

"I love you so much, Isolde Maria. I take joy in your presence. Yet I am lost here. Yeshua is dead, and I mourn for him."

"Did not our Lord promise that those who mourn shall be comforted?" Isolde Maria smiled. "Before today is over, your mourning will cease, and you shall find comfort."

"But my husband and my mother do now know my whereabouts." A tear fell from Rivka's eye. "I know that they suffer horrible distress because of me."

"Your mother is a believer. She has the comfort of the Holy Spirit. Yes. Your husband's anguish torments him. Yet we have plans for him. You are most precious in the eyes of the Angels and God himself. We would not have opened the door for you to marry a pagan unless we had a plan for him." Isolde Maria smiled and chuckled. "Heaven only opened the door for you to be with Magnus. It's you who opened your heart. The mystery of love is greater than the mystery of death. Today, we will reveal to you the mystery of death. But your love for Magnus shall remain a mystery."

"What are you planning for Magnus? I love him so much. I am his wife and his helpmate. I shall remain his partner until death do us part."

"You are a wife of epic worthiness, Rivka." Isolde Maria beamed at her. "Before I reunite you with Magnus, I must reunite you with someone else. Now for your little problem of being lost." Isolde Maria extended her long, toned arm. She had a gold and ruby band around her upper arm and a thin, golden bracelet on her wrist. "Take my hand."

Rivka complied.

"Follow me. I will lead you to where you must go. Only you can see me, feel me, or smell me. But people will sense my presence. You are safe from criminals. Come, Rivka."

Rivka beamed. She walked away, hand in hand with the angel Isolde Maria.

Chapter 16

Mary Magdelene and the Virgin Mary both awoke at dawn on the first day after the Sabbath. "Good morning, Mary," Mary Magdelene wiped a tear from the Blessed Virgin's face with her sudarion cloth. "Let's go to the tomb so that we may honor and mourn for him and pray together."

They walked together to Yeshua's tomb. They next heard a rumbling. The ground buckled and shook. Mary Magdelene fell. The Virgin Mary staggered but kept her feet by grabbing a sapling. "Are you alright?" The Virgin Mary extended her hand to Mary Magdelene and helped her stand. "It must have been an aftershock from the earthquake."

"Thank you. I am fine." Mary Magdelene brushed the dust from her garment. "A bit shaken, but fine." As they approached the tomb, another aftershock rolled the stone from Yeshua's tomb. An angel of the Lord came down from Heaven and sat upon the stone. His appearance was like lightning, and his clothes were white as snow. The guards were paralyzed with fear.

The angel said to the women, "Fear not. I know why you come. You are looking for Yeshua, who was crucified. He is not here." The angel raised his hands. "He has risen, just as he said and just as the prophets foretold. Come and see the place where he lay. Then go quickly and tell his disciples: he has risen from the dead and is going ahead of you to Galilee. There you will see him. Now I have told you."

The women looked at each other, still pale from fear, they beamed at each other. "Hurry! Let's go tell them!" Mary Magdelene took the Virgin Mary's hand. Together they ran. "Huh!" They gasped and froze.

Yeshua stood before them. "Greetings."

The women fell to their knees, clasped his ankles, and worshiped him.

"Do not be afraid. Go tell my brothers to go to Galilee; there, they will see me."

***

"Mendacium!" Pontius Pilate prodded at Caiaphas, Annus, and Itzhak. "You're here to tell me that my guards slept through an earthquake mighty enough to move a huge stone? Don't you know that a Roman guard can be put to death for a second of slumber? Yet you're here telling me that they slept so soundly that, after an earthquake, Yeshua's disciples simply walked in and stole his body?"

"Yes, Dominus Prefect." Caiaphas squeaked. "That's what happened."

Pilate stood and squeezed his temples. "I knew crucifying this man would be nothing but trouble." He paced back and forth. "My wife warned me. She saw it in her dream."

"But they did steal his body." Annus raised his palms.

"Enough out of you," Pilate prodded. "What if he did rise from the dead? What if he now seeks revenge?"

"Why should you worry, Governor?" Itzhak stepped forward. "You have an entire Legion to protect you."

"Are you not spiritual leaders?" Pilate collapsed onto his throne. "If he truly is the Son of God as he claims, he can put a curse on us and our families. If he does that, the entire Roman military can't help us."

"Yes, but they did steal his body." Caiaphas pointed at him. "Shouldn't you act before this gets out of hand and the people start believing that he did rise from the dead?"

"Ha! Ha! Ha! My military is proficient enough to keep order under any situation, including a bunch of religious fanatics claiming that their messiah rose from the dead." Pilate prodded back. "The biggest losers are you. How much will your words be worth when up against a man who rose from the dead?"

The three Pharisees blanched.

"Oh, very well." Pilate steepled his hands, fingertips touching. "I can stop an uprising at any time. Nevertheless, it's in my best interest to prevent it from happening. I will send reinforcements to smother the situation."

The High Priests looked at each other and nodded.

***

The angel Isolde Maria led Rivka to the garden near Golgotha. "Goodbye, Rivka." Isolde Maria braced her shoulders. "I leave you to your sister. I love you, Rivka. I love you with a love that can only come from an angel and Heaven above." The angel kissed Rivka's forehead and then disappeared.

"Rivka!" Mary Magdelene shouted and ran toward her.

'Her smile! She looks so happy. She practically glows. I've never seen anyone look so happy.'

"Rivka!" Mary Magdelene ran up and hugged her. "At first, I was worried, but the Holy Spirit comforted me and let me know that Heaven was watching over you."

"You look so happy, Mary!" Rivka again beheld her beaming smile, bright eyes, and flush cheeks.

"Rivka." Mary Magdelene braced her shoulders. "Someone wants to meet you." She then took Rivka's hand. "Come."

***

Leganus Octavius stood before Pontius Pilate. He punched his chest and extended his right arm. "Hail Ceasar!"

Pilate remained slumped in his chair, hunched slightly forward. His head remained lowered; his jaw trembled. He failed to return the salute.

Octavius could see that he was sweating. *'Cinaedus. I ought to slap you. You overpampered hare.'*

"I called you in because there's been a serious security breach at the garden near Golgatha. It seems that Yeshua's disciples stole his body."

Leganus Octavius narrowed his eyes, *'If you weren't so afraid of the Jews, you never would have had an innocent man crucified. He had more courage in the tip of his little finger than you have in your entire body. Prefect Cinaedus.*

Pilate stood and started pacing back and forth. "I need you to get your best men on it right away." He stopped pacing and turned to the Leganus.

Octavius could see the fear in his eyes. "I have just the right man for the job." He punched his chest and extended his right arm. "Hail Ceasar!"

Pilate's arm dangled slightly as he extended it. "Hail Ceasar," he said with a tepid voice.

***

Leganus Octavius met Centurion Magnus in the Antonnio Fortress courtyard. "Centurion Magnus. I have everyone in the Legion looking for Rivka. I still need you to conduct your duties as a professional soldier and commander. Go to the garden near Golgatha. It seems there's a security breach. Secure the situation and get back to me."

***

Magnus galloped toward Golgatha, sometimes stopping to inspect earthquake-damaged buildings, praying to whatever God would listen that Rivka did not lay dead in the ruble. After arriving at the Garden near Golgatha, he dismounted his horse and tied him to a tree. *'Seems quiet enough. I don't see anyone. I'll get to the bottom of it.'* Magnus turned a corner. Suddenly, he saw a man. *'He's of ordinary stature and build, I think in his early thirties.'* Magnus stood still. *'He's looking at me, but he's not staring. There's a strange glow about him.'* Magnus walked closer. The man spread his arms. Magnus saw the spike wounds on his wrists. The Centurion looked into his eyes. His heart paused and then palpitated. He dropped to his knees and bowed his head.

Yeshua reached out and touched Magnus's shoulder.

"I believe in you, and I accept you into my heart. Forgive me."

"You are forgiven and now belong to my kingdom. Please rise."

Magnus stood.

Yeshua then turned sideways.

Rivka never looked more radiant. Her olive eyes glowed. Her honey hair was uncovered and flowing.

"Rivka? Rivka!"

"Magnus!" They ran to each other and embraced. Magnus lifted her and cradled her. She braced her arm around the back of his neck. They kissed.

Yeshua smiled.

End of Part II

Part III

Chapter 1

Macedonia 58 AD

Rivka held her eight-year-old daughter Sarah's hand. The little girl pointed to the distant mountains. "Mommy, someday I want to go to those mountains. I want to play in the snow."

Rivka chuckled, "Oh, my little angel, someday soon. For now, we can run up and down our rolling hills right here."

"Yes, Mommy! I love sliding down them when we get snow, but we only get a little bit. I want to play in lots of snow." She then looked up at Rivka. "Someday, I hope to be as pretty as you, Mommy."

"You already are more beautiful than anything we will find in those mountains, the snow, and beyond, even to the distant sea." Rivka lifted Sarah and cradled her. "You have my honey-colored hair, and that pink ribbon makes it even prettier. And be careful, my little angel. Your smile alone is warm enough to melt all the snow on those mountains. Your father earned our sheep ranch as a retirement gift for service to the Roman Army. You are my gift from our Father in Heaven and more precious than the air that I breathe." Rivka placed Sarah back on her feet and took her hand. "Come, Sarah, let's go home. Dinner is almost ready. Tonight, your big sister Ruth is bringing your Uncle Argus and your baby niece Mariam to our feast." Rivka pointed. "Look, my little angel. Here comes Daddy and Big Brother."

Magnus and their twenty-year-old son, Samuel, rode on horseback. Two domestic dogs trained to help herd sheep trotted beside them. Samuel was taller than his father but not as stocky.

"Daddy!" Sarah ran toward them.

Magnus dismounted his horse. "Well, hello, my precious one." He picked up his daughter and hugged her. "Have you been helping your mommy?"

"Yes, Daddy!"

Magnus put his daughter down and looked into his wife's bright eyes and smiling face. He strolled over and embraced her. They then shared a long kiss.

"Mommy? Daddy?" Sarah tugged at Rivka's hem.

Magnus lifted and hugged her. "If Daddy and Mommy didn't love each other so much, you wouldn't be here."

Rivka then hugged both her husband and daughter.

"Daddy, when will you take me to play in the snow? The snow makes the mountains look so pretty, and it's so much fun to play in."

"Well, my little angel," Magnus beamed. "This winter, I will ask it to snow more right here. The shiny white snow and bright blue sky sure look pretty, but not as much as this streak of gray." He ran his hand through his wife's tress of hair.

"How about I just pull out a clump of this gray hair." Rivka clutched a handful of his hair, gently pulled on it, and laughed. "And feed it to the sheep." She kept her fingers locked in his hair while planting a long kiss on his lips.

Samuel smirked. "And here you two tell me to restrain myself with the young ladies."

"We may have gray hair on our heads," Magnus pointed to Samuel, "but how about you shave off that black hair on your face."

Samuel laughed. "Are you forgetting that I have a Jewish mother?" Samuel walked over, put his arm around Rivka, and pecked her cheek. "So, I am going to honor her side of the family and keep this." Samuel pinched his beard.

"I don't see a beard on her." Magnus looked at his wife.

Rivka blushed, lowered her head, and giggled.

A young female servant exited the kitchen. "The lamb is almost ready."

"It sure smells delicious." Magnus smiled. "We're waiting for Ruth, Argus, and little Mariam. And we must give my shepherds and other staff time to clean up."

Rivka walked over and touched her arm. "For your sake, I sure hope that you cooked it right." Rivka beamed at her cook. "After all, you're going to eat it with us." Rivka chuckled.

The servant lowered her head, blushed, and smiled. "Thank you, Domina."

"Domina?" Rivka smiled and threw up her hands. "Back in the day, Magnus would've made you bury a dead horse or go on a twenty-mile forced march for that." She chuckled, "It's Rivka."

"Yes. Thank you, Rivka." The servant beamed.

The shepherd dogs barked by the door.

"Quiet, you two." Rivka managed to shout through her laughter. "We'll save something for you, but you two eat last."

***

A Roast lamb surrounded by lentils, chickpeas, carrots, and turnips was placed on the table head. Visible smoke rose from the lamb. Its fragrance wafted about the dining room. Rivka, Sarah, Samuel, their oldest daughter Ruth, son-in-law Argus, and their granddaughter Mariam sat at the table. All six of their domestic staff and ranch hands had joined them. Magnus had also invited his banker, Josephus, and his wife.

"Before we enjoy this feast," Magnus stood, "Let us pray. 'We thank you, Heavenly Father, for your ultimate love of sacrificing your son as payment for our sins so that we may enjoy eternal life with you in Heaven. We also express our gratitude for providing this meal. May you bless it to our bodies and let it nourish our spirits. And may you keep Nero. Keep him as far away from here as possible. We thank you in the name of Yeshua and the Holy Spirit. Amen."

The table responded with Amen. All except Josephus. He narrowed his eyes and half smiled under his hooked nose.

Chapter 2

Rivka stopped wearing a head scarf after Magnus retired from the Roman army and moved them to Macedonia. She did cover her hair for religious services. Seven children and her daughter Sarah sat around Rivka. They had gathered in a wealthy villager's wine cellar. It had a musty odor but was comfortably cool. The rural, outlying parts of the empire were far safer from Nero's persecution than the urban enclaves closer to Rome. Nevertheless, with the penalty for belief in Yeshua being torture and public execution, every precaution was in place.

"So, you met Yeshua for real?" A young boy asked Rivka.

"Yes, James, I not only met him and his mother, I met him after he rose from the dead."

"Did you see him walk on water?" A little girl Rivka's younger daughter asked.

"No, Esther," Rivka chuckled. "But I did meet the men who saw it. I have seen and experienced his other mighty miracles."

"Really? Which ones?" A little boy asked.

"I helped him feed five thousand people with just five loaves of bread and two fish."

"How did you do that?" Esther asked.

"We will never truly know until we meet him in Heaven. That is why it's a miracle and requires our faith and trust in an all-mighty God who is above us as mere humans. If we knew everything and saw everything, we would not need faith. Some who even saw him after he rose from the dead chose not to believe. Do you believe?"

"Yes, Mother Rivka. Because you of what you tell me."

"No, Esther, don't believe because of what I say." Rivka chuckled. "You believe because his spirit lives inside your heart." She picked up Esther and sat her on her lap. "I can tell you of my experiences and teach you his words. It's up to you to believe in him and take his spirit into your heart."

"I do. I promise I do." She looked up at Rivka.

"I know Esther, I know. Best of all, Yeshua knows. He knows you personally, and he knows that you believe in him." Rivka put Esther back on her feet and stood. "Yeshua loves all of you, and he dwells in your hearts. He loves the children most of all. King David wrote in Psalm 127, 'Like arrows in the hands of a warrior are children born in one's youth. Blessed is the man whose quiver is full of them." Rivka held Esther's right hand and James's left hand. "Let's all hold hands in a circle." After the children held hands and made a circle, Rivka continued. "Nothing is more valuable to a warrior than his arrows. Likewise, nothing is more valuable to God and your parents than all of you. His children."

***

Magnus met with the other men upstairs in the atrium and addressed them. "We must step up our caution. Nero is possessed by Satan. He acts crueler and more insane by the day. He is no longer satisfied with persecuting Christians in Rome. His reign of evil and persecution will soon reach us."

"I hate to say this, Brother Magnus." The owner of the house, an older man with a long, pointy white beard, raised his hands. "But your status as a retired Centurion may have put you high on his list."

203

"Yes. I understand that Georgios. We are doing the right thing by having the women and children meet in your wine cellar."

"I know that you have met the resurrected Christ." A young Greek man wearing a white chiton with a large, rectangular red himation draped over his torso spoke. "Did you ever meet Judas?"

"You do understand his reason for asking, don't you?" Georgios added.

"Yes. Magnus stood. Judas Iscariot was at my wedding party. My legion commander was paying him for information on the Sicarii. At the same time, he would sell the Sicarii information on us."

"Our point is that If he can sell out the Son of God for thirty pieces of silver," Georgios touched his beard, "there are others like him who will sell us out to Nero."

"He is right, father." Samuel folded his hands. "I know that you and Mother are strong believers. I share your faith, but I am afraid not with your passion. I know that you want to spread the word." He raised his palms, "I do too. But, with all due respect to you as my father, we need to be more cautious of whom we invite for prayer."

"Point well taken, son." Magnus slapped Samuel's shoulder. "Our Lord told his disciples that I am sending you out as sheep amid wolves, so be wise as serpents and innocent as doves."

"We will have to be in constant prayer for wisdom." Georgios steepled his fingers. "Indiscretion will end our ministry, and witness will end in the jaws of lions. On the other hand, our Heavenly Father sacrificed his son for us. The son willingly laid down his life for us. We must not proceed as cowards but be bold in the word."

The young Greek added, "Magnus, you and your wife are among the very few living people who have witnessed the resurrected Christ. Tell us more."

"I met the living Yeshua before his crucifixion." Magnus nodded. "I had heard him speak and witnessed some of his miracles. Even one of his angels had twice appeared to guide me in Rivka's defense. I confess that I didn't truly believe until I saw him after the resurrection. In a way, I envy all of you. You believe out of faith. I only believed after I saw for myself."

"Don't diminish yourself." Georgios sat up straighter. "I heard that over five hundred people had seen the resurrected Christ but still didn't believe."

"All of you are a wonderful witness to the faith. You all face persecution up to a violent death." Magnus stood. "I can't speak for God, and I don't know all his plans. After all, who would have dreamed that Saul of Tarsus would become the Apostle Paul? Nevertheless, I am sure Nero has a hot place in Hell waiting for him. Maybe the next Ceasar will halt the persecutions; maybe he won't. I do hope that future generations that don't face persecution will appreciate it, will support those who are under persecution, and will remain vigilant of the forces of darkness who want persecution to resume.

***

A Roman Optio soldier handed Josephus a small, purple velvet pouch with gold coins. "Thanks. Here is your reward." The soldier patted Josephus's back.

***

Rivka and the children continued to link hands. "Children let's keep our chain of hands. Let's all go down on one knee and pray." Rivka and the children kneeled on one knee and lowered their heads. "I thank you Father in Yahweh's name for these wonderful children and the opportunity to share your word and your love with them. I lift them to your saving grace and ask for Heaven to shield them from all danger." Rivka raised her head and opened her eyes. "Would you like to thank Yeshua for your parents and the love and care that they give you?"

Esther prayed aloud, "Thank you, Yeshua, for my Mommy and Daddy, for all the food that I eat, and I thank you for Mother Rivka."

***

The next sound that Magnus and the children's parents heard was the rumble of galloping horses and soldiers, spurring them onward. Samuel peered out the window. His pallid expression spoke a thousand words.

"Quick!" Magnus commanded. "Move that shelf in front of the wine cellar door." He pointed. "Put everything you can grab on the shelf so they can't see behind it."

With a loud scraping, the men moved the shelf in front of the wine cellar door. The wives joined the men in the atrium and put various items on the shelves. They also remained silent.

Magnus moved to the center of the room. "Repeat after me. 'The Lord is my shepherd; I shall not want. He makes me lie down in green pastures; He leads me beside the still waters. He restores my soul; He leads me in paths of righteousness for his name's sake. Yea, though I walk through the valley of the shadow of death, I will fear no evil, for you are with me; your rod and your staff, they comfort me. You prepare a table before me in the presence of my enemies; You anoint my head with oil; My cup runneth over. Surely goodness and mercy shall follow me all the days of my life, and I will dwell in the house of the Lord. Forever."

***

Rivka felt her stomach rise into her chest. Her heart stopped before erupting into a syncopated beat. She gasped for air. "Children, children, please don't cry. We must remain silent. Bow your heads in prayer to our God. Rivka said aloud to the children, "My lord is my refuge and my fortress. My God, in him I will trust." Rivka took three deep breaths and held back her tears. "He shall cover you with his feathers, and under his wing, you shall take refuge; You shall not be afraid of the terror by night nor of the arrow that flies by day."

***

The Optio kicked in the front door. Seven other soldiers barged into Georgios's home. "Centurion Magnus. You are hereby under arrest by order of Nero for treason against Ceasar."

Magnus sang a hymn as the soldiers bound his arms behind his back and then firmly held them.

"Where are the others?" A soldier demanded.

The Optio replied. "We don't want any of these people. For now, anyway. We do want the Centurion's wife. Nero says she is for our pleasure. He wants the traitor to watch."

"She's gone far away." Georgios stepped forward.

"You lie!" A soldier put him in a chokehold. "Tell the truth or die."

"Forget him." The Optio pointed at the soldier and Georgios. "We got who we want."

The soldier threw Georgios to the ground. He lay on the floor, clutching his throat.

"You bastards." Magnus struggled vainly against his restraints. "My Roman Army was professional. You're an insult to Barbarians. Pigs have more honor than you!"

"Shut up!" The Optio slapped him across the face.

Magnus remained stolid.

"Oh, so you're turning the other cheek?" The Optio struck the other side of his face.

Tendrils of shock and pain surged from his skull to his eyes. Blood dripped from his mouth. He looked straight ahead and said nothing.

"How about his youngest daughter?" A soldier wearing a red cloak suggested. "I'm sure if we use her, he'll get a show that he won't ever forget."

Magnus stomped on the ankle of a soldier holding him. Breaking free, he spat blood in the other soldier's face, making him release his grip. Two other soldiers grabbed Magnus before he could attack the red-cloaked soldier. The Optio then slugged Magnus in the gut.

Magnus keeled over and gasped.

"You waste my time, traitor." The Optio prodded at Magnus and then said to his soldiers. "We got what we came for. Get this traitor out of here." He scowled at Magnus, "I hope to be in the arena to see what Nero has planned for you." As the soldiers brusquely pulled Magnus from the house and left, the Optio looked back. "Let this be a warning. Worshiping any God but Nero is blasphemy and punishable by death. The walls have eyes and ears. We know who you are. You could be next."

The soldiers tossed Magnus into a wooden carriage and locked him inside.

***

Rivka dropped to her knees. She put each arm around two children and pulled them close to her. Suddenly, the Angel Isolde Maria appeared. She knelt across from her and put her arms around the other four children. Rivka and the Angel linked hands. "Children," Isolde Maria's melodic voice soothed them. "Keep in silent prayer with me and your Mother Rivka." After five minutes of fervent prayer, the Angel stood and took Rivka's hand. "Come. It's safe to go upstairs. Children. Keep holding hands. We will go upstairs in a chain."

Samuel and the young Greek moved the shelf from the door.

Rivka entered the room. "Magnus? Magnus?" Her blurry vision saw only pale, blank faces. The crying of Georgios's wife sounded like a distant echo. She looked her son Samuel in the eyes. Seeing his tears and jittering jaw, Rivka felt her skull shatter like glass, and her heart drop into her stomach. Vertigo overwhelmed her. She fell to her hands and knees. "Magnus! Magnus!" She wailed.

Her eight-year-old daughter Sarah ran up to her and dropped to all fours next to her mother. "Mommy! Mommy! I want Daddy! Daddy!" She hugged her mother and bawled.

The Angel Isolde Maria knelt on the other side of Rivka. She put her right arm across Rivka's back and held Sarah's little hand. The Angel wailed with them. With her free hand, she wiped away Rivka's tears with her hair while kissing her cheek.

Chapter 3

The slats of the wooden carriage stank of urine, feces, and body odor. The blindfold intensified the stench. He tried laying on his side to ease the pain of his arms bound behind his back, but that only drove the pain to his shoulders. Each bump on the pitted dirt road hit him with a wave of agony. He prayed fervently, "Oh, Lord, my hands and feet aren't pierced, and I can breathe. I thank you, Lord Yeshua. Your heart agonized as you bore the sins of mankind. My heart is also in agony. In the name of the Father, protect Rivka and comfort her. Ease her anxiety and grief. Please watch over her and our little Sarah. Give Samuel, Ruth, and Argus the strength to carry on in my place." Magnus prayed nonstop for his family and his home church for the next interminable limb and nerve-jarring hours. Each jolt of the carriage rocked into the next. After what seemed like an eternity, it halted. He heard the rattling of the lock being released. *'Creak'*, the door opened. Magnus winced in pain as a soldier grabbed his arm and yanked him from the carriage. His mind felt like mush as they dragged him into a building and threw him into a dank cell. "You don't deserve this, traitor." They unbound him and took off his blindfold. "It's orders from the governor."

Circulation returning to his limbs gave him his first sense of relief in what seemed like a different age. He paced back and forth in his cell to restore blood to his upper and lower extremities. Each step animated Rivka, Sarah, and Yeshua. Pangs of hunger and thirst tormented him. Yet anxiety constricted his throat and stomach, stifling any desire to eat or drink. An hour later, a guard gave him a husk of stale bread and a dish of cold gruel. Magnus prayed, "Dear

Lord Yeshua, forgive me. I recognize the pain, death, and suffering that I had inflicted on others while a soldier in service of Rome. You endured far greater suffering to wash my sins away. I willingly bear this pain for you. But please protect Rivka and Sarah. Please be with them." Magnus then felt the comfort of the Holy Spirit.

A comforting inner voice spoke to him. *'Eat and drink what they have given you. You will need your strength to face your ordeal. I will be with you. An angel will protect Rivka and Sarah.'*

Magnus steepled his hands and thanked God for his provision. He ate and drank, but sleep's mercy evaded him.

***

"Time to go traitor." Two guards entered his cell, shackled him, and put a blindfold over his eyes. "You have an appointment with the governor. And not just any governor, but a proconsul. Ha! Ha! Ha! Put a smile on your face. The next stop will be Rome and Nero."

The soldiers returned Magnus to the wooden carriage. After interminable bumps and jolts, they reached their destination. The soldiers yanked him out of the carriage. They took off his blindfold. He squinted in the intense solar glare but relished breathing fresh air. Magnus's eyes adjusted enough for him to ponder a large official building. His knees buckled as the soldiers forced him to climb 127 steps, walked him between its Doric columns, and through a huge atrium with a high domed ceiling. A huge statue of Nero sat in the center.

The Proconsul sat behind a huge cedar table. Busts of Roman Gods, past Ceasars, and warriors sat on pedestals lined along the wall. "Unbind the prisoner." Although the Proconsul was elderly and worn, he carried himself like a

211

warrior in his prime. "Nero has taken a special interest in you." He then tilted his head and squinted at the disheveled, exhausted prisoner. "Magnus? Guard. Please wait outside. Close the door and make sure no one enters." The guard snapped to attention and then carried out his orders. He stepped forward, punched his chest, and extended his right arm.

Magnus did likewise. "Leganus Octavius."

"Now it's Proconsul Governor Octavius." He moved a padded chair toward Magnus. "You've had quite an ordeal. Here." He pointed to the chair. "Sit."

Magnus sat. The chair was comfortable; his limb's nerves, tendons, and muscles ached.

"I hope Rivka is doing well. She is a wonderful woman. I am above the governor of your region. I will do all I can to spare her from persecution." Octavius returned to sitting behind his desk. "Unfortunately, I cannot guarantee it."

Magnus inhaled deeply. His thoughts remained muddled. "You must know why I am under arrest."

Octavius looked around. "Yes. I do. I admire you now more than when you were my best soldier." Octavius closed his eyes and looked upward. He took a deep breath and returned his gaze to Magnus. "Is it right that you are here as a criminal being treated as a traitor? While I live in luxury?" Octavius twitched his head back and forth. "You will be rewarded in Heaven for your courage. I have no crown waiting for me. I have received my reward here on Earth. My only eternal hope is for mercy and forgiveness. Yeshua taught us the parable of the mustard seed. My faith got tangled in the thorns. I, too, believe. But I am a coward. Yes. I fought in many campaigns and gained the admiration of many for my courage in combat. I rose to the military's highest rank. But I put my life and my ambition ahead of our Lord." Octavius stood and walked over to Magnus. "We fought many battles. We have seen the whites of the enemy's eyes. They tried to kill us, but we killed them first. But were they evil? Or were they only following the orders of their command? How often were they defending their countries, tribes, and families from us?"

"Throughout my ordeal, I have come to realize that. I have even participated in crucifixions. I have caused much pain and suffering. Now, it is my time to suffer. I can only pray that God will spare Rivka, my children, and my grandchild."

"Yes. You have looked the enemies of Rome in the eye and defeated them. Yet you have never come face to face with true evil. Yes. We met Judas, the betrayer. I am talking about evil from the pit of Hell. The evil that controls weak men like Judas." Octavius walked around the room, assuring all doors and windows were sealed. "That evil is Emperor Nero. He is evil incarnate. I can only beg our Lord's forgiveness for following his orders. I have a wife, four children, and eight grandchildren. Nero would have them all tortured and killed if he were to discover that I am a believer." Octavius dropped his head. "I attend no Christian meetings. You are the first person that I have ever shared my faith with since Tiberius. Caligula was insane. Nero is just as mad but can institute his cruelty and insanity."

"I understand, Octavius. Many are called. Few are chosen. You will still find mercy and forgiveness."

"I can release you right now." Octavius raised his hands. "You don't have to renounce your faith. I'll just put in my report that you renounced your faith and pledged to worship Nero." He put his hand on Magnus's shoulder. "You can return to Rivka and your family."

"I cannot do that. I stand firm in my faith. I believe that our God will protect my family. I will die for our Lord."

Octavius inhaled deeply. He circled his table and sat. After two minutes of tense silence, he spoke. "Here is what I can do. I take great risk in doing this. Rather than send you to Nero, I will sentence you to Patmos. I once helped the Carcerarius Custos rise through the military ranks. I will have him appoint you as a prisoner carcerarii. You will be one step below a guard. You will not do hard labor; you will eat better food and have better housing."

"No. Dominus. Our Lord was beaten, humiliated, and crucified on my behalf. I thank you for sparing my life, but I will take the worst that Patmos has, and I will rejoice in my suffering."

"Magnus. You are far more worthy of a man than I." Proconsul Octavius steepled his fingers. "Take my offer. You can better serve Yeshua. You will have more influence on the guards. Perhaps some will treat the other prisoners better as a result. You can show them what our Lord is all about. Show them you must. You know too well that worshiping our Lord is a capital expense, and many on Patmos are loyal to Nero."

Magnus closed his eyes, yet he experienced brightness rather than darkness. "You are closer to him than you think, Governor. You can further his will. He trusts in your wisdom to do what is right." Magnus punched his chest and extended his right arm.

Octavius did likewise. "Your courage and sacrifice have inspired me and made me see my shortcomings and strengths. I can't promise you a pleasurable journey to Patmos. But as a former war hero, centurion, and now a prisoner carcerarii, I can assure you an easier trip."

Chapter 4

Rivka and Sarah stood on a hilltop overlooking a valley. A stream rolling over boulders meandered between their hilltop and distant snowcapped mountains. Sarah squeezed her mother's hand. "Mommy, is Daddy over those mountains?"

A nightingale chirped from an olive tree branch.

"Daddy may be over the mountain; he may be across the sea," Rivka wiped a tear from her eye. "He may be beyond the blue horizon."

"I want Daddy, Mommy."

"Wherever he is, my little angel, he is still here in your heart." Rivka smiled at her daughter.

"But I want him here."

"I know sweetheart." Rivka picked up her daughter. She braced her hands so that Sarah could sit on her arms. Sarah wrapped her arm around her mother's neck. "Close your eyes and pray. You don't even have to imagine. Just believe in God and know he is keeping your Daddy."

"But I want God to give him back to me."

"He never took him from you." Rivka fought back tears. "He's here in your heart right now. He loves you, and he is watching over you."

"No, Mommy! I want Daddy." Sarah cried. "I want Daddy here right now."

Rivka kept one arm bracing her daughter's seat while wrapping her other arm around her back and hugging her. "It's okay to cry, my little angel. Cry. God can hear you. God will comfort you." Rivka then returned Sarah to her feet. "Look at the stream rolling over the rocks. Think of it as living waters. Hush, my angel. Can you hear it?"

"Yes, Mommy." Sarah sniffled and wiped her eyes. "I hear the waters. It's Daddy saying that he loves us."

"I love you too my Sarah. Mommy and Daddy will always love you. But God loves you most of all."

"Mommy, not only do I hear the stream. I smell beautiful flowers, but I can't see any flowers."

The Angel Isolde Maria then appeared to Sarah. "You are such a special child, Sarah." She kissed her forehead. "Heaven loves you so much. I promise that you will be with your Daddy again." The Angel hugged Sarah and again kissed her forehead before disappearing.

"Mommy! Did you see the angel!"

"No, Sarah."

"Don't you believe me?"

Rivka held both of Sarah's hands and looked at her with widening eyes. "Did she have long, flowing black hair and bright blue eyes?" Rivka's breath quickened; a subtle grin played at the corner of her lips.

"Yes, Mommy! She was beautiful, and she smelled like a flower garden." Sarah beamed. "And she said that we will be with Daddy again."

Rivka beamed back at her. "I know that angel, Sarah! She loves us. Oh, Sarah, I love you so much. I love you forever and ever, my darling. We will be with Daddy soon. If the angel said so, it will happen." Rivka and Sarah hugged and then walked hand in hand to their house.

***

Magnus leaned on a sick with a sponge on the end, taking a break from scrubbing the deck of the prison ship. *'I am blessed to be outside, doing this labor. Thank you, Lord Yeshua.'* Magnus inhaled and smelled a breath of salty air. *'Lord, some of my brothers, also convicted of following you,*

are down below in chains. Please bless and comfort them.'
Magnus gazed at the Aegean Sea horizon's glowing lapis under the afternoon sun. The rocky Island of Patmos lay ahead. *'The Sirens. Even before finding you, Yeshua, I knew those stories were myths. Yet if I were captain of this ship, and I heard Rivka's voice whistling through the rocks, I would risk my life, the crew, and the ship to get to her.'* Magnus grinned, tilted his head upward, and closed his eyes. He saw Rivka. The sea breeze drifted in his ear. He heard Rivka singing her song which Yeshua loved. *'Come and follow him. Open your eyes to a world of seeing. Come and follow him. He'll show you a whole new meaning.'*

"Hey, you! Get back to work! You may be a carcerarii, but you're still a convict. Unless you would rather join the others down below."

Magnus said nothing. He put his strength and energy into scrubbing the deck. He heard the sea breeze chime little Sarah's laughter.

Chapter 5

Magnus stood before Carcerarius Custos Klavian. A prominent vein ran from his bald pate to his temple. "I am unsure whether to say that I am honored to meet you or to dishonor you as a traitor to Ceasar Nero. I know of your heroics as a soldier and a centurion, and that Proconsul Governor Octavius holds you in high regard." Klavian prodded. "You still are guilty of blasphemy and treason. You stand before me as a carcerarii. Otherwise, you would be in chains. Never force me to remind you that you are still a prisoner. I will issue you a whip, and you will work with the guards. This is a prison. Our purpose, however, is not just to punish criminals. We mine marble for the good of Rome. The prisoners must work to achieve those ends. Therefore, we keep them alive. They do get water breaks. As we are on an island, fish is readily available. The fishermen sell us their trash fish, and the fish are too small for the market. We grind up the fish: bones, guts, scales, and all into a gruel and feed it to the prisoners. We also mix lentils into it. You will not eat what the guards eat, but you will get a better portion of the gruel and be housed separately. If you please the guards, they may slip you some of their rations." Klavian again prodded. "I know why you are here. One word of your heretical God to the other prisoners, and you will die. I do not have to formally execute you or send you to Rome to be torn apart by wild beasts in the arena. I only have to reassign you to the general population. The other prisoners will kill you for having been a carcerarii." Klavian pointed to a guard. "Take this carcerarii with you, show him his quarters, and then put him to work. Let him know what is expected."

***

Cold freshwater dripped from cracks in the rock; hot salt water oozed from the pores of the prisoner's skin. The sharp noise of metal pickaxes and hammers striking rock was enough to cause ringing in Magnus's eardrums. The temperature underground was mercifully ten degrees cooler than above ground. Body odor and minerals made a strange scent cocktail. A wispy guard stood next to Magnus. "That one there. He's an otium." The guard whipped him. The prisoner yelped in pain but stubbornly refused to work any harder. "Oh, it looks like we have a resister." The guard bore into Magnus with his deep-set, small brown eyes. "You show them who's boss. Whip him!"

Magnus froze. He thought of Yeshua. He thought of both the cruel beating he got before the crucifixion and the love and mercy he gave his tormenters. He remembered how he affected Centurion Longinus and especially hard-core Optio Flavius.

"Whip him! I command you!"

Magnus stood and stared at the prisoner.

"Whip him!"

Magnus cracked his whip. He made sure that he missed by a nano-fraction of an inch.

The prisoner made eye contact with Magnus. He kept his mouth sealed but raised the corners of his lips by the width of a hair.

"Look at him! He's not working! Whip him again! Harder!"

Magnus again cracked his whip and again, and with the deft of a master illusionist, missed by less than a millimeter.

"Ahh!" the prisoner screamed. He smacked the rock with his pickax rapidly as a watermill in a gale.

Magnus was housed in an open bay unit with the other carcerarii. He stayed in silent prayer constantly. God was his sole companion. Magnus remembered hearing the Apostle James speak. '*A small rudder steers a mighty ship. Likewise, the tongue is a small body part that steers the course of life.*' Magnus knew that some of the other carcerarii and open population prisoners would inform on him for even a faint hope of a Carcerarius Custos favor. One loose word could result in death. Each night, Magnus would close his eyes and silently pray, '*Lord Yeshua, I thank you in the name of the Father for this straw bed and that I am not harassed at night. I ask you to bless the prisoners who are suffering far more than I. I pray for the guards and staff that they may see the light of your mercy. Above all, I pray for Rivka and my family. Bless them and keep them. Let the Holy Spirit comfort them in the knowledge that I am alive and that you are keeping me strong.*'

The next day, Magnus helped the guards supervise the above-ground prisoners. He could feel hatred and contempt from every angle. The guards hated him because he rejected the Roman Gods and was a traitor to Nero. The prisoners hated him because they considered him a collaborator with their oppressors. Magnus wiped the sweat from his brow and winced at the glaring sun. '*I can only imagine breaking rocks with a hammer under this sun.*' Magnus turned to a guard, "Don't you think the prisoners should get a water break?"

"You make sure they work." The guard scowled at Magnus. "I don't need you to tell me how to do my job." The guard cracked his whip at the prisoners. "Okay. Water break!"

An elderly carcerarii named Marcus carried a water bucket supported by a shoulder strap. He served each prisoner with a ladle. Magnus stood in front of an Ethiopian giant. He glowered back at him. *'He knows me. From where? I sense that he hates my guts. Why?'* Magnus took a ladle from Marcus's water bucket and handed it to the giant.

The Ethiopian drank. "More. Traitor."

Magnus gave the Ethiopian another ladle of water. He spat it in his face. The guard yelled at the Ethiopian from a distance. "That will be enough out of you." He cracked his whip.

"Until next time." The Ethiopian scowled back at Magnus. "We have a score to settle."

Marcus stood next to Magnus, pretending to tend to the water buckets. "That's Abede. He's the most dangerous prisoner here. Even the guards fear him."

"I can see by the size of him. He's as big as Goliath."

"I was thinking Gigantes." Marcus wiped the ladle with a rag even though it was clean. "Don't worry. I know why you're here. I don't care. His name is Abede. He was the bodyguard and henchman of a rich and powerful Judean merchant. He's here for killing his boss's enemies. The merchant had enough pull with Rome to have him sent here rather than crucifixion. The other prisoners are terrified of him and do what he says."

"Why does he hate me?" Magnus wiped the sweat from his brow. "I've never done anything to him."

"Who knows? There's not much love in this place." Marcus glanced about. "Keep your head down. Never move your lips when you talk. Another one to look out for is Carcerarii Shemcar." Marcus tilted his head and jutted his finger for a second. "Over there."

Magnus looked at carcerarii prisoner talking with two guards. "He looks rather chummy with the guards."

"That's because he acts as their eyes and ears. He thinks he's getting out of here alive. Right now, he has the guards distracted. That's the only reason that I can talk to you here. Even so, don't raise your head. The prisoners here have a word for an informant. Rat. And Shemcar would rat on his mother for the slightest favor. Too bad the guards don't know that he also rats on them to Klavian." Marcus again stared into the water bucket. "And speaking of rats. Even though you were a centurion and now a Christian, you're all right. Some of the boys have been saving a few of the four-legged kind. You're invited to our little feast." Marcus raised his head by two inches and grinned with his mouth closed. "You earned a break from fish bones and scales."

Chapter 6

Sarah knelt beside her mother. Rivka handed Sarah a bouquet to put on Hannah's grave. She placed it on the ground in front of her headstone. Samuel and Ruth stood beside them. Argus held Rivka's baby granddaughter, Mariam.

"I miss grandma," Sarah squeezed her mother's hand.

"Of course you do, my little angel." Rivka wiped away a tear. "She loved you too. God gives us only so many years here on Earth. Yeshua died and rose from the dead to give Grandma eternal life in Heaven. We all loved her. She made the lives of many better. I miss her terribly." Rivka leaned the bouquet on Hannah's headstone. "Let's not honor her with grieving and sadness. Let's try to share her joy in Heaven. Let's honor her by keeping the faith that one day we will be together again."

"I miss Daddy more."

Rivka could no longer fight back her tears. She bawled and held her daughter closer. "I love you so much, Sarah." Rivka kissed her daughter's cheek. "Nothing will ever replace your father. We must be strong as he is strong. He wants us to be strong until his return."

"I know that Daddy is alive and that we will be together again soon." Sarah beamed. "The beautiful angel told me so." Sarah beamed.

Rivka hugged her daughter. Her son, Samuel, put his flowers on Hannah's grave. He then squeezed his mother's shoulder. Ruth next leaned a bouquet on Hannah's headstone. She then kissed Sarah and then her mother's forehead. Argus leaned over with baby Mariam so that Rivka could kiss her cheek.

Rivka sat at the table head. Roast lamb surrounded by lentils, chickpeas, carrots, and turnips sat in the center. Sarah sat next to Rivka. Baby Mariam sat in a highchair flanked by her parents, Ruth and Argus. Samuel sat at the far end. "Today marks the birthday of our beloved, dear departed matriarch. We honor her with this feast." Rivka folded her hands. "Let us pray. Heavenly Father, in the name of Yeshua, we honor Hannah's life on Earth with this feast that you have bountifully provided. May we express our thanksgiving through prayer. We all gather in faith that Magnus is in your hands. We ask that you keep him strong and that the Holy Spirit comfort him and help him endure his persecution. Amen."

The family responded with "Amen."

***

After they finished their meal, their hired servant cleared the table. "I am sorry that we didn't invite you." Rivka handed her a plate. "This was a special, private family occasion."

"I understand, Domina."

Rivka half-smiled and skewed her eyes.

"Rivka," the servant smiled.

"I hope you won't find my offer insulting." Rivka held her servant's hand. "But there's plenty of food left. You and your helpers are more than welcome to have a feast of your own in the kitchen."

"Why thank you, Domin…Rivka." The servant beamed.

"Now that we have finished eating and are gathered around the table." Rivka steepled her fingertips. "We need to discuss family business. I have hired three workers to sheer the sheep. I had discussions with two different wool merchants. One bettered the price that the Karas Brothers pay. The Karas Brothers are willing to match their price. Out of loyalty and that we can trust them, we will continue our business relationship with the Karas's."

"I will make certain that the wool is baled and ready to go for their pick-up." Samuel nodded his head.

"Thanks, Samuel." Rivka placed her hands on the table. "As usual, sort out the sheep to take to the market and which to keep for breeding. The sheep auction is next week in Aigai. I have hired two shepherds to help you herd them during the trip, and," Rivka dropped her head. She steeled herself from crying, "Since Magnus is not here, I have hired a retired Roman soldier to help with security."

"Mommy!" Sarah tugged on Rivka's sleeve. "The beautiful angel. Remember what she said to me."

Knocking on the door interrupted her.

"It's the cursus publicus." Ruth pointed at the door.

Rivka walked over, answered the door, and took the note from him. She faced her family and read the message. Rivka's face glowed like a nova. Her smile stretched from ear to ear. Tears cascaded from her eyes. "He's alive! Magnus is alive. The message is from his former commander," She held up the parchment, "and now proconsul governor. He's in prison on the island of Patmos. The governor arranged for him to be a carcerarii.

The entire family cheered.

"Mommy! Mommy!" Sarah ran to her mother. "The beautiful angel was right."

Rivka picked up Sarah and hugged her.

"I know daddy's coming home."

"Praise be to God that he's alive and in a better predicament than we could hope for." Samuel's expression went blank. "Nevertheless, few prisoners have left Patmos alive."

"Gather around me." Rivka's hand gestured toward herself. "Let's all pray."

The family held hands and touched heads. Rivka led them in prayer, "Lord Yeshua, in the name of the Father, we thank you for Magnus's safety, and we pray that you continue to bless him and keep him. If it be your will, may you return him to us."

The family responded with, "Amen."

"Mommy," Sarah pulled on Rivka's hem. "I'm so happy! I want you to sing for us." She looked up at her with wide eyes and a smile. "Please, Mommy, please."

Rivka made eye contact with Sarah and then went to another room. A moment later, she returned with a lyre. She smiled at her family before strumming an opening chord and singing,

"Praise the Lord." She strummed an instrumental interlude.

"Praise him in all his glory;
praise him for our bounty.
Praise him for his power;
praise him for his charity.
Praise him for his unsurpassed greatness.
Praise him with trumpets and our voice.
Sing praises to him in whom we rejoice."

"Thank you, mama." Sarah hugged Rivka around her legs. She looked up into her mother's eyes. "Will you please sing the song that you wrote for Yeshua?"

"Yes, yes, please do," Her older daughter Ruth chimed in.

"It's my favorite too." Samuel tapped the table with a utensil.

"We sing and rejoice to his glory." Rivka started playing her lyre.

"Come and follow him." "Open your eyes to a World of seeing." "Come and follow him." "He'll show you a whole new meaning."

"Hear what he has to say; let him show you the way." "Trust in him and obey, and he will wash your sins away."

"See Heaven through the son, living waters soft and sweet." "You will find eternal life, believe, and he will set you free."

"His love flows upon the shores of time, From oceans deep to mountains high." "He'll lift your spirit far and wide, for his love is true and divine."

"The seed that he plants today, Tomorrow will grow into a tree."

"See Heaven through the son, living waters soft and sweet," "You will find eternal life. Believe, and he will set you free."

"His love flows upon the shores of time, From oceans deep to mountains high." "He'll lift your spirit far and wide, for his love is true and divine."

The entire family sat still and silent. No dry eye could be found.

Chapter 7

Abede cornered two prisoners, "I know the guards' routine. Tomorrow, Magnus and Shemcar will be assigned Mineshaft two. Shemcar is in tight with the guards. He'll be with them when they break to eat. It's then that you two will stage a fight by the opening of the hidden cave. I will be waiting inside. When Magnus comes over to break you two up, step aside. I will pull him into the cave and give him what he deserves."

"Abede, Shemcar is the one you should hate." A prisoner, half Abede's size, spread his palms. "Magnus is one of us. He has never whipped any of us. He fakes it. And he never rats us out."

"Do you think I don't know that?"

"Then why do you hate him? He takes great risks to spare us punishment. It's Shemcar who lashes us and rats to the guards."

"This has nothing to do with the guards or prison. This is personal." Abede flared his python-like arms.

"Abede, the other prisoners, and even the guards both respect and fear you. Need I tell you that the penalty for killing a carcerarii is death by beheading in the prison yard. "I'm an old timer. I've seen it more than once?" He put his palms in front of his face. "If they think we helped you, they'll chop off our heads too." He ran the edge of his hand across his neck. "Please, Abede, reconsider. It's not much of a life here, but at least it's living. We can at least dream of the outside and cling to the hope of leaving alive. When we join Pluto in the underworld, all hope is lost."

Abede lurched forward. With each hand, he grabbed the scruff of the prisoners' shirts. "Do it, or I'll rip off your heads with my bare hands right here and now." His eyes bore into them with solar flare intensity.

***

Abede briefed his two lacqueys, "Shemcar is with the guards eating their meal."

"I saw." One of the prisoners glanced in the other direction. "He must've ratted and ratted good. They're sharing some of their food with him."

"Magnus is now the only one watching the prisoners. The time is now. I'll hide in the cave. Count to sixty, then come to the entrance and stage the fight. Make as much noise as possible so that you will draw Magnus." Abede cracked his knuckles. "I will take it from there."

Abede strolled over to the cave. It was not empty. He heard several voices singing. Abede marched toward the entrance. '*Time to clean house.*' Clenching his ham-sized fists, he marched toward the cave entrance. He stopped. The men inside were singing hymns to Yeshua. Abede smiled and pinched his chin. He signaled to his Lacqueys. "New plan. Stage your fight. Wait until Magnus is about ten steps away. Then you both disperse. Abede grabbed one of his lacqueys. "You. Afterward, go straight to Shemcar and tell him that there's a commotion. Point him to here." Abede walked away.

***

Magnus heard prisoners yelling and swearing. He ran to the commotion and saw two prisoners fighting. Before he could intervene, they fled in different directions. Magnus next heard singing from a hidden cave entrance.

"We praise you, Lord, like a surging wave."

"May your mercy wash our souls to save."
"The stars stay silent for us to sing out loud."
"Only you rose from death's burial shroud."

Magnus walked into the cave. The prisoners nodded to him and smiled while continuing to sing. Magnus joined them.

After Abede's lacquey alerted him, Shemcar investigated the cave area. He heard singing. *'That's a Christian hymn.'* He clenched his teeth. He spotted the entrance and looked inside. *"Carcerarii Magnus is singing with them!'* His grin exposed his four remaining teeth. His eyes met the bridge of his snout-like nose.

***

Early the next morning, two guards pulled Magnus from his straw bed.

"What's going on? Why are you doing this to me?"

The guards bound Magnus's wrist behind him and brusquely ushered him into Carcerarius Custos Klavian's office. He prodded. "You are hereby charged with another count of blasphemy and treason against Ceasar Nero. What do you have to say for yourself before I pass sentence."

Magnus sang,
"We praise you Lord like a surging wave."
"May your mercy wash our souls to save."
"The stars stay silent for us to sing out loud."
"Only you rose from death's burial shroud."

"Stop it!" Klavian leaped up and smacked Magnus's face.

Magnus didn't budge.

"Silence! The penalty is death by beheading." Klavian faced Magnus. "The Governor Proconsul Octavius does have a special liking for you. Besides, you were once a

Roman hero. Octavius has also helped me advance in my career in the service of Rome. Anyone else gets beheaded in the yard with the entire prison watching. If I return you to open population, the other prisoners will kill you as a collaborator. I would still have to answer to Octavius. Here is what I am going to do. I am sure this isn't news to you. Once a year, we stage gladiatorial games in the main quarry. It is tiered to accommodate three thousand spectators. Roman officials and civilians from both the island and the mainland attend. It is secure enough that the prisoners can also watch. The main event pits the prison's two most formidable fighters in a battle to the death. The loser dies. The winner gains his freedom. Each opponent gets a dagger. No shield. No armor. You were once a legionnaire and Centurion. You had a reputation as a fierce and skilled fighter. Congratulations. You are fighting in the main event."

***

That night, Magnus prayed in his holding cell. "Oh Lord, in the name of the Father, let me glorify you. Tomorrow, I will stand before hundreds of people. Do I stand down and accept death like you in submission to the Father's will? Or do you have a plan for my life, and I fight to defend it, even if it means taking another's life?" After an hour of fervent prayer, Magnus saw a bright light. A sensation of euphoria and weightlessness swept over him. Magnus had his answer.

***

Rivka held Sarah's hand as she stood by four bales of wool. An ox-drawn cart pulled up to them. The driver

231

disembarked. "Good day, Rivak." He doffed his hat. "I see that you have the bales of wool ready for me."

"Yes, Kurios Karras." Rivka continued to hold her daughter's hand. "I prayed for you to have a safe trip, and I will pray for your safe return."

Karas ticced his head, surveying the surroundings, "May God bless you too, Gyne Rivka." He looked around again. He lowered his head and spoke without moving his lips. "And we pray for your husband's safe return."

"Thank you, I appreciate that, and little Sarah here appreciates it too." Rivka nodded. "Did you bring what we agreed upon?"

"Well, actually, I only could come up with twenty gold coins."

"Then you only get three bales of wool."

The other Karas stood with his hands on his hips and glared at his brother.

Karas shifted his feet and looked away from Rivka. "Hmm...It seems that my brother found the other five coins."

"That's a good thing." Rivka lifted Sarah and held her. "My workers will help you load the bales."

***

The trumpet blasted twice. An overweight man wearing a tunic shouted through a laryngophone. "Ave, spectatores! This is your main event! A fight to the death! The winner will be set free. In the south end of the quarry, he was a legionnaire and a centurion. He once fought for the honor of Rome." The Master of Ceremonies paused for effect. "He now fights for his freedom as a traitor. Magnus!"

The crowd booed and hissed. "Infamia!" a spectator yelled. Some threw rotten food. "Boo! Shame!" They next chanted in unison, "Kill the traitor! Kill the traitor! Kill the traitor!"

"Now, entering the quarry…"

The crowd gasped as his opponent entered the quarry from the north. He stood taller than the tallest draught horse. His shoulders were broader than an oxen yoke. His skin was blacker than a panther's fur.

…He is a triple murderer now paying the price to Rome. One more killing and he's a free man. He hails from Ethiopia. Abede."

The crowd cheered and shook their fists.

The master of ceremonies stood between them. "At the blast of the trumpet. Fight. There are no rules. May the best man win."

"You may not remember me." Abede glowered at Magnus. "You cost my boss his wife. He paid a generous dowery to her father. You seduced her before he could even touch her. He never recovered. As a result, he later had me kill three men. Now I kill you."

The trumpet blared. The master of ceremonies scrambled to safety.

Abede held his dagger overhead and roared. He lunged his dagger downward. Magnus raised his arms, crossed at the wrist, and blocked his strike; he countered by slamming his knee into the side of Abede's thigh.

Abede was more surprised than hurt as he stumbled sideways. He then lurched forward and swung his dagger at Magnus with a roundhouse swipe. Magnus evaded him, grabbed his wrist, and pinched his ulnar nerve. Abede dropped his dagger as Magnus flung him to the ground.

The crowd groaned.

Abede rose, faced Magnus, and snorted like an enraged bull. Magnus held his dagger low and close to his side.

Abede charged Magnus. Magnus thrust his dagger at his gut. At the same instant, Abede used his long leg for a front kick. With the dagger an inch from his gut, Abede's kick struck Magnus in the stomach. The pain and shock caused Magnus to drop his dagger. Abede moved in and lifted him by the armpits. He ran a few steps and heaved him into the wall. Magnus felt an agonizing thud and saw sparks ricocheting about his cranium. The impact stole his breath. He collapsed on the wall. Abede lunged in, lifted him overhead, and slammed him to the ground. Abede recovered the dagger. He stood over Magnus and looked at Carcerarius Custos Klavian.

"Kill the traitor! Kill the traitor! Kill the traitor!" the crowd chanted.

Klavian turned his thumb down.

Chapter 8

Rivka sat cross-legged on a pillow in her atrium. Sarah sat next to her. Rivka pointed to a scroll. "This time, honey. Try to read it in Greek."

"I will try, Mommy." Sarah put her finger on the scroll. "Stin archí, o Theós dimioúrgise tous Ouranoús kai ti Gi.

"Excellent, Sarah!" Rivka kissed her cheek, "In the beginning, God created the heavens and the Earth. The Earth was formless and void; darkness was over the surface of the deep. And the spirit of God hovered over the waters." Sarah pointed upwards. "And God said, let there be light!"

"Wonderful!" Rivka wrapped her arm around Sarah and squeezed her. "You got it, my little angel!"

"Mommy!" Sarah stood. "The Angel."

"No, Sarah." Rivka chuckled. "You're my angel."

"No, Mommy! The Angel"

Rivka then smelled a flower garden. She turned. Isolde Maria stood before her. "Our Lord, the son, promised that 'when two are more are gathered in my name, there I am with them.' Rivka, Sarah… Magnus is in mortal danger. I am not permitted to tell you more. He needs the power of our prayers. You, as two faithful mortals, and me, a Heavenly Angel, shall now pray together in Yeshua's presence."

Rivka, Sarah, and the Angel held hands and fervently prayed. A bright light filled the atrium.

Chapter 9

The sun gleaming from the blade of Abede's dagger stung Magnus's eyes; it roused a final thought. *'One chance.'* Magnus rolled over on his left side. With his right leg, he kicked the lateral side of Abede's right knee. Magnus could hear *'crack.'*

Pain caused the Black giant to drop his dagger and lift his leg by the ankle. Magnus followed with a kick to his left calf. Abede timbered to the ground. Magnus climbed to his feet, picked up the dagger, and put his foot on Abede's throat.

The crowd groaned.

Magnus looked to Carcerarius Custos Klavian.

He turned his thumb down.

The crowd silenced.

***

Isolde Maria stood and spread her arms. A glow blanketed Rivka and Sarah, and the aroma of a flower garden filled the air. "If Magnus obeys the spirit and does what is right, you will be reunited in this life." She raised her open hands. We must unite in prayer."

***

Magnus threw his dagger aside. He approached Carcerarius Custos Klavian. "I gave you sport and entertainment. I will not give you murder. If anyone is to be set free, it's Abede. He's the better fighter. If I must die here, I die for my Lord Yeshua."

Abede lay on the ground. The agony in his right knee and left calf muscle caused him to writhe.

Magnus walked over to him. "You're going to have to trust me. I am trained and experienced in combat first aid. Your knee is dislocated. I can put it back in place. It will hurt for a few moments. In about three weeks, it will be like new."

Abede grunted and nodded.

Magnus grabbed his right foot and twisted. *'snap.'* He put his knee back in place. "Your calf is only bruised. Let me help you stand on it." Magnus and Abede grabbed each other's wrists. Magnus pulled him to his feet. "Now brace yourself on my shoulder. We'll limp out of here together.

"Huh." The crowd stood and gasped. They were too shocked by what they saw to react.

Abede put his arm around Magnus's shoulder. Together, they limped from the quarry.

The crowd suddenly erupted. They prodded at Carcerarius Custos Klavian and shouted in unison. "Free them! Free them! Free them!"

Klavian ticced his head.

"Free them! Free them! Free them!"

Klavian turned pale. He started to sweat profusely.

"Free them! Free them! Free them!" Their chant reached fever pitch.

***

"You're a madman. Why didn't you kill me? I hate you and want to kill you." Abede winced from a wave of pain in his knee. "If you killed me, you would've been set free and able to go home."

"Do you hate me now?"

"Hate is all I've ever known."

"What about your boss? You killed for him, and you wanted to avenge him."

237

"All he gave me was a different kind of hate." Abede took three deep breaths. "He never did anything for me other than pay my wages. You were willing to die for me, and you gave up your chance at freedom for me. That's beyond my thinking. I want what you have."

"We better pray together and right now." Magnus looked to his left. "Because here come the guards. Repeat after me. "Yeshua, save me.""

"Yeshua, save me!" Abede said it with conviction.

***

"Free them! Free them! Free them!" Security was outnumbered and struggling to restrain the crowd.

Fear and nerves paralyzed Flavian. Two men broke past security and yelled in his face, "Free them! Free them!"

"I declare them free!" Flavian shouted.

***

That evening, Magnus stood before Carcerarius Custos Klavian's desk. Abede leaned on a crutch. An elderly man with a long white beard and an upscale robe stood beside Klavian. "I am Praetor Constinus. The Carcerarius Custos had declared you free in front of over three thousand witnesses. As a Roman leader, he is bound by his word. But Roman law takes precedence. Roman law only permits him to free one prisoner because of an annual game outcome. As a praetor, I am forced to make a ruling that honors both decrees. You two are free from the Patmos prison. You are not free to go to the mainland. If you do, you will be arrested and returned as an escapee. You will then be beheaded in the prison yard."

Chapter 10

"Kaa-kaw. Mew-mew." The seagulls circled above. "Kaa-kaw. Mew-mew." Fish filled the net. "Kaa-kaw. Mew-mew." The birds took turns diving for fish small enough to sift through the mesh. "Heave!" Magnus shouted as Abede and two other fishermen pulled on the net. The boat went over a sea swell, refreshing salt water splashed on their sweating bodies. "Heave!" They lifted the net over the gunnel. They then spilled the fish into a holding bay with the rest of the day's catch. The captain looked at the orange-red sun lowering on the horizon. "That's it for the day, men. We're heading home."

***

"Fresh sea air, nobody insulting us, and especially nobody whipping us," Abede walked next to Magnus on the wharf. "None of the other fishermen hate me or want to stab me in the back." His smile revealed ivory-white teeth. "No complaints here about a day of honest work."

"And we're paid a fair wage." Magnus smiled. "Let's thank the Lord for our every blessing."

"I know that you miss your wife and family. All those men in the prison." Adebe scratched his head. "I made them fear me. I never cared a speck of dust about them or if they had family on the outside. Since finding Yeshua, I realized that others have feelings and needs too. You'll never lose Rivka in your memory. Appreciate that you have both memories of the past and hope for the future. I never had either. I never knew the love of a wife or a family." Adebe raised his hands. "What's it like, Magnus?"

239

"You're never too old, Adebe. We're not free to leave this island, yet this is miles and miles better than the prison. Of course, the prison was leaps and bounds better than Hell, where all hope is abandoned. Yet this world can offer comes within a split hair width of Heaven." Magnus dropped his head and pictured Rivka's long, flowing honey hair with its gray streak. "I am not a betting man, but your odds of finding what you long for are far better now than inside the prison. You now have that hope. Keep it in your prayers."

"I see you're sad."

"Anything and everything make me mourn for my wife. My oldest son and daughter are adults now. That doesn't mean that I don't miss them. It's my little Sarah. My heart bleeds for her."

"I wish that I could say the right thing. The way you have spoken of them, and remembering how my boss in my other life described her, but you already know that story, I can almost imagine them. I wonder if they look anything like those two?" Adebe pointed to a woman with a child.

Magnus looked in the direction that Abede pointed. He made instant eye contact with the woman and child. '*Olive eyes.*' His mind froze for a second. Next, his heart skipped a beat. The mother and child beamed back at him. Magnus gasped. Suddenly, he ran toward them. "Rivka! Sarah!"

The woman squeezed her daughter's hand. Suddenly, the little girl broke free. "Daddy! Daddy! Daddy!" She ran to Magnus.

"Sarah!" Magnus picked her up and kissed her cheeks five times before placing her down. He then embraced Rivka. They shared a long, loving kiss. "I love you, Rivka. I love you. I love you. I love you. I thought of you every waking moment, and when I slept, I dreamed of you."

"I never lost faith, Magnus. Never. I love you; I love you forever." Rivka kissed him again. "This is the greatest moment of my life. This time, only death can tear us apart."

"I accepted his will. Yet this is the moment that I prayed for. This is the moment that I begged for."

"Daddy!" Sarah hugged Magnus around the legs.

"Come, Magnus." Rivka clutched his hand. "Let me take you to our new home."

Magnus looked back at Abede.

Rivka shouted to him. "Come with us, Abede."

Abede walked over to them. "Me?" He pointed to himself. "How did you know my name?"

"Well," Rivka smiled. "Your name is now written in the Lamb's Book of Life. Besides, an angel told me."

"Ahh," Magnus smiled at him. "I have met her angel. She glows with the beauty of Heaven itself."

"What's this Lamb's Book of Life?" Abede spread his palms.

"That has not been fully revealed to me. I do know that it means that you are saved by grace, and Heaven awaits you." After walking for ten minutes, Rivka pointed to a large house made of sun-dried brick and marble columns. "If the columns look familiar, it's because they were mined on this island," Rivka chuckled, "from you know where."

They walked through the entrance and into its courtyard. "Adebe, your quarters are over there." Rivka reached into her chiton. She grasped a key and handed it to Abede. "It's all yours."

"If it's all right with you. I would rather go back to the worker's dorm."

"I know what you're thinking, Abede." Magnus put his hand on Abede's shoulder. "You don't want a woman supporting you."

Abede pursed his lips.

"Nonsense." Magnus smiled. "It's from both of us. Besides, you do more work than all the other fishermen put together. You earned it."

"If you put it that way." He smiled. "It sure beats the worker's dorm. And I snore so loud that I must sleep with an eye open, lest someone cut my throat to shut me up." He laughed. "And I'm too beat to walk to the dorm anyway. Thank you." He shook Magnus's hand. "And thank you too." He bowed to Rivka. "Oh, if the walls shake, don't worry. It's no earthquake. Just me snoring."

Rivka watched Abede enter his quarters. "He had to duck to get through the door. "At least he didn't have to turn sideways."

***

Magnus and Rivka held hands while Sarah sat on her father's thigh. "Daddy, Mama, and I used to stand on our hill to pray for you. I would look at the mountains and imagine that you were on the other side. Mama said you might be over the sea. She was right. God is so wonderful to listen to my prayers. Whenever I was super sad, a beautiful angel visited me and made me feel happy. Now I am happy as can be. I love you, Daddy."

"I love you too, my precious Sarah." After kissing Sarah's cheek, Magnus realized that he had shed a tear. He quickly wiped it away. He then looked into his wife's olive eyes. Tears filled both of his eyes.

Rivka cried. "It's all right, my love. We know how strong and brave you are. We will face many more challenges. Adversity has made our love stronger and our faith stronger. Together, we shall overcome.

The three of them stood and embraced as family.

"And you've had quite a day." Magnus scooped up his daughter and cradled her.

"It's beddy-bye time for you, my little angel." Rivka kissed Sarah's forehead. "Daddy will carry you to your bed."

"May we all pray together before I go to sleep?"

"Of course, my precious little Sarah. We will all hold hands and kneel by your bed and thank the Lord that we are all together again."

After they prayed and Sarah fell asleep, Rivka took her husband by the hand. "It's beddy-bye for us too. Only sleep is the last thing on my mind."

Magnus hugged Rivka and kissed her. Hand in hand, they strolled to their bedroom.

***

The next morning their front door sounded like thunderclaps. Abede shouted. "Hurry up! Hurry Up! We'll miss the boat!"

"Oh no! He's right. We overslept." Magnus jumped out of bed and scrambled for his work clothes.

"Relax. I'll prepare us a big breakfast."

"Relax? Breakfast? We'll miss the boat and a day's wages." Magnus hastily donned his clothes.

"You two earned a day off."

"It's not just the money." Magnus put on his shoes. "You have no idea of how easily we can be replaced."

"That's a good thing." Rivka grinned slightly and tilted her head. "So, we're not letting anyone down."

"That's fine for today." Magnus headed for the door. "But we'll need work tomorrow."

Rivka stood between Magnus and the door. She hugged him and kissed him.

Magnus returned her kiss but only briefly. "I love you, and I wish to make love to you all day long, but a man has responsibilities."

"You have won great victories for our Lord and our fellow man. Nobody admires you more than me, little Sarah, and Samuel and Ruth." She put her hands on his shoulders, kissed his lips, then gazed into his eyes. "I ran the villa rustica in your absence and I bought us this house. I need you and Abede to trust me. Eat a big breakfast, and then we all go to the wharf."

***

"There she is." Rivka pointed to a twenty-foot-long, freshly painted blue navigium boat.

Four men were on board preparing nets. A stout, bearded man looked up at Magnus. "When do we set sail, captain?"

Magnus's jaw dropped. "Me?" He pointed to himself.

"Yes. You." Rivka smiled at Magnus. "She's yours. You better hurry up before the fish swim away." She winked at him. "Captain Magnus."

Abede walked toward the boat.

"Not so fast, you." Rivka tried to grab his arm. Although his arm was too big for her grip, she got his attention. "That's your boat." Rivka pointed to a similar twenty-foot-long navigium. This one was freshly painted green.

A crew member said to Abede. "Domina Rivka warned us that our captain was Black." He shook his head. "She never told us that you were a Titanes." He grinned. "You won't have to worry about us not doing what you say."

Rivka stood between Magnus and Abede. "We are officially a publicani. I will do the behind-the-scenes work.

Besides, you two can't set foot on the mainland, so I will also have to take care of the marketing and sales. That sun is not going to stay up there forever. You two better get going."

Stunned, Magnus and Abede looked at each other. They both then smiled. Magnus hugged Rivka. "You are an amazing woman and wife, the best any man could ever hope for."

***

Magnus's boat returned first. Rivka and Sarah waited for him on the dock. After paying the crew, she held Magnus's right hand and Sarah's left hand. The three walked home.

Abede's boat arrived thirty minutes later. After he and his crew tied the boat to the dock and secured the catch, he walked along the wharf. He closed his eyes, *'Thank you, Yeshua, for my good fortune.'* He bowed his head. *'It looks like it's just you and me.'* Abede lost himself in thought as he observed a passenger vessel enter the harbor and then dock. He squinted. A family of twelve Ethiopians disembarked. The four men wore a traditional knee-length linen kuta of various colors. The eight women wore white linen, ankle-length hamasha kemis dresses, and colorful netela shawls over their shoulders with matching headscarves. Adebe focused \on a female wearing a green netela and headscarf. She stood no taller than five feet and weighed no more than a hundred pounds. She looked back at him and smiled. He returned it. She then looked away and mixed with her family.

Adebe walked onto the boat and approached the captain. His size at first startled the captain. Adebe disarmed him with a toothy beam. "That Ethiopian family. Who are they?

245

"They're the Habte clan. The patriarch owned a copper and bronze refinery in Ephesus. He got fed up with the city and the business." The boat captain raised two fingers. "He sold it and purchased two sheep and goat rusticas up in the hills. He is combining it into one big operation."

"Who was the young woman wearing the green netela, the same color as my boat?"

"You must mean the petite one."

"Yes. She's the one."

 Her name is Stephanie."

"Is she married?"

"No. None of the Habte daughters are married or betrothed. But be careful. They're part of that cult of the Hebrew man who they say walked on water and rose from the dead. You know how much Nero hates them."

Abede's eyes widened; he grinned broadly.

Chapter 11

Patmos 63 AD

Magnus took the helm of his boat. Their catch secured; the crew manned and tied down the stays. They were homeward-bound. Their business had prospered enough that Rivka had acquired two more boats and hired two more crews. One was stationed at Patmos and the other operated on the mainland port city of Ephesus. Stephanie had proven an able administrative assistant. Magnus felt a foreboding. The scattered violet clouds on the horizon had darkened to indigo and mushroomed overhead like a shroud.

The Aegean Sea was glassy smooth but void of baitfish and birds, creating a spooky silence. The first bolt of lightning was distant. It spread across the horizon like a skeleton's hand, its peal echoing several seconds later. Magnus felt a gust breezing a metallic scent. The sea became choppy.

'Crackle.'

Lightning, looking like a bare tree branch, struck the sea only yards ahead.

'Boom!'

Its concussion rattled the boat. Next, a broad bolt and a roaring peal.

Magnus fought the wheel as a sudden gust and wave turned the boat. Rain now fell like steel pellets. The thunder and lightning were now constant as volleys of arrows. "Take down the sails!" Magnus yelled to the crew. The maelstrom grew in sound and fury. Rain and seawater drenched them in buckets. The gale made the rain and spray sting like shrapnel. A wave striking the side of the boat nearly capsized it. Sea water flowed over the gunnels. Magnus attempted to steer the boat into the waves. Another violent sea swell hit the boat's other side. The boat spun in a circle. It was out of control. A surge hit the boat head-on, driving it up to its crest and then crashing it into the trough. More water splashed into the deck. "That's it, men! Get below deck. Batten down the hatches."

Magnus and his four crew members sat helplessly below deck. The sea banging on the hull like an orchestra of tympanum and crotalum drums and the stench of vomit posed the least of their worries.

"I'm not ready for Pluto and the underworld." Crewman Dervis cried and shook his hands. "I want to see my children grow up. Please, Neptune! Make it stop!" The tall, lanky man clenched his fists. "Mighty Neptune! I beg of you!" He then looked at Magnus. "Why are you so calm, captain? Don't you care if we all die at the bottom of the sea?"

"I know the one true God. The one who created to sea. The one whose spirit hovered over the waters."

"His spirit is cruel captain!" Dervis shook his fists. "The waters are trying to kill us all!"

"My faith keeps me calm. That and prayer are our only choices. Panic can prove fatal." Magnus braced himself as the boat violently rocked. "His son didn't just walk the Earth; he walked on water. His disciples were also caught in a storm and thought that they would drown. He walked on the sea of Galilee and climbed into their boat. He then calmed the storm."

"The captain is correct. It happened. I am a believer too." Crewman Hadron bobbed his head. "I keep my faith secret. Yes." He dropped his thin, pointed-nosed head. "I fear Nero."

"Then, if your God's so mighty, make him calm the storm!"

"First, you must let him calm the storm in your heart and soul." Magnus nodded. "Accept him as the one true God and take him into your heart as your savior."

"Then will he make this end?" Dervis grimaced and shook his fists.

"Possibly. If it's his will." Magnus spoke calmly in contrast to the storm. "What he does promise is eternal life in the glory of Heaven rather than the grief of Pluto's underworld."

"All right! All right! I want to find your God. Neptune is doing nothing to help us."

"Ask For Yeshua's forgiveness and invite him into your heart." Magnus held Dervis's hand and looked into his eyes.

Dervis closed his eyes. "Yes, Yeshua. I want what Captain Magnus has. Forgive me and come into my heart."

"Crew." Magnus held up his palms. "Our lord says that when two or more are gathered in his name, he will be present. Let us link hands and pray."

"I will join you, but I don't know what to believe in." Crewman Antop pointed to Magnus. "But Dervis's right about one thing." Antop pointed to Nervo. "Neptune is doing nothing to save us." Next, he pointed to Hadron. "I want to believe too, but Nero's cruelty and his hatred of Christians have no limit."

Hadron replied. "Nero isn't here, and Neptune isn't helping. Join hands with us and pray. It's our only hope."

A wind gust and a sea surge struck the side of the boat, almost tipping it over.

"Ahh!" Antop screamed as a wave striking the boat hurled across the deck. "Now, I believe." He scrambled back to the group. "I will pray with you."

The crew linked hands. Hadron nodded to Magnus and then prayed aloud, "Heavenly Father, in Yeshua's name, you promise that if we have the faith of a mustard seed, we can move a mountain. We ask in faith that you calm the storm. Amen."

Magnus and the three other crewmen replied, "Amen."

"I know that he will calm the storm." Hadron raised his hands. "I no longer fear Nero. He can only end my life on Earth. I will boldly proclaim the one who owns my eternal soul."

"Amen!" The crew spoke in unison.

The boat suddenly was still and silent. *'Caw. Caw.'* A raven broke the silence.

Chapter 12

Patmos 87 AD

The lines on Magnus's face were stark as inscriptions in stone. His skin was ashen, and his hair no more than frayed white tendrils. His head rested deep in a pillow. Death's odor permeated the air. Rivka, her once glorious honey hair now gray and wiry, kneeled at his bedside and held his hand. Sarah stood at the other side of the bed. Samuel and Ruth stood at its foot. A single tear was in Rivka's eyes. Stephanie cried openly; her husband, Adebe, stood stoic, his massive arm covering his wife's torso. Sarah's husband looked after theirs and Adebe and Stephanie's children in another room.

Sarah squeezed her eyes shut; tears sluiced through her eyelids. She kissed her father's forehead and then nodded to the others. They left the room, leaving Rivka alone with her husband.

"Rivka." His once commanding voice reduced to a rasp, "You knew this day would come."

"I thank God for every second that he gave me with you."

"We will be together again." Magnus gasped for air. "Forever."

"We will find an even greater love in Heaven."

"You know that it won't be the same." His voice's volume weakened. "We will be as the angels, married to God himself."

"Magnus," she held his hand, brought it to her lips, and kissed it. "The mystery of love of greater than the mystery of death." She continued to hold his hand to her lips. Her tears rained upon his hand.

"Yes, Rivka, I know what awaits me after these final moments pass. Yet it will forever remain a mystery as to why we got to experience something denied even the highest angel."

Rivka wiped her tears on Magnus's hand. "God gave us something so grand, so lovely beyond human understanding." Rivka erupted into tears. "Why must it end? Why? Why?"

Magnus struggled to lift his head. "We experienced the greatest blessing accorded to humans: love. We must also endure the curse of humanity: death. Rivka, I was both blessed in life and now blessed as I look death in the eyes. Let's be grateful that I can die peacefully and in your arms. Our Lord Yeshua and his disciples were far less fortunate."

"He defeated death for us. We will live forever, and I will love you forever."

"I love you too Rivka." Magnus gasped for breath. "I will love you forever and forever more." He gazed into Rivka's moist, olive eyes. Her image went blurry although her eyes remained in sharp crystal clarity. Magnus lay still. His breathing ceased.

"Magnus? Magnus!" Rivka put her head on his chest. "No! Magnus!" Rivka wailed.

The aroma of a flower garden replaced the stench of sickness and death. The angel Isolde Maria appeared. She kissed Rivka's forehead and embraced her. Rivka buried her head in the angel's shoulder and wailed. After their long embrace, Isolde Maria held both of Rivka's hands. "Come now, Rivka." She kissed Rivka's lips. "Let your family and friends say goodbye to Magnus. They loved him too." Isolde Maria vanished.

Rivka opened the bedroom door for her family and friends.

***

Rivka, her extended family, Abede, Sarah, and their son and daughter, trusted crewmen and their families, and church members gathered in Cyclops Cove, named after the mythological one-eyed humanoid monster. The cove's shape and location created a powerful seaward current. Jagged rocks further made using Cyclops Cove as a harbor impossible. Magnus's body was placed on a raft of dried sponges covered by sackcloth. Three blazing torches were placed on each side of him. Nero's reign of insanity and terror had ended in assassination. Ceasar Domitian was not as depraved or cruel. Nevertheless, the persecution of Christians persisted. The funeral gathering took every precaution to keep outside eyes and ears away. Rivka stood by the raft and faced the mourners. "We stand at the door to eternity. As Magnus passes through that door to the glories of Heaven, we are not to grieve as those without hope. While this is a moment of sadness, our Heavenly Father has sent the Holy Spirit to us as our comforter. Let us rejoice in that our grief is only temporary. For one day, we shall pass through that door and reunite with Magnus. Our Lord Yeshua has prepared a glorious place for us in Heaven. By calling upon the name of the Lord, we shall one day be with our Lord and Magnus for eternity. Tonight, let us not mourn but celebrate Magnus's transition from mortal to immortal, from the corruptible to the incorruptible. Just as baptism in the name of Yeshua symbolized the cleansing of the soul by water, we commit Magnus's remains to the Aegean Sea."

Two of Magnus's crewmen pushed the raft into the current. As the funeral raft floated out to sea, Rivka sang to the mourners.

"Come and follow him."
"Open your eyes to a World of seeing."

"Come and follow him."

"He'll show you a whole new meaning."

"Hear what he has to say, let him show you the way."

"Trust in him and obey, and he will wash your sins away."

"See Heaven through the son, living waters soft and sweet."

"You will find eternal life, believe, and he will set you free."

"His love flows upon the shores of time, From oceans deep to mountains high."

"He'll lift your spirit far and wide; for his love is true and divine."

"The seed that he plants today, Tomorrow will grow into a tree."

"See Heaven through the son, living waters soft and sweet,"

"You will find eternal life, Believe, and he will set you free."

"His love flows upon the shores of time, From oceans deep to mountains high."

"He'll lift your spirit far and wide; for his love is true and divine."

As Rivka sang the final note, the raft, and its torchlights disappeared into the darkness.

Rivka dried her tears and departed with Sarah, Samuel, and Ruth.

Stephanie approached her. "I know this is not the best time. You can leave this island and return to Macedonia with Samuel, Ruth, and your grandchildren. Sarah and her family may also be better off leaving." Stephanie placed her hand on Rivka's shoulder. "I know that you are considering retirement as well. Yet the company needs you. You have taught me well, but this student can never surpass her teacher. The crewmen and their family's income depend upon your managerial skills. Can you at least stay here until you have taught me everything? Besides, the women's and children's ministry needs you."

Rivka looked to Samuel, Ruth, and Sarah. She then lowered her head in prayer. Her family nodded to her. Rivka tensed her lips. "Yes, Stephanie." She held her hands. "I will stay."

Chapter 13

Patmos 95 AD

    A wooden ox-drawn cart entered the Patmos prison. Two guards met the cart and unlocked the door to the cargo bin. The chains of four prisoners bound together at the waist clanged as they dragged themselves through the hatch. Their legs were wobbly. Their wrists bound at their waist prevented them from shielding their eyes from the sun's intense glare. The ruckus of pickaxes and sledgehammers striking rock racked their eardrums. One intake was eighteen years old. His pallid expression and wondering eyes oozed fear. A stout middle-aged man with straggly hair and a wild beard furrowed his brow, raised his chin, and tensed his jaw. Another older man stood gaunt and expressionless, resigned to his fate. The fourth man was nearly ninety years old. He still had a full head of white hair and a long white beard. His elbows jutted against his sagging skin. The harrowing journey from Rome put dark shadows under his eyes and added wrinkles to his cheeks. Age had reduced his stature. Yet his posture remained erect, and his eyes looked forward.

    "The old man on the end." The cart driver pointed him out to the two guards. "He's the one."

    "I know about him. Word travels fast. He was placed in a pot of boiling oil and climbed out unharmed. Rumor has it," the guard covered his mouth as he spoke, "that Ceaser is afraid of him."

    The other guard looked around before mumbling. "It makes sense. The Carcerarius Custos wants to see him right away."

***

Apostle John stood in front of Carcerarius Custos Ignatius. The stocky Carcerarius Custos had broad shoulders, thick limbs, and a huge girth. He had hair on the sides of his head but a bald pate. He looked Apostle John over. "You look harmless enough, old man, but I see far more in your eyes than any other prisoner ever brought before me. Is what I hear true? You were condemned to be boiled in oil but climbed out of the cauldron unharmed? What sort of magical powers do you wield."

"I only live by the grace of the one far greater than I. The one who beat death itself."

"Ahh," The Carcerarius Custos nodded. "Apostle John, they call you. You defeated the death sentence of Ceasar himself. Now I must deal with you. Blasphemy against Ceasar is a crime against the Gods and a crime against the empire. Of course, that doesn't float with the prisoners. Most of them blame Ceasar for their predicament. My prison is not a place of death. Its purpose is to mine marble for Rome. If I were to behead everyone here who rejects Ceasar as God, I would have no one to chop rocks and extract marble." He prodded. "But we do have ways of making you comply."

John silently nodded.

"This is a rough place. Some have converted to your faith and revere you as not only his final disciple but among the last human beings to see your Yeshua alive."

"I saw him after he rose from the dead. He never died. He ascended to Heaven." John raised his palms. "He even died for you."

"Silence!" He marched around the table and prodded. "That's the last time such words from your mouth will go unpunished."

John did not so much as flinch.

"Yes. Some here will revere you." He jabbed his finger in John's sternum. "Others will hate you and mock you. Congratulations, Holy man. Now you get to join thieves, rapists, and murderers. I am short of guards. It's hard enough for them to control the prisoners, much less afford an old man like you protection. That forces me to rely on prisoner carcerarii. They tend to treat their fellow prisoners worse than my civilian guards. I can control them, nonetheless. Returning them to open population amounts to a death sentence. So, what can I do with you?" Carcerarius Custos Ignatius pinched his chin. "Ceaser Domitian won't let me put you to death. An old man like you is little use with a pickax or sledgehammer." He raised his palms. "Ahh, I'll make you a waterboy."

***

Apostle John carried a bucket of water with a shoulder strap. He approached a muscular sledgehammer-wielding prisoner with a thick black beard. John offered him a ladle of water.

"If it's not John the Apostle. So, you can climb from a pot of boiling oil unharmed," he placed hands on hips with the sledgehammer at his side, "So, make these prison walls crumble? Ha! Ha! Ha! I get it. Turn the other cheek and let the Romans trample us underfoot? Well, turn the other cheek to this, old man." The prisoner drank a ladle of water and spat it in John's face. "Ha! Ha! Ha!"

John chose not to react.

Another prisoner carrying a pickax intervened. "Why don't you show the old man some respect." He hunched his shoulders.

The black-bearded prisoner brushed him off.

"He may turn his other cheek. But I have something that will turn your cheek." He dropped his pickax and slugged him in the jaw. The prisoner fell to the ground.

A guard ran over, blowing a whistle. "What's going on here?" He cracked his whip.

Five prisoners pointed at the black-bearded prisoner. "He slipped."

"Break's over. Get back to work. Or…" The guard cracked his whip.

The prisoner with the sledgehammer took a ladle of water from John. "The name's Hosea. It's an honor to meet you, Apostle. You're going to hear plenty of mockery from the other prisoners. Let them insult you. If they assault you, we've got your back."

"I have all the protection that I need from my Father in Heaven."

Hosea chuckled. "In here, you'll need a lot more than…" He again laughed. "All right. Consider us as not your father but your big brothers. Ha! Ha! Ha! I said big, not elder."

John laughed with Hosea.

The guard didn't laugh. "I told you to get back to work!"

Crack!' His whip stung Hosea before he could resume breaking marble.

***

"You have supple hands for a woman in her eighth decade." Stephanie cut a sea bass into bits. "I'd hate to take you on in a knife fight." She chuckled.

Rivka chuckled. "How else can two poor widows make a living other than to cut a big, delicious sea bass into something that will resemble undersized trash fish."

"Poor?" Stephanie guffawed. "We own six boats. That airtight container that you invented made us the wealthiest fish merchants in Eurasia."

"I am a potter's daughter, remember." Rivka pushed the fish pieces aside. "That should do it. You and your son did wonderfully to get us the contact to sell fish to the prison."

"They are paying us for our excess catch and trash fish." Stephanie smiled. "Only you would take the best of our catch and disguise it as detritus on behalf of prisoners."

Rivka chuckled. "I think that you're forgetting where our late husbands met."

Stephanie laughed. "Great point." She stood. "Hi there, Abede."

Abede the Younger, Stephanie's son, entered the kitchen. He stood Six foot, five inches tall, still shorter than his father and not as robust. "Hello, Mother," He kissed Stephanie on the cheek. "Rivka. Have I got news for you." He beamed. "The other day, when delivering fish to the prison, the kitchen carcerarii told me that Yeshua's final living disciple, Apostle John, is in the prison. The kitchen carcerarii is a believer. He seems to have a lot of pull. Perhaps he can find a way for you two to meet?"

Rivka gasped, her jaw dropped, her mouth a circle. Stephanie then clutched her arm and beamed. Rivka returned her smile.

***

Abede the Younger lugged a ceramic cast of fish chunks into the Patmos Prison kitchen. "Good afternoon carcerarii Parcibian. Another load of good fished sliced up to look like bad fish." He chuckled. "I hope the Carcerarius never catches on."

"Why should he care?" Parcibian was medium height and slender build. He had brown hair with gray sideburns. "He's paying the same for sea bass as he would undersized trash fish." He laughed. "Besides, he enjoys the meals that I cook him far too much to punish me or mess with our little arrangement."

"You're still talked about in Ephesus as the best chef in all Eurasia." Abede laughed. "Too bad you couldn't stick to slicing fish instead of slicing your wife and her lover."

"If we were under the law of Moses, they could have dragged her out to the town square and stoned her for me." He grinned. "Unfortunately, that doesn't float by Roman law."

"You're lucky the judge sympathized with you." Abede chuckled. "Roman law is the death penalty for double murder. And you know that the Romans have creative ways of executing double murderers." Abede looked Parcibian over. "It sure helps that you were a famous chef. Running the kitchen as Ignatius's most trusted carcerarii must kick the stercus out of breaking rocks in the hot sun or toiling underground in the mine."

"I'd rather not be imprisoned at all." Parcibian smiled. "Nevertheless, I count my blessings every moment." He opened the cask of fish. "This is quite something that your boss invented." He tapped the side of the cask. "The prisoners used to eat spoiled fish. I could never cook the carcerarius the delicious meals that gain me his favor without it. I heard that its inventor and your boss is a woman."

"Yes. She and my mother." He laughed. "My mother, Stephanie, is almost seventy years old and is less than five feet tall. She doesn't weigh but ninety pounds soaking wet." He chuckled. "But I surely don't mess with her." He pointed upward. "You were telling me that Apostle John is confined here. Did you know that the owner of the company knew John personally and, along with John, may well be the final living eyewitness to the resurrected Christ? Her name is Rivka. Tell John about her."

"Let's do even better. You know where Ignatius lives. Bribe him to have John re-assigned to my kitchen. Rome doesn't pay stercus to even the Carcerarius. He will appreciate a little gratuity. Trust me." Parcibius pointed to himself. "Once John is here if you can come up with an idea to bring Rivka, they can meet."

***

Apostle John winced in the sun. He wiped the sweat from his brow with a rag. Prisoner believers had shown him their secret cave. Here, John preached and testified to the prisoners of the risen Christ. After word got around that Patmos's toughest prisoner, Hosea, had his back, the pagan prisoners left him alone. A guard blasted his whistle, signaling a water break. John spotted an exhausted-looking prisoner, walked over to him, and handed him a ladle of water. John had to help him steady the ladle so that he could drink. "Thanks, Old Timer." He panted for air.

"Believe in the one who created the water, and living waters shall flow from within you."

"You're talking that Yeshua, aren't you?"

John nodded.

"What do I have to lose? What's Jupiter done for me? Look at what Ceasar has done to me." The prisoner braced his sledgehammer on the ground and used it to lean over. He gasped. "What do I have to look forward to in Pluto's underworld? I know about your meetings in the cave. Can you clear it with Hosea for me to attend?"

"Yes, my new brother."

"You!" A guard pointed as he marched over to John. He grabbed his arm. "You're coming with me."

'Lord Yeshua, in the name of the Father, if I am to endure more punishment for testifying in your name, give me the strength to endure it joyfully.'

The Guard said nothing as he ushered John away.

***

Parcibian sliced fresh onions, leeks, and radishes to sauté with garlic and sea bass filets. The guard escorted John into the kitchen. "Look at what I'm preparing for you." Parcibian pointed at the guard.

The guard released John, wet his lips, and sat. The sizzle and scent of the meal filled the kitchen as Parcibian sauteed and stirred the sea bass blend over a low wood flame. He then served it to the guard. He zestfully gobbled. A minute later, he wiped his lips with a rag. "I brought you a new assistant. I don't know what this ancient old wreck can do for you here, but it's the Carcerarius's orders."

Parcibius waited for the guard to depart. "I am honored to serve the last living disciple of our Lord. Let me prepare you what I made for the guard. I bet you never had a meal like it in years." He folded his arms and grinned. "If ever."

"No. No." John shook his head. "I can't. The other prisoners never get to eat fresh, chef-prepared meals, so nor shall I. I am but a sinner saved by the blood of Yeshua. I am no better than the others."

"I'd say you are better than that pagan guard who called you an old wreck," Parcibius chuckled. "But who am I to judge? Yes. You can eat it." He arched his eyes. "Eating my little recipe won't exactly make your entering the gates of Heaven as difficult as a camel going through the eye of a

263

needle. After all, you sleep in a straw cot and live in barracks carved out of a cave. And your mission is far from over. You need your strength." Parcibius started chopping vegetables with his carving knife.

A glint from the blade caught John's eye. "All things considered; I am surprised they trust you with that thing."

"Did not our Lord teach us about being more grateful for being forgiven the greater debt?" Parcibian put the mixture in a pan. "You're insight is accurate. I stabbed and killed two people. I can argue that it was in hot blood and not cold blood. Nevertheless, it's murder just the same. The penalty is death. Not only was my life spared, but I have it better here than any other prisoner. Yet I still sleep in a cave, and I will never leave alive. I found Yeshua within these walls. He has saved my spirit for the next life." Parcibian put the pan in front of John.

"How true. And I remember Apostle Peter was no slouch with the knife." John chuckled. "I don't know if this is a temptation that I must resist or a blessing for me to be grateful." John imbibed the aroma. "If at my age I can smell this, maybe that is my answer." John prayed over the meal. "I thanked our Lord in prayer. I now thank you in voice." He ate the meal of sauteed sea bass.

"John. You knew our Lord in person and were eyewitness to his resurrection. You are far more learned than I and you have suffered far more travail for the faith. Moreover, you're not a double murderer. Yet I got an epiphany. Tonight, God is going to give you a mighty revelation."

John glanced out of the iron-barred window. He noticed a puffy, white cloud taking human form. Three seconds later, it glowed golden.

Parcibian walked over to a table. He returned and gave John papyrus sheets, a reed pen, and ink. "This evening, when I cook the Carcerarius his dinner, I will make extra for Hosea. Even though he is also a believer, bringing him a small blessing can't hurt. He will take you to our secret cave. Spend the night in it and ask Hosea to ensure no one disturbs you."

"Look at that cloud." John pointed to the window." What do you see?"

"I see no more than a Merino wool pillow." Parcibian smiled. "In the meantime, you can rest up or make yourself useful by helping the kitchen workers cook the prisoner's evening meal."

John helped the kitchen prisoners.

***

Hosea sat on a rock by the secret cave entrance and devoured sauteed sea bass from a ceramic jar. John noticed his biceps bulge as he spooned each portion. "I haven't eaten like this in ages." Hosea laughed. "Actually, I have never eaten a meal that tasted this good." He smiled at John. "Well, if ever you were to spend a night in the cave rather than your assigned cot, this is the night. Today is a Roman holiday on the island. Most of the guards are off duty. It will be just carcerarii watching the barracks. Even though they're carcerarii, they're still prisoners. They wouldn't dare rat out Hosea or any of his friends." He patted his chest and guffawed.

***

Apostle John sat with his legs crossed in the cave's corner. The cave was void of all light. He prayed in the

265

darkness, '*Lord, I thank you for my travails as you have honed me for this moment. May I serve you, Lord, and bring you glory, never to myself, but to you and the Kingdom of Heaven alone.*' He then went into deep meditation, clearing all thoughts.

A blinding light filled the darkness. John squinted. A figure stood before him amid seven candle sticks. Clothed in a spotless garment down to the floor, he was girded with gold. His head and his hair were white as Merino wool. His eyes flared like torches. His feet shined like brass in a furnace. He spoke in a voice sounding like mighty surging waters. In his right hand, he had seven stars. Out of his mouth went a double-edged sword. His countenance was as the sun: shining in power, strength, and glory. "I am the Alpha and the Omega, the beginning and the end. I am what is, what was, and what is to come. I am he that lived and died. Behold, I live forever more. I have the keys to hell and death. Write the things that you shall see, the things that are, and the things to come."

***

Ceasar Domitian sat on a plush Persian pillow amidst dishes of dates and nuts and lamb and poultry on spits over a wood fire. A fourth dancing girl cavorted before him, salaciously moving her abdomen, hips, and breasts. The females, even with the strategic torchlit shadows, fine wine, and risqué music, failed to excite him. He rather bit into a turkey leg. He turned, dropped it, and gasped.

A man, not fat or thin, not short or tall, sat next to him. Yet his facial features were striking. Ceasar Domitian first noticed his unusual beard. His mustache did not connect to his beard. It ran in a thin line from just below his earlobes, along his jawline, to a well-trimmed point on his chin. His dark, deep-set, piercing eyes both scared him and intrigued him.

"Where did you come from? How did you get here? Why didn't the Praetorian Guard stop you?" Ceasar Domitian stood and tilted his head, about to shout.

The intruder grabbed Ceasar's sleeve and yanked him down. "No need to shout. Your Praetorian Guard let me in. They knew how important I am and how much I can do for you. Moreover, I brought you a most exquisite gift." He pointed to a draped statue. "You are a great man. The greatest who ever lived."

Domitian grinned.

"Let me make your reign greater and last forever."

"Just who are you?"

"I go by many names and rule kingdoms beyond even the understanding of a great and powerful ruler such as yourself. You can call me Drago."

"You did get past the Praetorian Guard, and I can sense something both unusual and powerful about you. What is it you want from me?"

"I want nothing from you. You are a great man, and I want you to rule forever. Service to you is my reward."

Ceasar Domitian raised his head, tilted his chin, and grinned.

"I understand a certain follower of that subversive cult troubled you. You tried boiling him in oil, but he climbed out of the cauldron unscathed. Do you know how much that incident hurt your legacy as the World history's greatest Caesar and man? Do you know how many converted to that blasphemous cult as a result?"

Domitian furrowed his brows, his complexion reddened.

"Don't get angry at the messenger. Look to the one who can solve the problem."

"I take it that's you." The Ceasar pointed at Drago.

"I can't undo what has been done. I can prevent it from happening again."

"So, I should kill him? What if he survives again? Then what? This Yeshua that they worship." He scratched his bald pate. "His followers, and even our historians, say that he rose from the dead three days after death by crucifixion. Now look at the trouble it's causing."

"He had twelve disciples. You tried to boil his final living disciple to death in oil. You now have him imprisoned on the Island of Patmos. You can't kill him. Nevertheless, I have inside information that he is writing a document so dangerous and subversive that it can bring down the entire empire, end your rule, and even end your life." Drago looked piercingly into Ceasar Domitian's eyes. "Do you want to die a painful and humiliating death and go down in history as the Ceasar who lost the empire?"

"How do you know all of this? Why should I believe you?"

"Ahh, ahh, ahh," Drago prodded. "How about if I can show you that I know you even better than you know yourself."

"I've had enough of this." He prodded at Drago. "I'm calling my Praetorian guard. You can prove your power when facing hungry lions in the arena."

"Ha! Ha! Ha!" Drago bent over with his hand on his stomach. "You'll do no such thing. Not until after I show you your gift. Come." Drago nodded toward the draped statue.

Domitius paused, then followed Drago.

"Behold." Drago pulled the drape from the statue. "Apollo."

"Huh!" The Ceasar gasped. "I've never seen anything like it. He looks so real." He ran his fingers over the contours of the statue's face. "He's beautiful beyond measure." The Ceasar rubbed the statue's pectorals and biceps. "He's amazing."

"You do notice that his handsome face and grand muscles are not the only fantastic features of this artwork?"

The Ceasar panted and sweated.

"Before I show you just how powerful I am and how much I want to serve you as the god that you are, and as Rome's greatest ever Caesar, I want you to commission the full force of your military to go to Ephesus and make sure they seize John's document."

"This is a wonderful gift, and I will spare your life because of it. But Ephesus is over twelve hundred miles away. I can't make my military take such an undertaking just because you gave me a statue."

"What of your life, Ceasar Domitius? You've never experienced what you truly want. You're bored with your wife; none of the dancing girls excited you. But I know what you want, and I can give it to you." Drago snapped his fingers. The statue of Apollo came alive. The Ceasar froze. The vivified statue stepped off the pedestal. He planted a long, wet kiss on Ceasar Domitius's lips. He hungrily returned the kiss. "Ahh, ahh, ahh," Drago waved his finger. "You know what you have to do first."

"Yes, yes." Domitian panted and sweated. He loped over to a guard, spear at his side, standing by the door. He whispered in his ear. The guard sprinted away.

Drago nodded to Domitian. He took Drago's *Apollo* by the hand and led him away.

***

269

Rivka and Stephanie sat together in their company kitchen. Abede II entered. "It's done. I went to the Carcerarius's home and, shall I say, gave him a little gratuity. He transferred Apostle John to kitchen duty."

"A lot of good that will do, Rivka," Stephanie folded her hands. "You know, and under no circumstances is a woman permitted inside the prison."

"You know it," Rivka smiled at Stephanie, "and I know it." Rivka grinned. "I've got a plan, so they won't know it."

***

The dimension of time ceased to exist for John. A stack of writing sat before him. He could not stop to contemplate the wonderous and fantastic things that an Angel and Yeshua had shown him. He remained in a trance. Yeshua again stood before him. John's awe increased with every second of the Lord's presence. "Behold! I come again soon. My reward will be with me. I will reward every man according to his works. I am the Alpha and the Omega, the beginning and the end. The first and the last."

The Holy Spirit continued inspiring John. He wrote, 'And the spirit and the bride said, '*Come. And let him who thirsts come. And who that comes, let him take the water of life freely.*' For I testify to every man who hears the prophetic words of this book, if any man shall add to these things, God will add to him the plagues that are written in this book. Any man who takes away from the words in this book, God shall take away his part out of the Book of Life, out of the holy city, and from the things written in this book. He who testifies these things says, 'Surely I come again soon.' Even so, come, Lord Yeshua. The grace of our Lord Yeshua be with you all. Amen.'

Exhausted, John lowered his head and fell asleep. Hosea marched into the cave, grabbed his arm, and lifted him. "Wake up, Brother! The guards are back. It's shake-down day. They're going to tear the entire place apart and body search everyone."

John had trouble balancing. Hosea had to brace him. He pointed to the stacks of papyrus. "Let's gather that up. The guards will destroy it and then punish you for writing it." Hosea gathered up to the manuscript. He hid half under his tunic. John hid the other half. Hosea led John by the arm. "Hurry. Let's get you to the kitchen. If Parcibian cooks the guards breakfast, they probably won't shake it down."

***

"Back when I first met Magnus, this would've been unthinkable." Rivka chuckled. "The lush honey tress of a nineteen-year-old girl is a long time ago and a far cry from the fragile gray strands of this elderly woman."

"Those brittle tendrils may not be as pretty." Stephanie clipped another lock of hair from Rivka's head. "But never were they so useful."

Abede further chopped up the gray hair clippings. Stephanie applied some vegetable-based adhesive to Rivka's cheeks, jawline, and chin. She next stuck the hair clippings to it. "Perfectus!" Stephanie beamed. "How does it feel to transition from an elderly woman to an old man."

***

Abede pushed a wooden cart with a cask of fish to the prison gate. Gray-bearded Rivka, dressed as a man, walked beside him.

271

"I know you." The guard exited his kiosk. "But what's with the old man."

Abede deliberately dumbed down his speech. "I be big and I be strong to bring you fish." He scratched his head. "But ya know I don't be readin' or writin' so good. He's gonna be readin' and writin' for me."

"Oh, very well. He looks harmless enough." The guard returned to his kiosk. "You both can pass."

***

Dazed, confused, and exhausted, John needed Hosea to help him into the kitchen. Abede and a bearded Rivka entered the kitchen. "John! It is you!"

John's thoughts took five seconds to codify the strange-looking, gray-bearded old man. He staggered over and looked Rivka in the eyes. "You may look like an old man with a beard, and I haven't seen you in almost sixty years, but I have met only one person with those olive eyes."

"Yes, John." Rivka beamed. "It's me!"

"Your voice aged, but those eyes and smile are timeless." John laughed. "It really is you! Rivka!" He raised his palms and looked upward. "Yeshua loved you. He loved you so much that he assigned one of Heaven's highest angels to guide and protect you." John nodded to Hosea. He handed John his half of the Revelation manuscript. He then took his half from under his prison tunic and combined them. "These are to be the final words of our Lord Yeshua's New Testament. You and I are the final living eyewitnesses to the resurrected Christ. Last night an angel and our Lord appeared and showed me what will come. He also addressed seven of our churches. An angel told you years ago about the Lamb's Book of Life. It's revealed in this book. The Angel also told you that Heaven had chosen you to be among the first to read God's Revelation of what is to come and that you would be tasked to take this final book to the church. Take this to the elder of the Church of Ephesus. Have him make six more copies and have them distributed to the churches of Smyrna, Pergamon, Thyatira, Sardis, Philadelphia, and Laodicea." John looked at her with straight lips and intensified eyes. "It will be dangerous, especially for an elderly woman. The powers of darkness will do everything to stop you." John furrowed his brow. "You may not survive."

"You two can catch up on old times in Heaven." Hosea pointed out the window. "Here come the guards. Ignatius is with them. They look like they mean business."

"Quickly! Here," Parcibian carried over an empty cask. "This is from your last delivery. The workers cleaned and dried it. Put those papers in here."

"Great idea." Abede put the manuscript in the cask.

"You two go. Now! Ignatius and the guards are almost here."

Adebe put the cast on his shoulders and grabbed Rivka's hand. Once outside, they put the cask in their wooden card and marched it toward the gate.

***

Carcerarius Custos Ignatius and four guards barged into the prison kitchen.

"You got here just in time, Carcerarius Custos." Parcibian grinned. "I am about to scramble those eggs that you brought me from the market and mix in just the right blend of garlic and parsley. And I about to grill lamb botuli on the side."

"Not today, Parcibian. And you," Ignatius prodded at Hosea. "What are you doing here?" The Carcerarius Custos lurched toward him. "You are in an unauthorized area. Every one of you, hands against the wall. Now! Guards. Tear this place apart. Find what they're hiding."

The guards turned over Parcibian's desk, dumping the contents of its drawers. They turned over pots and cleared out pantry shelves. The guards then frisked John, Hosea, and the rest of the kitchen prisoners. While getting searched, Parcibian spotted Rivka and Abede approaching the gate.

"They're all clean." The guard finished frisking Parcibian.

"Now that you know that we're not hiding anything and that we are model inmates reforming our ways for Caesar," Parcibian kept his gaze away from the window, "how about that egg and botuli breakfast."

Ignatius put his hands on his hips, hunched his shoulders, and glowered at Parcibian. "Reforming your ways for Ceasar?" He smirked. "Taurus stercus! You sliced up two people on the outside, and you would do the same to me if I turned my back to you." He licked his lips. "At least I know that you murder by stabbing and not poisoning. I'll take that breakfast."

"I know that you bought the eggs and botuli with your own money, but don't you think your hard-working guards need some added nourishment for the shakedown?"

The four guards dropped their jaws, half-smiled, and gazed at their boss.

"Oh, I suppose."

Two of the guards picked up the overturned table and put it upright. All four sat at the table, grabbed a spoon, and watched Parcibian's every move with anticipation.

***

Rivka and Abede reached the gate. They blanked their expressions and fixed their gaze straight ahead. The gatekeeper looked toward the kitchen for a signal from Ignatius.

***

"Here you go, men." Parcibian served the guards and the carcerarius custos. "I once prepared this egg recipe for the Ephesus elite. Thank my former wife for cheating on me. Now I am serving it to you."

***

The gatekeeper waited for a signal from the carcerarius custos.

'What's he waiting for?' Rivka caught herself biting her fingernail. She quickly lowered her hands to her waist and touched her fingertips. *'Lord Yeshua, cover me with your power. Don't let the forces of darkness stop your words in this document from going forward to the seven churches.'*

***

John and Parcibian stole a glance out of the window. The gate guard was looking at the kitchen. Ignatius started to stand.

"Carcerarius. It's ready. I've been marinating your lamb botuli in cumin, colander, and saffron for days."

John prayed silently. *'Let your will be done; let your name be glorified.'*

An unexpected draft blew the aroma of the marinated botuli toward the *carcerarius*. He sat. Parcibian strolled over and placed a plate with the botuli and wheat flatbread on the table. Ignatius devoured it.

***

'No signal or sign of the carcerarius custos.' He looked at Rivka and Adebe.

They looked forward, not returning the gate guard's gaze.

He shrugged and opened the gate.

Chapter 14

"It's finished, Rivka." Stephanie beamed and raised her chin. "Your new kuttonet. Not just any kuttonet. It's a cold day and it will be colder on the Aegean Sea. That's a good thing. Your clothes are double layered with waterproofed leather lining and," Stephanie winked, "special padding in between. And, not to tempt anyone with your new haircut. I made a matching takrik."

"You're going to make me the most beautiful smuggler in the empire," Rivka took the kuttonet and takrik from Stephanie. "Even if I'm in my eighth decade."

***

"A perfect fit." Rivka stepped into the atrium of her house. "Even with the extra," she winked. "Padding."

Stefanie, Abede II, Sarah, and her grown son and daughter applauded.

"Well, this is it. I have no more time. I need to leave now. I wish that you could see me off at the boat, but we can't arouse any suspicion."

"Why don't you go in one of our fishing trawlers?" Sarah walked over to Rivka.

"A woman in her eighties departing a commercial fishing boat will surely catch the eye of the Roman authorities. Rather, I take the passenger boat and mix in with the other travelers."

"Mother," a tear welled in Sarah's eye. "We all know how dangerous this is." She openly cried. "We may never see you again."

"No matter what happens. Have faith. One day we will be reunited. My time on Earth is almost up. You, and especially my grandchildren and my great-grandchildren in Macedonia, have your entire lives ahead of you to serve the Lord."

Stephanie started wailing. She embraced Rivka. Sarah and her son and daughter also embraced her. Abede II wrapped his long arms around all of them.

***

The Aegean Sea looked like gray alabaster under an overcast sky. Rivka sat in a corner. She had to brace herself each time the boat pitched over a white cap. She prayed constantly to include thanking the Lord for a cool day, lest she appear overdressed for the weather.

***

Centurian Maximus led his century of a hundred soldiers into Ephesus. He had his unit break up into Auxiliary units. He stationed them in every harbor in Ephesus with orders to search every boat, crewman, and passenger. A unit awaited at the dock as the boat transporting Rivka arrived. Rivka stooped and bowed her head. She walked between two large men, past a soldier. "Hey! You! Old woman." The soldier loped toward her.

"Stop!" Another soldier stood in front of a married couple. "Everyone gets searched." The soldier walked behind the wife, patted her torso, and then cupped her breasts.

"You filthy dog!" her husband shoved the soldier. "Nobody touches my wife like that!" He prodded at the soldier; his finger hit the soldier's nose. He shoved the husband. They then grappled.

"Hey!" The soldier yelled to the other soldier. "Forget that old woman. Help me!"

Rivka marched on. She saw Roman soldiers stopping and frisking pedestrians. Rivka ducked into a clothing shop. She went to a rack of garments and hid behind the clothing. Rivka sat and prayed. Her right knee had locked up; her left knee felt like someone was prodding it with a red-hot poker. Her ankles were swollen, and her knuckles felt stiff and sore. Each moment felt like an hour. As the store closed for the evening, Rivka exited unnoticed. She limped along the avenue. Exhaustion, hip pain, and knee stiffness forced her to stop every several yards until the pain subsided and she could catch her breath. *'Everything is blurry. I feel lightheaded. Don't pass out. Don't pass out.'* She at last arrived at the home of Elder Jacobson.

"Praise God! Rivka. You look exhausted." He took her hand and led her to a plush chair.

"Before I sit. Help me take off this cloak."

He helped her doff her cloak. "It's lumpy and heavy. What do you have in here."

"Shh!" She put her finger before her lips. "It's a manuscript from the hand of Apostle John, inspired by the Holy Spirit. It's a Revelation of things to come from Yeshua himself."

"Yes. Of course. That must be why the Roman soldiers are shaking down everyone and everything in Ephesus. It's a miracle that you made it."

John wants you to keep the original. He wants you to make copies for the churches of Smyrna, Pergamum, Thyatira, Sardis, Philadelphia, and Laodicea. It is to be the final book of the New Testament of Christ."

Elder Jacobson hugged Rivka's cloak. He felt a power surge through his body. "God bless you, Rivka. The Holy

Spirit is affirming that it's God's revelation to all mankind. I wish it could be known as Rivka's Revelation, but I know you humbly serve our Lord." He chuckled. "So, I know that you will have none of that."

Rivka laughed with him.

"You have just experienced an ordeal for anyone of any age. But an elderly woman? Each second, I admire your courage and fortitude more. Let me get you something to eat to build back your strength."

"I am too worked up to eat."

"I understand. How about a glass of wine to take the edge off your nerves?"

Rivka nodded.

Elder Jacobson walked over to a counter and poured wine from a bottle. He handed the glass to Rivka.

"Thank you, Elder." Rivka sipped the wine. "I at last feel drowsy."

"Let me help you to my guest room." The Elder helped Rivka stand. "Sleep for as long as you need. I will have my staff write copies of this and get it to the six other churches right away. A big meal awaits when you wake up."

Rivka fell into a deep sleep, deeper than she had ever slept. She awoke in a cloud feeling refreshed, vigorous even. Her limbs felt supple and strong. Her vision, hearing, and smell were sharper than ever. She smelled a floral fragrance and then an image of ethereal beauty. The angel Isolde Maria took her right hand.

"Isolde Maria!" Rivka placed her left hand over their hands. "I am so happy to see you! I have always admired your raven hair. It flows like a river and even sheens a shade of indigo. Now look at me." Rivka laughed. "What little brittle gray hair that I had is chopped off."

"Your hair is my envy." Isolde Maria chuckled. "Many prefer hair the color of honey." She stroked Rivka's tress while showing it to her.

"Huh! My hair. It's lovelier and lusher than the day I met Magnus." Rivka beamed. "You are still the most beautiful angel in Heaven."

"I was." Isolde Maria chuckled. "Many will now see me as first runner-up." Isolde Maria pulled a gold, jewel-encrusted hand mirror from her white gown. "Look."

"Huh!" Rivka covered her face with her fingers, feeling smooth, taut skin. "I'm, I'm…Beautiful and, and, young again! I love you so much, Isolde Maria." Rivka's face was flush; she beamed, "I love you, my wonderful angel."

"But I'm no longer your angel." Isolde Maria chuckled. "But I will always love you. Now, I am your sister, and we will be sisters forever. Come, Rivka. Take my hand. Fly with me. Let me take you to Yeshua. He will take you to the Father. Magnus, Hannah, and your brother Samuel also await."

Rivka and Isolde Maria flew together to the throne of Christ.

The End

www.ingramcontent.com/pod-product-compliance
Lightning Source LLC
Chambersburg PA
CBHW051508120626
46551CB00012B/826